Neversuch House
Mask of the
Evergones

ELLIOT SKELL

Neversuch House

Mask of the Evergones

SIMON AND SCHUSTER

First published in Great Britain in 2011 by Simon and Schuster UK Ltd,
A CBS COMPANY

Simon & Schuster UK Ltd
1st Floor, 222 Gray's Inn Road, London WC1X 8HB

A CIP catalogue record for this book is available from the British Library.

ISBN 978-1-84738-744-8

1 3 5 7 9 10 8 6 4 2

Typeset in Plantin Light by Hewer Text UK Ltd, Edinburgh
Printed in the UK by CPI Cox & Wyman, Reading RG1 8EX

www.simonandschuster.co.uk

In Memory of
Everard Waldo Kidd
whose early disappearance has never been explained.

1

Under the House

The oars dipped in the water. The boat glided smoothly forward, trailing faint ripples in its wake. In it was a man dressed in black with a hooded cloak over his shoulders.

A lantern hung from a pole at the front of the boat. Its light moved as the man rowed, sending a glow into the darkness ahead, leaving in darkness the area behind. All around was rock, rising directly out of the water on either side and closing in a roof overhead, yellow and pink in the lantern light. Cracks ran through the stone, giving the impression of patterns, outlines, as if the shapes of various creatures had been carved there. If you stopped and stared at one place long enough, you would see whatever figure your imagination chose to create, whether evil or good.

But the man didn't stop to examine his surroundings. He rowed steadily, in silence, an oar in either hand. The only noise was the rhythmic plunking dip of the oars. The underground river flowed slowly, its surface as smooth as a lake. The boat moved forward into the ever-advancing glow of the light, leaving its trail of ripples disappearing into the ever-following blackness behind it.

Eventually the boat came to an area where the river widened. The man saw a stretch of flat rock at one side of the river. Another boat lay on the bare stone, out of the water. Behind it was a tall crevice in the wall, big enough for a person to enter.

He rowed towards it. The front of the boat bumped on the rock and the lantern shook. The man pulled in his oars. He stood up and balanced for a moment as the boat rocked, then stepped out on to the stone and pulled the boat up behind him. He unhooked the lantern from its pole and went to look at the other vessel. It was longer than the one in which he had arrived, and narrower, and a single long oar lay inside it. The boat was bone dry. A few curling flakes of black paint clung to the wood, but the rest of the paint that must once have covered it had disappeared, revealing bleached, cracked timbers. It looked as if it hadn't been used in years. The man peered closer. He doubted it would still float.

He went back to his own boat and dragged it further on to the rock, making sure it was completely clear of the water. Then he reached in and took something out, an object about the size of a human head.

The man raised his lantern and peered into the crevice in the rock. Cautiously, he went in. The walls of the crevice twisted and turned and then he saw a set of steps carved into the stone. They spiralled upwards, disappearing into the darkness above him.

He went to the steps and began to climb.

He had never used these steps before, but he had been told about them – not by someone who had used them themselves, but by someone who had heard about them, in turn, from somebody else. Exactly where they would come out, he didn't know. The steps were bare stone, damp. At the top he found a narrow passage and followed it until he came to a pile of fallen rubble that half blocked his way. Still clutching the object he had taken out of the boat in one hand, and with the lantern in the other, he scrambled over the rubble, stooping to get under the roof. Then he followed the passage further and went up another flight of stairs until, finally, he found a door.

It was only about chest-high, and made of timber which had rotted and split away in places near the top and bottom, as if some kind of hungry animal had chewed at it. Light filtered through the gaps.

He put down the lantern. This man hadn't done the things he had done – and survived – by taking chances. He made a mental note of exactly where he placed the lantern so he would know if it had been moved before he returned. He took off his long, hooded cloak and set it down as well. Then he raised the object he had brought from the boat and began to fit it carefully over his head.

It covered his head entirely, front and back, right and

left, every centimetre of his face and every strand of his dark, curly hair. He took a few moments to adjust it, ensuring that the eyeholes were in position for him to see through them. The mouth, which had a set of gleaming fangs, could open and close by a mechanism built into the jaw, and he tested it now, the sharp teeth opening and snapping shut as his own mouth moved.

When he was satisfied with the fit, he approached the door. Crouching, he pushed it open a fraction, then further, and peered cautiously out.

Through the eyeholes he could see a narrow, empty alley. He didn't immediately recognise the location. Not far away was the corner of another alley and high in the wall at the corner was a stone carving of a dancing clown. He made a mental note of it.

The alley in front of him was empty. The man came out, crouching to get through the opening, his head now not that of a human, but of a beast. He closed the door behind him. His fangs gleamed in the sunlight that filtered down between the alley walls.

He stepped past the carving of the dancing clown, turned the corner and went quickly away.

2

In the Meantime

This is the second book in the story of the extraordinary events that befell Omnia Halibut at the age of twelve and a quarter. So extraordinary were those events, and so numerous, that one book certainly wasn't enough to contain them, and sometimes I wonder whether two books will be enough either. I have been asked by some people who read the first book whether a series of events so extraordinary could possibly be true, and if so, how I can possibly know about them. Some people even doubt that there ever was such a place as Neversuch House, and seem to think that just because they have never heard of it before, it couldn't exist – which seems to me a peculiar way to think, because when you're born, for instance, you haven't heard of anything and yet there's a whole world around you, and it certainly doesn't stop existing just because you don't know about it yet. So all I can say is that there certainly was such a place, and the events that happened there certainly are true, or at least they are to the best of my knowledge, and anyone who knows me will tell you that I rarely make things up, and when I do, they don't turn out to be very interesting, let alone extraordinary. As to how I know about them, well, that would be another tale in itself, and since we've already begun Omnia's story, I think we should concentrate on that.

So to return to Omnia . . . Almost three months have passed since the events I described in the first book about Neversuch House, and Omnia's age is now closer to twelve and a half than twelve and a quarter, but we needn't quibble over the details. We all get older, and if time passes, what else can we expect? No, the interesting thing isn't the fact that Omnia is three months older after three months have passed, but what has happened in those three months. And the answer to that is quite simple. Nothing.

Or, to be more accurate, I should say nothing *unusual*. Because things have happened, of course. The world of Neversuch House has gone on with its feasts, its rituals, its traditions, its obsessions. Breakfast, lunch and dinner have been served every day in the Tempered Hall, where the food arrives from the kitchens below in gusts of hot air. Bracketball games have been played in the great Bracketball Courts. The daily lessons for the Halibut children on subjects without the slightest importance have continued in the Hall of Leaning, overseen by the poet and unofficial headmistress, Pedagogia, while the Halibut adults have remained engrossed in their own individual fascinations. Everfine D Halibut has continued to plot the shadows of the architecture of the House, Deliria Halibut has continued to study the growth of moulds on the north face of the Great Tower, Eversink I Halibut has continued to study their growth on the south face, Farinia Halibut has continued to bake ever more elaborate cupcakes in her private kitchens, Evernear K Halibut, Omnia's father, has continued to study the butterflies in the meadow below the Long South Range, and a thousand other obsessions have been pursued by a thousand other Halibuts in studies, libraries, observatories and laboratories all over the House. The feasts of the Halibuts have continued at their usual intervals. Songster's Day has taken place, when every Halibut has the right to take part in a singing competition in the Theatre of Sound no matter how bad their voice and how appalling the noise that it produces, followed by a feast in the Purple Nave. Leverall Day and Morrel Day have come and gone, each with their feast and each involving competitions so ridiculous that they would make the game of Planque, played with quoits and reindeer antlers, seem like the greatest sport ever invented. Two weddings have been celebrated in the Hall of Vows, and three funerals have taken place in the Field of Dreams, watched by Omnia and her friends from perches in the trees. Evermay L Halibut, the painter, has held an exhibition of his works in the Grand Marble Court, in which his new masterpiece, *The Death of the Loyal Servant Tobias Hildegrew*

While Grappling with the Black Condor, has been widely praised as the greatest pictorial work of a Halibut since Evermay's great-uncle, Everwill T Halibut, painted his magnificent *Planque Day under a Cloudy Sky, with Seagulls*.

And yet those of you who read the first book about the extraordinary events that befell Omnia Halibut might think that something else *ought* to have happened. Some kind of response, some kind of action, to prevent such things happening again. After all, the Captain of the House had been murdered, as had the Hereditary Butler, the keys to the Treasure Room had been copied and the perpetrator of these crimes had turned out to be none other than Tobias Hildegrew, one of the most trusted servants in the House. And Tobias wouldn't even have been discovered but for a gust of wind that took the hood off his head as he made his escape from the top of the Great Tower. Omnia had been there when Hildegrew had shouted: 'The Evergones *will* win!' – whatever that meant – as he flew away into the night. But none of these things had been revealed to the rest of the Halibuts, who were told that Hildegrew, the loyal servant, had fallen tragically and heroically to his death. Only the new Butler knew the truth, and the three UnderButlers, and of course Omnia, who had been marched to the UnderButlers' room immediately after seeing Hildegrew escape and sworn to silence about what she had witnessed.

As far as Omnia could tell, the three UnderButlers – Trimbleby, Withers and Dish – seemed to think that was the end of the matter, as if Tobias Hildegrew really had died that night at the top of the Great Tower rather than escaping. He could never come back, they said, never dare to show his face in Neversuch House again. Omnia realised there must have been instances like this before. She had worked out that outside the House were the Evergones – whoever they were – and from Hildegrew's last words as he flew away, it didn't seem likely that they would give up whatever it was that they were trying to do. Yet the UnderButlers seemed less concerned about that than about making sure she kept her promise to keep silent.

Omnia received regular reminders from them. Dish, with his drooping, basset-like jowls, would happen to bump into her when she was by herself in a corridor. Or Withers, with his wispy hair wafting in the breeze, would fall into step beside her as she was walking to the Hall of Leaning. Or Trimbleby would happen to come down one arm of the Splitted Stairs just as she came down another and thrust his huge pickle of a nose in her face. *Did* she remember the promise she had made on the night of Tobias Hildegrew's escape? *Had* she kept quiet about what she saw and not told a soul? Not really a question – more of a threat. Omnia felt as if she was the criminal, not Hildegrew. She was fairly certain the UnderButlers were having her followed. Sometimes she would look around and catch sight of a young woman wearing the green smock of the servants whose job was to polish the various things that needed to be shined in the buildings of Neversuch House. The polisher always seemed to be watching from a distance, but as soon as Omnia took a step towards her, she would disappear.

So the weeks passed. Apart from the UnderButlers bumping into her, and the polisher watching her, Omnia's life went back to normal. She spent her time with her friends, her cousin Evergrow, the twins Artesia and Evesia – although Evesia was more of an enemy than a friend, and disliked her, for some reason, to exactly the same extent as Artesia liked her – Eversmart O Halibut, the prankster of the group, Sororia Halibut, the most kind-hearted child in the House, Everright F Halibut, the cleverest child, and various other children of her age. But when she was completely honest with herself, she had to admit that there was a part of her that missed the adventure of those days when Tobias Hildegrew was on the loose. Not that she would ever wish that he was back, and anyway, he could never show his face again, as the UnderButlers had said. But life just wasn't as exciting. Omnia had to remind herself that people had been killed – almost including herself – and that during most of the adventure she had been in a state of sheer terror, thinking she was about to die. That was nothing to miss, even slightly.

But if, despite this, Omnia is missing the excitement, she is about to rediscover what it was really like. As she goes to the Tempered Hall each day to eat lunch with her friends, as she sits in the Hall of Leaning or swims in the Pallid Pool, things are happening. People are on the move. The series of extraordinary events that came to a stop three months earlier is about to start again. Omnia has been right all along, and the UnderButlers have been wrong. The plans of others can't be prevented just by ignoring them. And someone – and perhaps more than one person – is about to pay for this mistake with their life.

After Leverall Day and Morrel Day comes Flip Day, one of the great feasts of the House. On Flip Day, for one day only in the year, the Halibuts and the servants swap places. The Halibuts serve and the servants sit. But since no Halibut wants to be known to have served a particular servant – in case his or her friends see that it's a particularly unimportant one – and since no servant wants to be known to have been served by a particular Halibut – in case his or her friends have been served by a more important one – there is another tradition on Flip Day that makes it unique in all the Halibut festivals.

On Flip Day, everyone, Halibut and servant alike, wears a mask.

3

The Flip Day Feast

Omnia and her friends sat on the roof of the Narrow Range. Below them, on the Long Terrace, a line of tables had been laid, as tables had been laid every year since the first Flip Day. All morning people had been coming and going, bringing food from the kitchens under the Great Kitchen Court.

They wore masks of every possible description. Some of the masks were small, just covering the eyes and hardly obscuring the identity of the wearer. Others covered the whole face, and some were like full helmets over the head, especially designed for Flip Day with mouths that opened for eating. There were faces of animals and faces of people and faces of imaginary beasts that were a combination of the two. Some of the masks showed a smile, some a scowl. Some were ancient, prized masks, dating back many years, and others, worn by people who liked to have something new every year, had been recently made by the Lombardis, a family of servants who were the traditional hatters and mask-makers of the House.

The people bringing food and drinks to the tables all wore the scarlet tunics that were traditionally worn by the food servers of the House, but if you had been watching, you would soon have noticed that they didn't handle the trays and dishes with the air of people who knew what they were doing. They took too many things, and had to stop halfway up the stairs to the Terrace and leave something and come back, or they took too little, and arrived with only one little plate or a small tray of dishes. They spilled things or bumped into each other or knocked things over and tried clumsily to pick them up. They weren't servers at all, of course, but Halibuts.

No one trusted the Halibuts to be able to prepare a feast of this magnitude, or of any magnitude, at least not with food that was edible, so the food itself had been prepared by the cooks overnight and left to keep warm in the ovens. But there was no rule against a Halibut cooking his or her own food, and some of them brought dishes they had prepared in their own private kitchens, which they were desperate to put in the best positions. They swept other dishes carelessly out of the way in order to put their own creations in pride of place. Two minutes later, someone else would come along and do exactly the same to their dishes.

All around the tables such manipulations were taking place. Accustomed to being presented with perfectly laid tables at every other feast of the year, the Halibuts had no idea about the planning and care required and inevitably ended up with dishes thrown higgledy-piggledy and slap-dash across the tables. Five bowls of sausages would sit at one end of a table and none at the other, or six trays of jellies would be placed on one table and the spoons for them on a second. A number of the more officious Halibuts, led by Pedagogia in a mask with a dolphin's snout, were trying to direct things, telling people to put one dish here or another there, but since they had no right to be in charge, no one listened to them unless it suited them, in which case it usually didn't suit someone else. People jostled and pushed. Fights broke out as they vied for the best places for the dishes they were carrying.

The Halibut children could have helped, but since so many of the adults were eager to be involved, it was much more entertaining to sit on the roof of the Narrow Range and observe the fights and arguments that broke out below them. A long line of children sat along the roof and watched. Omnia wore a small blue cat's-eye mask, sitting between Evergrow, who wore a mustard-yellow lion's mask that he had worn every year since he was five, and Artesia. Evesia was next to her sister, and the twins each wore a parrot mask – one orange, one blue – that covered their hair with feathers and came halfway down their face, ending with a curved beak over their nose. On top of that they wore a pair of matching lime-green sunhats.

Below them, a lady in a pelican mask marched up the stairs to the Terrace carrying two baskets of cupcakes, accompanied by a devil and a walrus, who were carrying another two baskets each. She proceeded to extract a series of plates from one of her baskets, together with metal stands that would position them above everything else. She handed plates and stands to the other two and sent them off to one end of the tables, while she began to set out her cupcakes at the other end.

As soon as she had set up her first plate and moved on, someone in a unicorn's mask crept up behind her and replaced the cupcakes with a dish of chicken. Evergrow and Omnia glanced at each other and smiled, then watched with interest to see what would happen. The pelican-lady set out a second plate of cupcakes, and the unicorn, following along and waiting behind her, did the same thing to it. Suddenly the pelican turned around, saw what had happened and let out a shriek. She threw herself at the unicorn, whose plates of chicken went flying. Pelican beak clashed with unicorn horn until the pelican sent the unicorn sprawling, breaking its horn in the process. Then she looked around, beak in the air, went back to the first table, put her plate of cupcakes on its stand and shoved the chicken under another dish.

'She's strong, that pelican,' said Evergrow.

'It must be Farinia,' said Omnia. 'She'll defend her cupcakes to the death.'

Under her lime-green sunhat, Artesia laughed. Even Evesia couldn't suppress a smile.

Elsewhere another scuffle had broken out between a big-bellied leprechaun and an ostrich.

Eventually the tables were set. Dishes stood crowded against each other, overlapping, tilting at angles, the gravy of one dripping into the juice of another. The masked Halibuts stood in a mass at one end of the tables and eyed each other suspiciously. Only one would have to move to set the whole lot of them swarming over the tables again.

The bells in the Hatted Belfry chimed four times.

'We'd better go down,' said Omnia.

Masked children climbed down from all along the Narrow Range. They filed on to the Long Terrace and joined the Halibuts at the end of the tables. At the front of the crowd was Everdean P Halibut, who had been dragged away from his geological obsessions and made Captain of the House three months previously when the preceding Captain had died without nominating a successor and no one could think of an alternative but to appoint the oldest Halibut living. Everdean's mask, in keeping with tradition, was a portrait of the first Butler, and he wore a butler's coat of dark-green velvet. He was too frail to stand by himself and a monkey and a goblin stood on either side of him, holding him up.

The chairs at the tables were unoccupied. But instead of lunging at them, as they would have done at any other feast, the Halibuts waited.

They glanced at each other impatiently and threw longing glances at the food. If you had been there, you would have felt that if something didn't happen soon, whatever was holding them back would disappear and they would throw themselves at the tables.

Then a low rumble began. It was like the sound of far-off thunder coming from somewhere beyond the stairs that led to the Long Terrace. The Halibuts gazed at the top of the stairs. The rumble grew louder, as if now a giant wave was roaring towards them. Suddenly a masked figure appeared at the top of the stairs, and an instant later a mass of masked servants erupted on to the Terrace. They ran for the chairs, elbowing each other, tripping each other up and generally playing all the tricks they had learned from watching the Halibuts at their feasts. In seconds, the chairs were taken. The rest of the servants – the slow, the weak, the infirm, those who had been tripped and trampled – stood behind the chairs and pushed to get close enough to reach the food.

Still no one ate.

At the end of the tables opposite Everdean stood the young Butler, Digby, in front of the chair that was reserved for him. His mask was a portrait of the First Captain of the House, and he wore a blue Captain's coat.

The waiting went on. People started to mutter. The goblin beside Everdean gave him a nudge.

'What?' said Everdean. He looked round, blinking in confusion at all the masked people surrounding him, having forgotten why he was here.

'The servants of today welcome the Halibuts,' hissed the monkey who was helping to hold him up.

'Why?' asked Everdean.

'Just say it!'

'What?'

'What I just said.'

At the other end of the tables the Butler had already started speaking, on the assumption that Everdean, who always spoke so softly that no one could hear him, must have finished. It was his first Flip Day as Butler of the House, but he had been instructed in the custom. 'The Halibuts of today thank the servants,' he said loudly. He paused for a moment. 'Let's eat!'

Everyone lunged for the food, servants and Halibuts alike. Masks were bent out of shape or knocked off altogether in the crush, but you weren't allowed to eat on Flip Day unless you wore one, so people were soon on their hands and knees scrabbling after them, coming up with masks that were torn and dented or hanging loose from one ear – anything so that they could continue with the feasting.

It was one of the great annual sights of Neversuch House, a vast collection of animals, people, goblins, elves and just about any other creature one could imagine, all at feast on the Long Terrace.

And amongst them was a tall, grey panther with gleaming fangs.

Omnia and her friends carried their food to the roof of the Narrow Range, where most of the children were eating. When they had finished, they went back for more, plunging into the sea of masked feasters on the Long Terrace. There was so much noise and so many extraordinary faces, and it took so much effort and concentration to get to the tables through the crowd, that Omnia hardly noticed the individual feasters around her.

But the man wearing the grey panther mask noticed her. Omnia and her friends walked straight past him. He turned his head and watched as she went by. Omnia's cat's-eye mask wasn't designed to conceal her face and anyone who knew her could easily see it was her.

She walked straight past the grey panther again with her friends on the way back. He beckoned to a smaller, brown panther who was standing nearby with a plate of food. The grey panther whispered to him and looked up towards the Narrow Range where Omnia was now sitting. The brown one looked up, nodded and then headed for the Range.

There were other people in panther masks on the Terrace that day, a red one, a blue one and an orange one. From time to time, each of them happened to stop by the grey panther, who whispered something in their ears before they melted back into the feasting crowd. Very few people, if any, took notice of them, and if they did, they soon forgot them. There were too many faces, too much noise and laughter. A panther, or even a pair of panthers, whether red or blue or orange, short or tall, was no more remarkable than a short red giraffe, or a thin blue pig, or a triplet of gerbils in orange veils, or a skull with a diamond tiara, or any of the hundreds of odd apparitions that appeared on the Long Terrace, all innocently enjoying the feast.

Omnia wasn't the only person who was of interest to them. Eventually the grey panther spotted a man with a half-mask of a dog's snout and long, hound-like ears above the man's own basset-like jowls, sitting at a table between a lizard and a gnome. The grey panther knew those jowls. He whispered in the ear of the red panther, who went to watch him.

Omnia came down for more food and went up again. The brown panther constantly kept his eyes on her. But Omnia was with her friends every minute that day, whether on the roof of the Range or when coming down to the Terrace, and there was never any chance to catch her alone.

That was what saved her.

The feasting went on, for two hours, for three, for four. People were beginning to wish that night would come, marking the traditional end of the feast. They sat slumped in their chairs, or lay flat on their backs on the stone of the Terrace, bellies bloated, groaning with fullness. Some removed their masks as a sign that they couldn't eat another thing. Only the greatest gluttons of the House managed to keep going. Everfull V Halibut, his wife Insatia, Everround Y Halibut and a few others in various disguises had taken over a set of chairs from a group of servants who had walked away and collapsed, and they continued to munch and crunch as the sun dropped.

At last, people began to stagger away, clutching their bellies, leaving the tables covered in dishes and bowls of half-finished food. The grey panther moved in the shadows now, still waiting his chance. Omnia left with her friends, watched by the brown panther until she had gone.

At the table, the gnome next to the man in the dog's mask got up and shuffled away. The lizard eventually left as well. The man in the dog mask continued to sit, too full to move, waiting before he tried to get up. Soon there was no one left sitting near him.

The red panther signalled to the grey one. Night was falling. The shadows across the table were deep.

The grey panther moved quickly.

Eventually even the gluttons were finished and got up from the tables, pausing only to stuff a last morsel into their mouths. The moon rose, casting its light over the scene. The Terrace was a chaos of overturned chairs and emptied plates and leftover scraps. No one would clear it tonight. Tomorrow, masks would be set aside. The servants would be servants again and the Halibuts Halibuts, and the servants would clear the feast that the Halibuts had staged in their honour.

That would be tomorrow. Tonight, birds landed on the tables and chairs and pecked at the food.

But there was something at one of the tables that didn't consist of leftover food. It was dark in the moonlight and completely still. Birds landed on it, but it didn't interest them and they left it alone.

The servants came back in the morning. Thirty of them arrived and still the gigantic mess in front of them would take all day to clear. Some headed off to start on the roof of the Narrow Range others began at the end of the long line of tables. They had already started working when one of them noticed someone apparently still sitting far off towards the other end of the tables.

'Who's that?' asked one of the servants.

'Not sure,' said another.

They went to investigate. A man sat in a chair, his head slumped forward in a big bowl of lamb cutlets.

'Had a bit too much to eat, eh?' said one of the servants.

The other laughed.

The servant put his hand on the man's shoulder and pulled him up.

The man's head rolled back, hit the chair and then rolled forward into the bowl again.

The servants stared.

'Who is it?' said one of them.

The servant who had pulled the man back reached out gingerly. He raised the man's head again. His face was half covered by a dog's mask and was wet from the gravy in the bottom of the bowl.

The servant pulled off the mask, revealing the cold, basset-like features of the UnderButler Herbert Dish.

4

Something Somewhere . . .

Eldred Sturgeon, the Chief Physician of the House, looked at the UnderButler from one side, looked at him from another and then felt for the pulse at his neck to make sure he was dead.

'This is exactly how you found him, is it?' he asked the two servants, using his most severe tone, so as to let them know that he wouldn't tolerate any lying.

They nodded quickly.

'In the bowl? Face down?'

They nodded again.

Eldred Sturgeon glanced at the Butler, who, together with the two other UnderButlers, the eight UnderUnderButlers, the thirty servants who had come to clean up the Long Terrace and an ever-growing crowd of noisy onlookers, was watching his examination.

He peered into the bowl of lamb cutlets. There was a

puddle of gravy at the bottom. He poked a finger into it to measure its depth.

A death at a feast wasn't something that particularly concerned Eldred Sturgeon. Deaths at the feasts in Neversuch House weren't uncommon, and anyone taking part in them should have been aware of the dangers. In fact, given the massive amounts of food that were eaten – not to mention all the choking that went on as people ate and talked at the same time, a habit to which the Halibuts seemed particularly prone – Eldred Sturgeon was surprised there weren't more fatalities. At one feast in the days when Evertrue V Halibut the Second had been Captain, it was said that seventeen people had died of overeating, a feat so much admired that a new annual feast was established in its memory, the Feast Feast. Naturally, Eldred Sturgeon was never happy when one of his patients died, but since Herbert Dish hadn't been one of his patients – having been perfectly fit and healthy, as far as anyone knew, until the moment he was found dead with his face wedged in the gravy at the bottom of a bowl of lamb cutlets – there was no particular reason for the doctor to be upset.

He checked the pulse at the UnderButler's neck again, just to be absolutely sure. There was nothing more embarrassing than pronouncing someone dead only for them to sit up two minutes later and ask why everyone was crying. It had happened to Eldred Sturgeon a number of times in his career and he didn't want it happening again. Sometimes he suspected people played tricks on him just to make him look like a fool. Surreptitiously, with his other hand, he gave Dish's arm a powerful pinch, to see if that would wake him. But the UnderButler remained cold, still and silent. In other words, dead.

And that was the end of the examination. Anything more seemed unnecessary to the doctor, who didn't like having anything to do with dead bodies and rarely did more by way of examination than glance at them and give them a couple of pinches to see if he could make them sit up. Besides, the case seemed obvious.

'Take him away,' said Sturgeon. 'I've seen enough.'

'Do you know what he died from?' asked the Butler.

'Of course I do,' retorted the doctor, as if the very question was an insult. 'It's clear that Mr Dish died from a sudden attack of something somewhere in some part of his body, almost certainly brought on by overeating, causing him to keel over, drop forward and end up nose down in a bowlful of gravy. Now, whether he died from the attack, in the first place, or from drowning nose down in gravy, in the second, is something we will never be sure of. But that's neither here nor there, Mr Digby, is it? He's dead. And dead is dead.'

The Butler frowned. 'I suppose so.'

'Indeed it is.' The doctor turned to the two servants who had found the UnderButler. They were gazing uncertainly at the body. He snapped his fingers. 'Take him away, I said. You found him, so you can carry him!'

The doctor waited until they had picked him up, then

set off himself. He went back to his office and sat down to write the UnderButler's death certificate. Eldred Sturgeon really had no idea whether the UnderButler had died from an attack of something somewhere in some part of his body which had caused him to keel over, or from drowning in the gravy into which he had keeled, and he didn't particularly care. But since he had never written a death certificate saying that someone had died from drowning in gravy – but had written a good number saying that someone had died from an attack of something somewhere in some part of his body – he decided to put drowning on the certificate, if only for the sake of variety.

As for the Halibuts, when they heard about it, the death of the UnderButler raised no eyebrows, even amongst the few who paid attention to it. The average Halibut barely knew what happened amongst the servants and cared about it even less. As long as the things they ordered from the outside world were promptly delivered, and their meals appeared three times a day in the Tempered Hall, and they were otherwise left to pursue whatever particular obsession possessed them, they were content. Besides, there were three UnderButlers, so one could hardly complain about the loss of one of them. And if a replacement was needed, surely there must be a candidate among all the clerks and filers and messengers and various other officials who did whatever they did in the Butlery in the Bright Tower.

As for Omnia, she wasn't sure what to make of it.

It wasn't a freakish accident, like those which had killed

the Captain and the Butler three months previously. People *did* die at feasts, she knew, and she had seen a number do precisely that with her own eyes. Perhaps Dish had got carried away with his eating and had succumbed as a result.

But Omnia knew that things in Neversuch House were rarely as they seemed. Basilica Halibut had explained that to her three months earlier, after Basilica saved her life when Tobias Hildegrew hurled her off the Slate Tower. Basilica lived in the Tower together with her servant, Winnicott, although Omnia had never seen a door into their apartment. The only way she knew to get in was by falling past her window and being caught by Basilica in a net. Basilica also told Omnia never to tell anyone that she had seen her, but Omnia had. In fact, she had told both the UnderButlers and Pedagogia, although she hadn't meant to. But a lot of extraordinary things had been happening back then and it was only to be expected that occasionally something might just come out that one hadn't intended to say. When those extraordinary events had been taking place, when 'accidents' that were really incidents seemed to be happening all around her, Basilica was the one who had helped Omnia understand what was really going on.

Omnia had tried to find her again after Tobias Hildegrew's escape. Early on the morning after Planque Day, Omnia went back to the Slate Tower. She climbed the stairs to the top and stood on the parapet, balancing herself against the wind, and called out Basilica's name. But for some reason, this time, Omnia couldn't bring herself to jump. Last time,

Basilica's net had come out to catch her as she plummeted past Basilica's window. But now it was as if being caught previously by Basilica was a kind of dream, and she didn't know how or if it could possibly have happened. She stood on the parapet and peered downwards. The ground below seemed far, far away. She called again. Still the net didn't appear. If she had already jumped, Omnia thought, by now she would be dead. Or maybe the net would come out only if she actually stepped off the edge, and you had to take that chance. Maybe Basilica somehow knew if you had actually jumped. Omnia called out Basilica's name a third time. Still nothing happened. But having had the thought that she would already be dead if she had stepped off the parapet, Omnia couldn't bring herself to do it. Suddenly, the sight of the drop and the noise of the wind howling in her ears were terrifying. She climbed down from the parapet and ran down the stairs.

Omnia went back the next morning, telling herself that this time she really would jump, but she found the door at the bottom of the Tower barred with a huge, metal grille. It was firmly fixed to the stone of the Tower and there was no way to open it.

She didn't give up. When Omnia had left Basilica's rooms in the Tower, she had slid down a chute that delivered her into a tunnel that ended opposite the Purple Nave, so she went back along the tunnel to see if she could find the opening. But when she came to the area where she thought the chute must have opened, she found not one but fifty holes in the tunnel wall. Just about every apartment in the Slate Tower must have had a chute that came down here! She realised that each time she had come down from Basilica's apartment, she had never stopped to look around before heading away, always having her mind on other things, and consequently she had no idea which of the openings she had come out of. She called into each in turn, listening for a reply above the sound of her own voice echoing back at her. By the time Omnia was finished, she was hoarse and had heard nothing in reply from any of them.

For days after that, Omnia had walked around the House looking for places from which she could see the Slate Tower from one angle or another. She went late at night to see if she could spot a light in one of the windows, or early in the morning to see if she could catch sight of Basilica's net. But none of the windows in the Tower showed any sign of life, some firmly covered by shutters, some empty and dark. She didn't know how else to find her. Omnia's cousin Evergrow, who had seen Basilica as well, couldn't think of any other way either. Nor could Cornelius Slinker, the messenger who had saved her life above the Silent Cloister. Omnia trusted Cornelius as much as she trusted Evergrow. Cornelius kept watch on the Tower as well, but had no more success than she did. The UnderButlers had told Omnia that Basilica didn't exist, that she was a ghost. Omnia didn't believe that, but she couldn't find a way back to her.

Now, more than ever, Omnia wished that she could talk to her. Very little in Neversuch House was as it seemed, and that might very well include the apparently unremarkable death of an UnderButler at a feast.

But Omnia was no closer to finding Basilica than she had been the morning after Planque Day, and was beginning to think she might never see her again.

5

The Funeral in the Meadow of Rest

There was no expectation for a Halibut to attend the funeral of an Under Butler, but something made Omnia go. She knew she wouldn't discover any facts at the funeral about Dish's death – she had learned that what was said in public in Neversuch House was what the Butler and his UnderButlers wanted people to think, not necessarily what had actually happened. But she felt some kind of connection to the basset-jowled UnderButler. Only four people had been with her at the top of the Great Tower the night Tobias Hildegrew flew away, and Dish was one of them. Now there were only three others left who knew what had really happened.

Servant funerals took place at night. Omnia sat in one of the trees around the Meadow of Rest, as the Halibut children had the right to do. She could see only one other Halibut child there, Everglum L Halibut, a boy of fifteen who was sitting on a branch nearby with a lantern hanging from another branch just above him. Everglum had a fascination with funerals that, Omnia suspected, would take over his life in one form or another as he reached adulthood. He had brought a small notepad and as the funeral commenced, he began to take notes in the glow of his lantern.

A crowd of servants stood round the grave. A woman sat on the Mourner's Throne beside the coffin, her face lit up by a candle in her hand. Omnia had never seen her before, but she assumed it was Dish's wife. Next to her, holding on to the imps carved on the arms of the Throne, were two small children, who must have been junior Dishes. The Butler stood on the other side of the coffin, flanked by the remaining two UnderButlers, all of them holding candles, as were a number of mourners in the crowd. The Butler spoke, and then each of the UnderButlers added a short speech, by tradition no more than eighty words.

Omnia glanced at Everglum, who was scribbling on his pad.

'What are you writing?' she asked.

He ignored her.

'Everglum?'

He glanced at her impatiently. 'Shhhhh! I've never seen an UnderButler's funeral before!'

Omnia rolled her eyes. Everglum was watching the funeral again, taking more notes. He would probably end up writing a great history of the House's funerals, thought Omnia, that would take him forty years to research and which no one would ever read. She could just imagine the lessons from him in the Hall of Leaning that future genera- tions of Halibut children would endure.

Not far from where the funeral was taking place, Omnia could see where the old Butler had been buried three months previously. His grave appeared as a kind of darker stain under the moonlight in the general darkness of the Meadow. On that night three months before, Omnia had watched the old Butler's funeral from the roof of the Middle Range, hiding from Tobias Hildegrew.

Soon Dish's coffin was being lowered. Then it was gone into the blackness of the hole that had been dug for it.

The Mourner's Throne was raised by four of the serv- ants. Dish's wife stayed seated, holding her candle, as she was carried away. The other people moved off, their candles floating through the darkness.

Everglum remained in the tree, scribbling in the light of his lantern.

Omnia climbed down and headed across the dark Meadow. Shadowy figures were lit up here and there by the flickering of candles. Omnia glimpsed the face of Cornelius Slinker. He waited for her as the others left.

'Is that the death certificate?' asked Omnia, pointing at the pale corner of an envelope that poked out of the pocket of Cornelius's cloak.

Cornelius nodded. 'Take it tomorrow. First thing.'

It was easy to imagine that Cornelius Slinker was someone who just carried out other people's errands. But

Omnia knew that he was more than that. When she had been in danger, he had realised she needed help and decided to protect her. No one else had. The scar which ran down the left side of his long, thin face was the result of that decision. Tobias Hildegrew's knife had left it there when Cornelius fought him on the roof of the Silent Cloister, saving Omnia's life, and he was lucky he hadn't lost his own life in the process.

A few days after that, Cornelius had given Omnia a small white stone, with a smooth, polished surface and a star carved into one side of it, and told her that if she ever needed help, she should put the stone in a little hole that he showed her in the wall of the Captain's Keep, hidden behind the trunk of a vine that grew against it. Then she should come at five o'clock in the afternoon to the courtyard beneath the Granite Arch where he would meet her. Omnia had used the stone when she wanted to ask Cornelius to help find Basilica. She had used it a couple of other times as well, and each time Cornelius had appeared at the Granite Arch at five o'clock, just as he said he would, and he gave her back the stone so she could use it again if she needed to.

'What do you think?' asked Omnia, looking towards the open grave at the bottom of which Dish's coffin now lay.

Cornelius shrugged.

'You think all of this could be suspicious?'

'Could be. No way to know.'

'But it could have been a natural event, is that what you mean?'

'*Could* be,' said Cornelius quietly.

Cornelius never said much, but Omnia knew what he meant. He was aware, just as she was, that things were rarely as they seemed in Neversuch House. Omnia looked round the field. The glow of a lantern moving in one of the trees showed that Everglum was finally coming down. Omnia noticed two people standing near the edge of the Meadow, lit up by a candle that one of them was holding. The one with the candle was a short young man wearing the clothes of an apprentice mason. The other was the polisher Omnia had often seen following her.

'Do you know them?' she murmured to Cornelius. 'Behind you.'

Cornelius looked.

As Cornelius turned, the light of the candle was snuffed out. The two figures, now shadows, melted away under the trees.

'One of them's a polisher. I think she's been following me for the UnderButlers.'

Cornelius scanned the edge of the Meadow, but whether the two young servants were still there under the trees, or had run off, it was impossible to say.

'Wouldn't be surprised,' said Cornelius. He turned back to her. 'You've still got the stone, haven't you?'

Omnia nodded. She always carried it with her. It was in her pocket right now.

'If you need me, you know what to do. Leave it at the

Captain's Keep.' The messenger looked at her seriously. 'Don't hesitate, Omnia.'

'I won't.'

Cornelius gazed at Omnia with his deep-set eyes. 'I don't know what happened to Dish. Natural or not – time will tell. Whatever happens, Omnia, you can trust me. Always. If you need me, leave the stone.'

Slinker gazed at her a moment longer and then turned and moved away. He fell into his quick, silent, messenger's trot. Soon he reached the edge of the Meadow and disappeared.

Where he would go that night, Omnia couldn't say. Back to the Warren probably, where the servants lived. But in the morning, she knew, he would trot for three miles at his fast messenger's pace until he reached the gate in the wall that ran around the estate, and once the gate had been opened for him, he would step into the streets of the city of Pettifog to deliver the death certificate of Herbert Dish.

But what the UnderButler had actually died from – whatever the death certificate said – was something that Omnia still didn't know.

6

Stalks in the Ice Cream

The fires in the kitchen blazed. A teeming brigade of cooks, peelers, washers, boners, choppers, dicers, slicers, kitchen hands and pot-scrubbers had been at work since dawn, all under the ferocious gaze of Thomas Coffier, the High Chef, who strode through the kitchen in his tall, white hat, his enormous belly straining the buttons of his white coat, stopping, tasting, prodding, poking, yelling at a kitchen hand here or a pot-washer there as he added salt to a dish with one hand and pushed a cook out of the way with the other.

Lunch was being served. Cooks ran to deliver their dishes to the serving station, where a team of straining, red-faced, scarlet-uniformed servers loaded the dumb waiters and hauled on ropes to send the food up to the Tempered Hall, where another team of scarlet-uniformed servers unloaded the food and sent the dumb waiters back down for more. Coffier glanced at the servers and yelled at one of them to load faster. He spied a pan full of chicken livers that were about to burn and yelled at a cook to get them off the fire, then swung around, thrust a spoon into a pot of soup and demanded more pepper. He watched as a cook ground the pepper into the pot, then grabbed the grinder impatiently out of his hands and used it himself, spraying thick clouds of pepper into the soup with vigorous turns of his enormous, meaty fists. 'That's how you do it!' he said irritably, shoving the pepper mill back at the cook. Off he went along the line to find someone else to shout at.

Everything in the kitchen was on an enormous scale, in keeping with the enormous amounts of food that had to be produced. The kitchen itself, with its butcheries and pantries, was as big as a cathedral, covering the whole area under the Great Kitchen Court, the Tempered Hall and another half a dozen buildings nearby. Soup bubbled in huge cauldrons. Gigantic ovens took dozens of trays for roasting. Pans were vast. The heat was extraordinary, the noise tremendous. In this maze of benches and boilers the High Chef was assisted by six Lesser Chefs who prowled the kitchen to enforce his orders.

Part of the kitchen was devoted to the cooking of special orders. The Halibut gluttons competed with each other in demanding the most exotic dishes they could imagine. The most experienced cooks worked here, and sometimes the High Chef himself pushed them aside, grabbed a pan, thrust it into the flames and went to work on a particularly complicated dish. But not often. Mostly he stomped around the kitchen, pushing and shouting and keeping an eye on everything that went out.

It was the chief job of the High Chef, Thomas Coffier believed, to prevent the hundreds of mistakes that were sure to happen if he wasn't there to watch. In his opinion, the cooks and other kitchen workers were the laziest people in the world, always looking for short cuts and taking naps under the chopping tables if they thought they could get away with it, although in reality they worked twelve hours on a normal day and eighteen when there was a feast, which was at least once a fortnight. That didn't impress Thomas Coffier, who had worked that hard, and even harder, since he was a boy. He loved the kitchen. He loved the fearsome heat, the clattering noise, the steam, the sweat, the flash of knives, the slapping of butter, the sizzling of fat. As far as he was concerned, if anyone didn't love it as much as he did, then they could get out and find themselves something else to do, and he was happy to let them know it. Up and down the kitchen he marched, breakfast, lunch and dinner, looking for laziness, carelessness, sloppiness, spite, sniffing them out and burning them up in the fierce fire of his rage.

Now he came to a halt, staring at a young kitchen hand who was churning a tub of ice cream.

'Stop,' he said and drew a small spoon out of the twenty-two different tasting spoons and forks that he carried in the pockets of his jacket. He put the spoon in the ice cream, then tasted it. 'What flavour is this?' he demanded.

'Strawberry,' replied the kitchen hand.

'Then make it taste of that!' snapped the High Chef. 'It tastes of nothing! Get more strawberries.'

The kitchen hand didn't move. He muttered something. To the High Chef, it sounded very much as if he had muttered, 'Get them yourself.'

The High Chef stared at him in amazement. '*Get more strawberries!*'

'Why should I? I used what the recipe said.'

The cooks nearby, who had heard what the kitchen hand had said, fell silent. Anything even approaching rebellion against the High Chef was unheard of.

'What's your name?' demanded the High Chef.

'Owens,' said the kitchen hand.

'Well, *Mister* Owens, I don't care what the recipe said. I can't taste the strawberries. Can't taste 'em, do you understand?' The High Chef grabbed a box of strawberries. 'Put some more in, before I put *you* in!' he yelled and flung the box at Owens. It hit the kitchen hand and strawberries scattered over the floor.

Now just about everyone in the kitchen was staring. Pots were boiling over, meats were singeing. At the serving station, the servers watched, dumb waiters standing empty behind them and the dishes in their hands going cold.

'*Back to work!*' yelled the High Chef.

There was another instant of silence and then work in the kitchen recommenced.

The High Chef turned back to Owens. 'Pick those

strawberries up and wash them. And next time you answer back to me, I'll have you peeling potatoes with a fork handle. Do you fancy that?'

Owens was silent.

'*Do you?*'

'No, Chef.'

'No. You're lucky I don't do it now. Now make that ice cream so I can *taste* something.'

Owens began to gather up the strawberries. The High Chef stomped off, but Owens saw one of the Lesser Chefs watching him. He washed and trimmed the strawberries, crushed them into a pulp and poured it into the ice cream. When the Lesser Chef turned away, he threw in the stalks as well. He churned the ice cream, silently cursing it and every Halibut who would eat it.

Nearby, standing in front of a chest-high pile of carrots, one of the peelers was watching him.

'What, Carrot Boy?' hissed Owens.

'Nothing.'

'Soon we won't be doing this.'

'Who will?' asked the peeler.

'The Halibuts, that's who! Soon they'll be doing this for us.'

The peeler looked at him disbelievingly.

Owens glanced at the Lesser Chef, who was watching him again, and put in more strawberries. He churned the ice cream. Eventually the Lesser Chef walked off. Owens threw the rest of the stalks in.

'You listen to me,' muttered Owens to the peeler. 'Things are going to change.'

'When?'

'Soon.' He smirked knowingly. 'Just you wait and see.'

Upstairs, the Halibuts ate in the Tempered Hall, unaware of Owens or the High Chef or the noise and heat in the kitchens below them. A hum of conversation filled the air. Now and then someone shrieked with laughter or surprise at something someone else had said. For the past hour, Everfull, Insatia, Everround and a table of other gluttons had been tucking into the delicacies they had ordered, accompanied by plates of roasted meats, buttered vegetables and salty chips. Not far away, Omnia was eating with her friends. Eversmart was whispering something to Evesia, which was making her giggle. Her yellow sunhat bobbed up and down. Then Eversmart noticed a bowl someone was carrying back to another table.

'Ice cream!' he said.

Half the children at the table jumped up.

Evergrow brought a bowl back for Omnia. He tasted his own ice cream as soon as he sat down. He frowned, put his fingers to his lips and pulled out a strawberry stalk. Across the table, Eversmart pulled out a stalk as well. And another. He stuck one in each of his eyebrows, which he obviously thought was funny. Evesia giggled. Artesia glanced at Omnia and rolled her eyes.

'*What in the name of ice cream is this?*' came a bellow from the gluttons' table.

'I think Everfull just found a stalk,' whispered Evergrow.

So did another couple of gluttons. Soon they were deep in discussion about the stalks, and shortly afterwards, they had convinced themselves that they were a special delicacy that had been thought up by the High Chef for their enjoyment, designed to contrast in their woody bitterness with the ice cream's velvety sweetness. They called out to one of the servers to bring them the vat of ice cream, and were soon picking out the stalks and chewing them with expressions of deep delight on their faces.

Omnia found a couple of stalks in her ice cream as well. She didn't think they were much to chew on.

Afterwards Omnia and her friends headed for the Pug's Palace, a round building that was decorated with huge paintings of tiny dogs. Two Halibuts who were both obsessed with woodcarving, Evercut L Halibut and Everchip P Halibut, had decided to hold a competition on its roof that afternoon. On their way, Omnia and her friends passed Evertwitch N Halibut, the House's bird expert. He was sitting high above them in a kind of cage that he had had constructed on the side of the Hatted Belfry, from where he could watch a pair of grey-spotted lesser eddles which had built a nest on the top of the Storied Stack. These were the first grey-spotted lesser eddles he had ever seen, and the first ever recorded in the House, which made some people wonder if he hadn't mistaken a pair of common doves for the elusive birds, as they apparently looked remarkably similar. For the last three weeks, Evertwitch had been there in his cage from before dawn each day until well after dark, and sometimes slept there as well, being supplied with food and water by a servant who climbed a rope ladder that dangled to the ground.

Omnia called out to ask what he had seen today.

'They've got a chick!' his voice came back faintly. 'Either that or it's a mouse they've killed that they've brought back. I can't quite tell.'

'He'll find out if they eat it,' murmured Eversmart and everyone laughed – except Evertwitch, who couldn't hear him from the cage, and probably wouldn't have thought it was very funny even if he could.

By the time they arrived at the Pug's Palace, the roof was crowded with Halibuts who had come to watch the contest, many of whom had brought picnic baskets with afternoon tea. In front of Evercut and Everchip stood two enormous logs, each as tall as the woodcarvers themselves and twice as thick. In keeping with the chosen location, they were going to carve pugs. Chronolia Halibut, one of the most pedantic inhabitants of the House with a collection of over three thousand clocks, watches and metronomes, was over-seeing the event. A pair of servants had carried one of her stopclocks up to the roof, a huge, green clock with a face a metre wide, and had set it up on a table beside the logs. The cutters picked up their axes. Chronolia asked if each of them was ready. They were. She hit a button on the top of the clock.

The two cutters hacked into the logs. Chips flew. Soon the assembled Halibuts began to chatter among themselves, pouring cups of tea and handing out scones and jam. After a while, most of them seemed to have forgotten about the two cutters who were straining, sweating, chipping at the logs with all their might.

Evercut broke a blade and had to stop to find another. Everchip grinned in delight and kept going.

It took over an hour for the first pug to be finished. An hour, twenty-three minutes and thirty-three seconds, according to Chronolia. But it was actually quite interesting to see the pugs taking shape, and there were plenty of scones. At last, Everchip finished and then threw down his tools, collapsing in exhaustion. His pug was a short-eared, big-bellied creature with a long tail. Evercut's was a long-eared, skinny thing with short legs – or so it seemed, because it wasn't completed. Evercut collapsed as well and didn't look as if he had the heart to finish it now that he had lost.

On her way back to her family's apartment after the competition, Omnia passed the House of Arches. The two artists, Evermay and Everset, worked together in a studio on the top floor. While Evermay painted vast, sweeping canvases showing scenes from the House, Everset carved tiny sculptures that took months to complete and which you could see only under a microscope. Everset's sculptures were about as far from the big pugs that Evercut and Everchip had produced as a sculpture could be. Omnia went through the huge, arch-shaped doorway and climbed the eight flights of stairs to the studio at the top.

Evermay and Everset were chattering to each other as usual. The two artists hardly ever stopped, arguing and making up and arguing again. Evermay stood at an enormous canvas that must have been two metres high and ten metres long, wearing a paint-splattered smock and a purple cravat, while Everset sat at his desk in an elegant green suit, one of his tiny carvings under the microscope in front of him.

Evermay turned when he heard Omnia come in behind him. 'Well, Omnia,' he said, waving his paintbrush at the canvas. 'What do you think? I call it: *Death on Flip Day.*'

'I'm not sure about the name,' said Everset, not taking his eyes off the microscope.

'But that's what it shows!'

'Hardly. I think you've overstated it, Evermay, if you'll allow me to say so.'

'You can say what you like,' muttered the painter. 'Doesn't mean I'm going to listen to you.'

Everset looked up at him. 'That's not very nice, Evermay.'

'Well, you've irritated me, Everset. I'm sorry, but you have.'

'Unintentionally.'

'Maybe so.'

'I'm just saying—'

'I know what you're saying. You've said it already. It's ridiculous, if you'll allow me to say so.'

'Suit yourself,' muttered Everset. He glanced at Omnia. 'If he's going to call it something like that, at least he should call it *A Mysterious Death on Flip Day*, don't you think?'

'It's not mysterious!' retorted Evermay. 'It's just a death. If every death at a feast was a mystery, we'd be up to our necks in them.'

Everset shrugged, a shrug that left his hands perfectly still under his microscope.

'You and your *Mysterious*! Everything's got to have a mystery in the title.'

'I'm only trying to help,' replied Everset.

'I don't recall asking you to.'

Omnia coughed. 'I only came to say hello.'

'Indeed you did,' said Evermay. He waved his paintbrush at the canvas again. 'So what do you think, Omnia? Is it a masterpiece?'

Omnia looked. The painting was a riot of colour. Along the canvas Evermay had painted the Flip Day tables, laden with food. In the background was the Narrow Range. At the table, all over the Terrace, on the roof of the Range, people were eating, all in masks. It was an extraordinary painting, bursting with energy. If anything, thought Omnia, it was full of life, not death.

'You see,' said Everset, watching Omnia's face. 'She can't see it.'

'Of course she can!' exclaimed the painter. He pointed with his brush. 'See, Omnia? Do you see it?'

Omnia peered closer. Amongst the hundreds of figures in the painting, sat one slumped forward in his chair, his face in a bowl.

'The whole point,' said Evermay, throwing a glance at Everset, 'is that you have to look for the death. That's the whole trick in the title.'

Everset shrugged. He didn't think much of titles with tricks. He much preferred a title with *mystery* in it to give a sense of suspense.

Omnia walked along the painting, gazing at it. It really was an exceptional painting. Everywhere you looked, there was something to see. She searched for herself on the roof of the Narrow Range. But the figures there were very small, as if seen from far away. When you looked closer, you could see that Evermay had skilfully managed to create the impression of faces here with mere smudges of colour.

In the foreground of the painting, the figures were larger and the masks were well defined. Some figures faced the table or were at an angle. Omnia saw a pelican, a goblin, a toucan, a rabbit. One figure looked directly at her out of the canvas.

Omnia stared.

'What is it?' asked Evermay.

Omnia pointed. It was the figure of someone in the mask of a grey panther. Evermay had shown the panther staring at the viewer with gleaming fangs in a kind of twisted grin and with a burning look in its eyes. It was the largest single figure in the painting.

'I remember someone in a panther mask,' said Evermay.

Omnia stepped back. Once you had noticed the figure, you couldn't ignore it. It seemed to her now that the panther-man dominated the entire picture.

'Why did you paint him there?' she asked. 'Right at the front. And so big. And looking like that.'

'I don't know. I just did. It seemed right.'

'An artist doesn't *know*,' murmured Everset, who had gone back to his microscopic carving. 'An artist *does*.'

'And what about the shadows?' asked Omnia.

'What shadows?' said Evermay.

'The shadows. Look at them. The shadows.'

Evermay looked. His eyes widened, as if he had no idea what he had done. The panther-man's head threw a long shadow across the canvas, and the two pointed tips of the panther's ears elongated them even further.

In the exact centre of the gap between the shadows of the panther ears, as if they were framing it, sat the slumped body of the dead UnderButler.

The painter glanced at Everset. Carefully, the sculptor moved his hands from under his microscope and stood up. He came out from behind his desk and stared at the painting.

'Omnia's right,' he said. 'You've painted shadows, Evermay. Look at them.'

Evermay didn't reply.

Omnia remembered the picture Evermay had produced three months earlier, which he called *Expedition to the Top*

49

of the Great Tower to Snare the Black Condor. There had never been a black condor to snare, but Evermay had painted it anyway, and from its wings had extended two dark shadows over the background of Neversuch House. The shadows in that painting were a sign, he had said, and the painting didn't lie.

The panther face in the painting and the shadows of its ears framing the figure of the dead UnderButler sent a shiver down Omnia's spine.

From the look on Evermay's face, the realisation of what he had painted sent a shiver down his spine as well.

'Why did you do it?' asked Omnia 'Why did you paint the shadows like that?'.

'I don't know,' said Evermay, shaking his head. 'I really don't.'

'An artist doesn't know,' said Everset again, still gazing at it. 'An artist does.'

The painting brought back all of Omnia's doubts about Dish's death. The next day, she mentioned it to Evergrow. He said she was being too suspicious. It was just a painting, after all. Evermay could have chosen to show a red herring, or a white fly, or any of the other hundreds of characters that were on the Terrace that day. He happened to choose a grey panther. He had painted a few shadows. So what? Surely she didn't believe that Evermay – or anyone else, for that matter – had some kind of special knowledge that only came out when he painted something without being consciously aware of it?

No, Omnia didn't believe that. She really was being too suspicious about Dish's death, she told herself. In fact, she told that to herself so often she almost persuaded herself that it was true.

For about a week.

7

In the Shadow of the Faunal House

Eversnip T Halibut was a long-legged, spidery man who spent his time studying books on clothing and making old-fashioned clothes out of velvet and silk. He wore them on his daily walks, with matching silk cravats and leather gloves in a variety of colours. One of his regular walks took him along the side of the Faunal House, and there, early one morning in the week after Flip Day, wearing a suit of moss-coloured velvet, a blue silk cravat, purple boots and yellow gloves, was where he saw the fallen statue.

It was far from the first time that such a thing had happened and Eversnip wasn't particularly surprised. The roof of the Faunal House was lined with statues of animals – some real, some imaginary – that had been put up by the masons in the days when Neversuch House was built, and there were a number of gaps in the line where a figure had fallen and smashed on the stones of the narrow passage below. Others leaned at various angles – some forwards, some backwards, some to the left, some to the right – as if waiting their turn to topple over. According to the Chief Mason, Albert Gondolier, the tendency of the statues to plummet was because of a defect in the mortar that held the bricks of the wall below the roof. As far as he and generations of Chief Masons before him could tell, it was unlike any other mortar that had been used elsewhere in the building of Neversuch House. It had possibly been an experiment by the First Captain's masons, but if it was an experiment, it hadn't been a successful one, which would account for the fact that it hadn't been repeated elsewhere. Over time, the mortar had weakened so much that bricks occasionally loosened, eroding the support under the statues. Had the mortar experiment been performed at the bottom of the building, rather than the top, the whole thing would have collapsed long before.

Over the years, various attempts to repair the damage had taken place, none entirely successful. Albert Gondolier had even suggested removing the top storey of the Faunal House, along with its rooftop statues, and either rebuilding it or leaving it off for good. But Halibuts, being Halibuts, had grown fond of the gap-toothed, leaning line of statues at the top of the Faunal House and opposed the Chief Mason's suggestion. After all, no one was obliged to use the narrow passage that ran along the Faunal House, separating it from the Midges Mansion. There were ways to avoid it. And if you did use the passage, all you had to do was hug the wall of the Midges Mansion and you would probably be safe. Halibuts who enjoyed the thrill of a moment of danger, or Halibut children daring each other to run the gauntlet of the Faunal House, would scuttle hurriedly down the passage, one shoulder brushing the wall of the Midges Mansion, eyes turned up to the leaning line of animals that stood ready to fall above them. Others took a detour to avoid the place altogether. Eversnip Halibut, who wasn't otherwise a notably brave man, prided himself on walking the length of the Faunal House in one of his fine, newly made, old-fashioned suits every second morning – but never in the evening, for some superstitious reason – and never breaking into a run.

That morning, Eversnip spotted the pile of shattered stone on the ground as soon as he entered the passage. Eversnip knew each of the animals on the roof and even had his own private names for them, and he immediately realised which one had fallen as soon as he looked up and saw a new gap in the line. Rufus Gladbarker, as he called it – a gigantic statue of a chihuahua dog that had been leaning forward at a precarious angle for years – was gone.

He walked carefully down the passage, staying close to the wall of the Midges Mansion. Just because one statue had fallen it didn't mean another couldn't fall as well. Finally he came to the pile of rock.

A pair of legs poked out from under the rubble.

Eversnip stared at them. He nudged one of the legs cautiously with his boot.

Nothing. Not a twitch.

Eversnip took off his yellow gloves. Bending his long, spidery legs, and trying to keep the sleeve of his moss-coloured velvet jacket – which he had finished making only the previous evening – clear of the rock, Eversnip rolled away a piece of Rufus Gladbarker. Now he could see the bottom of a prune-coloured cloak. He pulled back another couple of pieces. He could see a head.

Cautiously, bending his long hand at the wrist to keep the cuff of his jacket clean, Eversnip T Halibut turned the head of the man lying beneath him and found himself staring into the lifeless features of the UnderButler Harold Withers.

Eldred Sturgeon didn't bother pinching Withers's arm to see that he was dead. The body was so crushed that there was no doubt. After it had been taken away, Albert Gondolier arrived with half a dozen other masons to investigate the roof. They climbed to the top of the Faunal House and examined the area from which the chihuahua had fallen, or at least the area very close to it, because there was no telling whether that part of the roof would give way entirely if they stepped on to it. An accident pronounced Albert Gondolier after an hour or so of investigation, and not even a freakish accident, since he had been warning for years that the statues would continue to fall, and if one of them had, that was only to be expected. At best, it was an unfortunate accident, and he filled out a form to that effect and gave it to one of the junior masons, who took it to Digby, the Butler, who gave it to Trimbleby, the only remaining UnderButler, who gave it to the Master Filer, who gave it to one of the clerks in the Butlery, who filed it away under 'Unfortunate Accidents' in one of the dusty boxes in one of the dusty rooms where the bills, invoices, receipts and reports of Neversuch House had been filed for over two hundred years. And that, as far as Albert Gondolier was concerned, was that. And that, for just about everyone else, was that as well.

But not for Omnia. The moment she heard the news, a shiver ran down her spine. The drowning of Dish in a bowl of lamb cutlets at a feast might just about count as a natural death, but there was nothing natural about being crushed to death by a falling chihuahua. It was an accident, as the Chief Mason said. Another accident? Like the one in which Everwise B Halibut, the old Captain of the House, had died? Like the one in which Digby, the old Butler, had met his end? Like the one in the Hall of Leaning in which she herself might have been killed three months earlier if she hadn't happened to move at just the right moment to avoid a falling tile? She had looked up then and seen a shadow move across the hole in the roof. It was only a week later, at the top of the Great Tower, with the wind howling in her ears, that she had seen the face of the man who had caused that shadow, the face of Tobias Hildegrew, who had been behind that 'accident' and all the others.

Had Withers looked up, she wondered, and seen the

stone chihuahua hurtling down at him? Had he glimpsed, for an instant, when it was too late, the face of a person on the roof who had pushed it?

But it could have been an accident, couldn't it? It *could*, but Omnia knew what Basilica would say. 'An accident, Omnia? Surely you're not foolish enough to believe that.'

She thought of the panther in Evermay's painting of the Flip Day feast. Was the person in that mask – whoever it was – connected with this? Had Dish been murdered, and was the panther the one who had killed him? And had he now killed Withers as well?

But apart from Omnia, everyone in the House seemed to want nothing so much as to forget about the death of Withers, who was quickly buried. The incident did create some interest among the Halibuts – not because an UnderButler had been killed, but because another statue had fallen. Did this mean the passage was now safer, because there was one less statue to fall? Or did it mean it was more dangerous, because it showed that the crumbling of the mortar under the remaining statues had accelerated? Much discussion and argument took place. Naturally, there was no agreement. As for the UnderButler, losing one was unfortunate said Evertell G Halibut, but losing two was beginning to look like carelessness. Evertell was the House's chief writer of plays and he got all his clever lines from other writers without admitting it. For his part, Everhale U Halibut, who liked to turn up to the Hall of Leaning and tell jokes to the assembled children, immediately remarked that this was the first time he had ever heard of a person being crushed by a chihuahua – which was just about as funny as most of the jokes he told.

Yet they couldn't ignore it, thought Omnia. Or simply tell jokes about it. Not if this death, and that of Dish, weren't accidental. Not if the murders had begun again.

She needed to see Basilica, who was the only one who had tried to make any kind of sense out of the things that had happened three months before. Omnia had had no luck in finding her and she knew that Trimbleby, the last remaining UnderButler, would never tell her where Basilica was. But the Butler probably knew as well, and he was a different type of person. There was something softer, almost gentle about him. If she could find the Butler when he was by himself, she thought, when he was out of sight of Trimbleby, he might tell her. He was her only chance.

The next morning, Omnia headed for the Butlery in the Bright Tower. As she hurried along one side of the Lofters Court, she thought she glimpsed the polisher, the one who seemed so often to be following her, moving behind the columns under the Studded Loft. But when she looked again, no one was there.

'You don't need to follow me!' she called across the Court. Her voice echoed off the stone walls of the lofts surrounding it. 'I'll save you the trouble and tell you where I'm going. To your masters! To the Bright Tower!'

8

Right Place – Wrong Person

The two men behind the high desk looked down at her.

'Yes?' said one of them.

'I'm Omnia Halibut.'

'And?' replied the man.

'I need to see the Butler.'

The two men glanced at one another. Both of them wore the walnut-coloured coats of Butlery clerks. One of them had a thick moustache and mutton chop whiskers and the other didn't, and aside from that, there was very little to tell them apart. They were the Clerks of the Entrance and they sat at the high desk all day in the anteroom to the Butlery, quizzing anyone who arrived about their purpose, deciding what to do with them and keeping a record of every case in two huge ledgers that lay open on the desk in front of them.

'I said I need to see the Butler,' said Omnia.

'We heard,' replied the clerk with the whiskers. His name was Fellowes. 'We're not deaf. Is that what you're trying to say, young lady? That we're deaf?'

'No, that's not what I'm trying to say.'

'I should hope not!'

The other clerk, whose name was Childes, nodded sternly and began to write in his ledger.

'If you're not deaf,' said Omnia, 'you'll have heard what I said.'

'Which was . . . ?'

'I need to see the Butler.'

'Oh, that,' said Fellowes. 'I heard it. I just couldn't believe it.'

Childes shook his head, writing steadily. 'Halibut children turning up to see the Butler? Wasn't there another one a couple of months ago, Mr Fellowes?'

'Indeed there was, Mr Childes. Name of Evergrow. Evergrow D Halibut, if I'm not mistook.'

'You're not mistook. They're making a habit of it, Mr Fellowes.'

'An unpleasant habit, Mr Childes.'

'Not to be encouraged, Mr Fellowes.'

'Who knows what they'll think of next, Mr Childes?'

'I need to see the Butler,' repeated Omnia through gritted teeth. 'You can either take me to him or I'll find him myself.'

Both the clerks looked at her.

'Will you just?' demanded Fellowes.

'Yes, I will.'

He stood up, hands on his hips, his face red with anger. 'Will you *just*?'

'Yes, I *will*.'

'Go on then,' growled Fellowes. He flicked a finger in the direction of one of the doors that led from the room. 'Find him if you can.'

Childes smirked. 'The last Halibut who went in there by himself didn't find his way out for a month.'

'Don't exaggerate, Mr Childes. Three weeks.'

'Went mad.'

'That's true.'

'I'll take my chance,' said Omnia, and headed for the door.

'Stop!' roared Fellowes as Omnia grasped the handle. He pointed to a chair beside the entrance to the room. 'Sit.'

Omnia looked around. A row of empty chairs stood by the entrance. Sitting on one of them was a young clerk with a freckled face and blond hair, wearing a short, walnut-coloured coat. He gave her a friendly smile and then shrugged slightly, as if to say that he knew all of this was ridiculous, but there was nothing he could do about it.

Omnia knew what was coming next. Evergrow had told her what had happened to him when he had come to the Bright Tower two months previously. She would be ordered to wait while one of the clerks went off for a couple of hours and the other wrote up her 'case' in one of the big books on the desk, hinting that the more she said the more complex her 'case' would become. Omnia had no intention of sitting through anything like that.

She turned back to the door, pulled on the handle and went through.

Childes, who had started writing again, jumped up. Fellowes, who was already on his feet, stared for a moment in astonishment. Then he went through the clerks' door behind the desk, slamming it behind him.

He came storming at Omnia around a corner.

'What do you think you're *doing*?' he demanded.

'I told you, I need to see the Butler.'

'What if he doesn't want to see you?'

'He will.'

'How do you know?'

'How do you know he won't?'

'Go back in there,' said the Clerk, nodding towards the door. 'Go *back in there* and wait as you're told and I'll go and see if he'll see you.'

'I'll come with you.'

'You'll wait!'

'I'll come!'

Fellowes frowned, fingering his whiskers and trying to decide what to do. If he grabbed this troublesome child and took her back to the entrance, what would she do then? She was obviously capable of anything. As soon as he left her to go to the Butler, she'd probably run through the door again and since the entrance could never be left unattended, Childes wouldn't be able to go after her and Omnia would be running loose in the Bright Tower. That was the last thing he wanted – the last thing anyone in the Butlery wanted. As a Clerk of the Entrance, the most important part of his job was to make sure that no one from outside the Bright Tower was able to run loose inside it, most of all a Halibut.

As for the other clerk who was sitting beside the door at the entrance, he was a very junior messenger clerk, very junior indeed, and Fellowes wouldn't trust him with a matter for the Butler's consideration. Short of tying Omnia up or locking her in a room somewhere – neither of which would necessarily be approved of by the Butler, who seemed to have an alarmingly lenient attitude to people in general, and almost distressingly lenient towards the Halibuts – the safest course of action was to take her with him.

'All right,' said Fellowes at last, 'I'll take you to the Butler, but you'll wait outside his door until I've spoken to him.'

Omnia smiled pleasantly. *That's what you say*, she thought.

Fellowes led her down the corridor. Soon they began to pass doorway after doorway and room after room where clerks were at work behind desks overflowing with papers and files, with shelfloads of more papers and files on the walls around them. Fellowes led her up stairs, around corners, down stairs and around yet more corners, and still the rooms with the clerks and the files and the papers kept coming. Omnia had no idea how so many corridors could fit in the Bright Tower and after a while, she thought she recognised some of the rooms and wondered whether Fellowes was leading her along the same corridors twice. But the rooms and the clerks generally looked so much alike that it was possible she only imagined that she recognised them. Finally Fellowes stopped in front of a red door. He knocked twice and waited, keeping his eye suspiciously on Omnia.

After a few seconds, he opened the door a fraction. 'Wait here,' he hissed and went inside, closing the door behind him.

Omnia waited – for about three seconds – and followed him in.

Fellowes, who was in the middle of saying something, turned to her in rage. Omnia ignored him. On the walls of the room were paintings of a series of small men with brown eyes, all shown sitting in this very room wearing green Butler's coats. Metal safes and big chests of drawers with padlocks stood on the floor below the paintings and in the middle of the room was an enormous desk covered in a jumble of in-trays and out-trays piled high with files, with an ancient chair in purple leather behind it.

It was obviously the Butler's room. A man was sitting behind the Butler's desk. But it wasn't the Butler. He wore a prune-coloured coat and had a huge pickle of a nose. It was the one remaining UnderButler, Horace Trimbleby.

'I told you to wait outside!' roared the Clerk. He clenched his hands as if it took all his willpower to keep himself from physically lifting Omnia up and hurling her against the wall.

'Mr Fellowes,' said Trimbleby from behind the desk, 'it's all right, I'll deal with this now.'

'But I *told* her—'

'I'm sure you did. She's not necessarily the easiest person to tell things to.'

Fellowes continued to stare at her, his anger almost beyond control.

'Mr Fellowes, you can go.'

Fellowes glared at Omnia a moment longer. Then he straightened himself up, threw back his head, cleared his throat, ran his fingers through his whiskers, smoothed the lapels of his walnut-coloured coat – which had become somewhat rumpled in the excitement – brushed past Omnia as if she wasn't there and left, closing the door loudly behind him.

There was silence.

Omnia took a few steps into the room. 'What are you doing here?' she said.

Trimbleby raised an eyebrow. 'What do you mean?'

'Where's the Butler? Why are you sitting in his chair?'

Trimbleby didn't reply.

Omnia looked at him suspiciously. 'Where is he?'

'Where do you think?'

That was exactly what Omnia was trying to work out. Was Digby dead as well? Was that why Trimbleby was sitting in his chair? If so, how had it happened and why had no one been told? And who would be the next Butler? Digby had only one child, who was three years old. A child of three could hardly be expected to buttle.

Trimbleby stood up. Omnia jumped. Suddenly everything fell into place. It was Trimbleby! He had killed Dish, he had killed Withers and now he had killed Digby and taken his place, all in the hope of becoming Butler himself.

'Stay away from me!' Omnia stepped back to the door. 'You'll never get away with it.'

'With what?'

'The Butler's a Digby. Always has been, always must be. The House will never accept it.'

'What?'

'You!'

'Me?' Trimbleby came out from behind the desk.

'Stay away!'

Trimbleby started to laugh. 'Do you think . . . Me . . . ?' Trimbleby could hardly get the words out through his laughter.

Still Omnia watched him, ready to turn and run. The UnderButler could laugh all he liked. That was no proof of innocence.

'Mr Digby is perfectly well,' said Trimbleby.

'How do I know?' demanded Omnia.

'You'll have to take my word for it.'

'Where's the proof?'

The smile went from Trimbleby's face. 'My word, I told you. That's all the proof you're getting.'

'Where is he?'

'Somewhere safe. With the Captain. They're in a place where they'll both be safe.'

'Where?' demanded Omnia.

'Somewhere. You don't need to know.'

'I want to know!'

Trimbleby shrugged. 'Think about it, Omnia. If I'd done something to Mr Digby, I'd have done it to you as well by now, wouldn't I? I wouldn't leave you running free, not knowing what you know.' He paused and came closer. 'Now, why have you come here? You can't see the Butler, so you'll either tell me or you'll tell nobody. It's your choice.'

Omnia considered for a moment. She came cautiously back into the room, still keeping her eye on Trimbleby, and sat on a chair in front of the Butler's desk. She thought about what the UnderButler had just told her. The Captain and the Butler had both been put in a place where they would be safe, he had said. That meant they thought they were under threat.

'You think Dish and Withers were murdered, don't you?'

Trimbleby didn't reply.

'You must think so, otherwise why put the Captain and the Butler somewhere safe?'

'Let's just say we're taking precautions.'

'I think they were murdered,' said Omnia.

'I wouldn't say you're wrong.'

'Why? Why would someone want to kill Withers and Dish?'

Trimbleby was silent. He leaned on the desk, watching her.

'I want to talk to Basilica.'

67

The UnderButler shook his head, as if there was something pathetic about Omnia's demand. 'Still on about Basilica? I told you three months ago—'

'I want to talk to her.'

'There's no such person. She's dead. I told you, and so did Withers, and so did Dish.'

'Well, they're dead, aren't they?'

'That doesn't mean Basilica's not.'

'Evegrow saw her too.'

'Did he just? You didn't tell us that before.'

Omnia shrugged.

'How can I believe anything you say, Omnia, if you don't tell us things like that? You mustn't tell lies, you know.'

Omnia almost laughed. No one in the House told bigger lies than Trimbleby.

'If Evergrow saw her,' said the UnderButler, 'then what he saw was a ghost, just like you did.'

'That's not true.'

'Isn't it? Where's your proof?'

'You'll have to take my word for it, won't you?' retorted Omnia.

'No,' said Trimbleby. 'I don't have to take anything from you.'

'No? Why did you bar the door then?'

Trimbleby stared, not understanding.

'The door to the Slate Tower. Why did you have it barred? If there was no one there but a ghost, why did you bother?'

68

The UnderButler hesitated. 'To stop people climbing up and falling from the top,' he said eventually. 'It's a dangerous place. We were worried someone might go to the top and jump.'

'Why would they do that?'

'Because they might think they could survive.' He looked at her intently. 'But they wouldn't. Do you understand me, Omnia? They wouldn't, I can guarantee you. So if you're thinking about it, don't try.'

Omnia's eyes went wide. 'She's moved, hasn't she?'

'Basilica? She's a ghost. Who knows what a ghost will do?'

'Where has she gone?'

Trimbleby didn't reply.

'*Where?*'

'Get up,' said Trimbleby. 'I've had enough of this. I'm taking you back to the entrance.'

Omnia stayed seated. She watched him thoughtfully. 'You're next, aren't you?'

Trimbleby's eyes narrowed.

'Of course you are. Dish is dead. Now Withers. If you didn't kill them, someone else did. And if someone else killed them, you're next on the list. One UnderButler, two UnderButlers . . . three.'

Trimbleby didn't reply. Omnia watched him. Trimbleby was the loudest, most overbearing of the UnderButlers and had been the most threatening to her after Tobias Hildegrew escaped. Yet now she almost felt sorry for him.

'Nothing will happen to me,' he said. 'I'm taking precautions. In the meantime, Mr Digby and Everdean are out of harm's way.'

'Was Withers taking precautions?'

'We weren't sure what was happening. Dish's death could have been an accident.'

'So Withers wasn't taking precautions?'

'Some.'

'Not enough.'

'Apparently not,' said Trimbleby. 'I'm taking more.'

There was silence.

'It's the Evergones, isn't it?'

The UnderButler didn't reply.

'Isn't it?'

'I can't tell you about that. Don't ask.'

'They've got someone else here, haven't they? Just like they had Tobias. Now it's someone else.'

'There's no one else like Tobias Hildegrew,' said the UnderButler. 'He was one of a kind – the most dangerous one I've ever seen. If they do have someone here, just be glad it's not him.'

'This one doesn't seem to have done too badly.'

Trimbleby smiled slightly. 'He had surprise on his side. He doesn't have that any more. Let's see what he can do now.'

'There might be more than one.'

'Let them try. I've got eight UnderUnderButlers to protect me.'

'And you trust them, do you?'

'I do. In the meantime, Digby and Everdean are safe. Whoever it is doing this, they made a mistake killing Dish. They made another killing Withers. In the end, they'll have to try to get the Captain and the Butler, and all they've succeeded in doing is giving us warning. Now the Captain and Butler are safe and we can wait. Time's on our side. The longer it goes on, the greater the chance they'll do something to reveal themselves. They always do. That's why we've always won.'

'What if they get you?' asked Omnia.

'They won't.'

'What if they do?'

'Then Mr Digby will decide what to do next.'

'Where is he?'

'I told you,' said Trimbleby. 'He's safe. So is Everdean. There's a place that's always ready when a Captain and a Butler need protection.'

A place that was always ready for the Captain and Butler's protection? Omnia had never heard about it. 'I don't believe you. Why didn't they go there last time?'

'After the old Butler was killed, Hildegrew persuaded the new Butler he didn't need to. Young Mr Digby trusted him, remember?'

Omnia frowned. Her suspicions returned. It all sounded too easy. Trimbleby had an answer for everything.

Suddenly Omnia stared at him. 'It's not in the House, is it? That's what you're saying. They've left! They've left the House!'

'I didn't say that.'

'Then where are they?'

'I'm not saying. It's a secret place. No one knows about it.'

'*You* do.'

'Of course I do. UnderButlers know.'

'Then what if whoever's doing this gets you like Withers and Dish?' demanded Omnia. 'Who'll tell the Butler?'

'There's someone else who knows as well.'

'Who?'

'It doesn't concern you,' said Trimbleby. 'Last time you got involved by mistake. Be thankful you're not involved in it this time round.'

'Then you can stop having me followed, can't you?'

'I haven't told anyone to follow you.'

'Of course you haven't,' said Omnia sarcastically. 'None of the polishers, for instance? Well, you can tell her to stop.'

'Omnia, honestly, I don't know what you're talking about.'

Omnia rolled her eyes. She wished, just once, that the UnderButler could be honest with her. 'All right. Whatever. Mr Trimbleby, they might get you. If they do, who else knows where Mr Digby and Everdean are? Who can take me to them?'

Trimbleby was silent.

'Please, Mr Trimbleby. If you're gone, who can tell me where to find them?'

'You know, you remind me of Basilica,' said Trimbleby softly. 'What happened to her . . . it was never what I wanted.'

'Where is she? She's not in the Slate Tower any more, is she? Tell me! Where is she?'

The UnderButler gazed at Omnia thoughtfully. 'The Master Filer,' he said at last.

'What? Who's that?'

'If I'm gone and you need to find Digby and Everdean, come back and ask to talk to the Master Filer. Apart from me, he's the only other person who can tell you how to find them.'

Trimbleby took Omnia back to the entrance. Behind the desk, Fellowes and Childes were writing in their ledgers. They barely looked up to acknowledge her. The junior clerk, who was still sitting there, caught her eye and smiled as she left.

Omnia walked slowly away from the Bright Tower. Who was it who had killed Withers and Dish? She stopped and watched a servant walking past her, heading for the Bright Tower. Could it be *him*? She saw another pair of servants. What about *them*? She thought of all the other servants in Neversuch House. How many were there? And it would take only one, one like Tobias Hildegrew, clever and brutal and quick.

But why kill the UnderButlers, one after the other? What was the point of doing that?

Suddenly she had second thoughts. *Could* it be Trimbleby after all? He had seemed very confident about his own safety. Maybe Everdean and Digby weren't under protection. Maybe they were dead already, like the two UnderButlers.

Or maybe their so-called place of safety that no one knew about – no one apart from the so-called Master Filer, who might not even exist as far as Omnia was aware – maybe this place was some kind of dungeon, and the Captain and the Butler would be dead just as soon as Trimbleby decided that the time had come to be rid of them.

At least she had let Trimbleby think she believed him. That bought her some time. If it was Trimbleby who had locked the Butler and the Captain away – or worse – he wouldn't be able to keep it secret for more than a week. People didn't know that the Captain and the Butler were missing because they had no reason to see them, but in a week it would be Rinque Day, and everyone would expect the Captain and the Butler to attend. If they were absent then, Trimbleby wouldn't be able to keep it quiet.

In the meantime, she was no closer to finding Basilica than she had been when she went into the Bright Tower. The UnderButler knew where Basilica was, Omnia was sure of that, and it wasn't in the Slate Tower, but Omnia didn't know how she could make him tell. The Butler would know, but Trimbleby wouldn't tell her where *he* was either.

Who else could help her?

She felt the stone that she always carried in her pocket. Running her fingers over its smooth surface, she could just detect the lines of the star that was cut into one side of it. If there really was a place that was kept ready for the Captain and the Butler when they needed protection, perhaps Cornelius knew something about it. As a messenger, he went to all kinds of places and must hear all manner of things.

Omnia headed quickly for the Captain's Keep. When she got there, she went straight to the hole behind the vine that Cornelius had shown her. She paused to look around. There was no one to be seen. Omnia took Cornelius's stone out of her pocket and put it into the hole and then walked rapidly away, wondering how she would fill the time until five o'clock, when she would meet Cornelius at the Granite Arch.

But so preoccupied had Omnia been with her thoughts that not once on the way from the Bright Tower to the Keep, before pausing to take the stone out of her pocket, had she stopped to glance behind her.

9

Surprise!

The Granite Arch was a gleaming black construction that rose four storeys in height, standing at the end of a courtyard between the Winter House on one side and the Summer Lodge on the other. The two buildings and the Arch itself were follies that had been built by the First Captain, structures conceived purely for the sake of amusement. The Winter House was stark, grey and bare, whereas the Summer Lodge was a bright feast of colours. A covered walkway ran along the top of the Arch connecting the two. At the foot of each end of the Arch was a door with a stairway to the top, and Halibuts sometimes joked that if you went up the Arch, you could walk from summer to winter without having to bother with autumn in between – or if you went in the other direction, you could skip spring. Yet very few Halibuts ever went to the trouble of doing it. As follies, the Winter House and Summer Lodge were amongst the First Captain's least popular. Omnia herself had never been into either of the buildings, nor had any of her friends.

Altogether it was an area of the House where hardly anyone ever came, which was exactly why Cornelius Slinker had chosen it as their meeting place.

At five o'clock, Omnia came up the stairs that led into the court. She stopped and looked around for Cornelius. She had met him here before and knew that you could miss him when you first looked, because he was always dressed in black which blended in with the granite of the Arch.

The Arch was directly opposite her at the other end of the court. On one side was the bare, grey wall of the Winter House; on the other side was the wall of the Summer Lodge, a mosaic of shimmering greens like a thicket of luxuriant foliage, studded with porcelain blossoms in white and red and yellow. Along the wall of the Summer Lodge ran a covered porch, and on the roof of the porch clustered thick grapevines carved in purple and green stone that tumbled down the gleaming marble columns supporting it.

'Cornelius?' called Omnia.

Her voice echoed.

Once before Cornelius had failed to appear, caught on an errand and unable to get back by five o'clock. He had met her that evening outside the door of the Long South Range and explained.

Omnia called his name again, still standing at the top of the steps. The echo of Cornelius's name rang around the court.

And perhaps at this point, if you stop to think about it, you might reach the conclusion that Omnia should turn around and leave, because apart from the one time Cornelius was unable to come, he has never been late, so if he isn't there, he has almost certainly been delayed and will find her later as he did before. What does she have to gain by going further into the court and calling his name a third time? Nothing, you might say – and I would agree. But sometimes curiosity takes over from logic. It happens to us all and Omnia is no exception. We can't stop her. All we can do is watch as she goes further towards the Granite Arch and whatever might be waiting for her there.

'Cornelius?'

Her voice echoed again. Omnia was about halfway into the court by now.

She looked up at the Arch. There was no sign of anyone on the walkway at the top. She looked carefully round the court. Out of the corner of her eye, behind one of the grape-clustered columns of the Summer Lodge, she glimpsed something move.

Omnia ran her eye along the columns.

'Cornelius?'

Silence.

Perhaps she had only imagined someone was there. Or perhaps it was some kind of an animal, a cat, perhaps, that had moved and had caught her eye. Or perhaps . . .

The panther! From Evermay's picture! It stood between two pillars under the porch of the Summer Lodge – its grey

78

head, black clothes – as if it had come to life off the canvas in the painter's studio.

For a moment, they stared at one another. Then Omnia turned and ran, not even aware of the scream that was coming out of her mouth. She raced for the first door she could see, the one at the foot of the Arch beside the Winter House, and leaped on to the stairs, one flight after another, until she came out on to the covered walkway at the top. At that same instant, the panther-man appeared from the stairs at the other end of the walkway. Omnia ran into the Winter House and down a corridor. She could hear footsteps chasing her. She saw a door and opened it. For an instant, she stopped, dazed. Whiteness. Dazzling. A huge space. Walkways and staircases ran everywhere, like an exploding star, shooting off into space and interlinking and connecting with each other, all gleaming white. She ran up a set of stairs in front of her, then down, then around, trying to get as far from the door as she could. Behind her, the panther-man was already on the staircases as well. She glanced back and saw him trying to find a route that would intercept her. She turned on to a staircase that would take her away from him. He leaped on to another staircase that would bring him closer. Up and down the stairways they ran. Again she looked back. He had stopped. Omnia stopped as well, panting. He was looking around, his grey panther's head slowly turning, fangs gleaming in the light reflected from the whiteness all around, as he tried to calculate how to get to her. Perhaps twenty metres separated them across space, perhaps double that distance by the staircases and walkways between them.

'Why are you doing this?' Omnia cried.

The panther's head turned to her.

The terror she felt was like the terror she remembered when Tobias Hildegrew had thrown her from the top of the Slate Tower, the terror she had relived in nightmares for weeks afterwards. It was strong, like a taste of metal in her mouth.

'Cornelius? Is that you? What are you *doing?*'

There was no reply.

It was the panther's mask, as much as anything, that terrified her, the animal face concealing the face of the person inside. And the silence. His refusal to answer her, to speak, as if whoever it was under there had been turned into some kind of machine, perhaps not a person at all under that mask, but a dreadful mechanical device that wouldn't stop until it had chased and caught her.

'Take off the mask! *Take it off!*'

The panther gazed at her for another moment, then began looking around again. Omnia looked around as well. For the first time, she noticed that some of the staircases ran to the edge of the space and ended in doors like the one through which she had come. Upwards and to her left, intersecting the staircase she was standing on, was one of them. Omnia had no idea where it led.

She heard a noise and glanced round. The panther-man was on the move.

Omnia ran for the door and pulled it open.

Red walls. She was in a space a couple of metres wide, a few metres long, with no obvious exit but the door through which she had come. But there was no going back. She ran to the other end and pounded on the wall to see if there was some way through. Nothing. Trapped! She turned, hands spread across the stone, fingers scrabbling at the surface, knowing that in another few seconds the panther-man would come through the door, her heart pounding as she tried to think of what to do next. She pressed back hard against the wall.

Suddenly she fell backwards. Before she could understand what had happened, she was on the floor and the wall that had apparently opened behind her back was closing in front of her.

Omnia heard footsteps. She glanced around. A formally dressed man with thick, grey hair, waxy skin and black, owl-like eyebrows looked down at her.

'Winnicott!' she said in amazement.

'Omnia,' said Basilica's servant. 'How nice of you to drop in.'

10

Basilica

The man helped her to her feet. Omnia looked incredulously at the wall that had closed in front of her. It looked just as solid as it had looked from the other side.

'Care to watch?' said Winnicott.

He removed a cover from a hole in the wall and beckoned to Omnia. She could just see into the hole by standing on tiptoe. Winnicott himself watched from another hole beside her.

Omnia could see the length of the space where only a moment before she had been trapped. The panther-man was in there, looking around.

'Peculiar disguise,' murmured Winnicott.

Peculiar wasn't the word for it, thought Omnia. The idea of being chased by a man with the head of a panther might have seemed comical, but the reality was terrifying. He hadn't said a word, not made a sound. Just kept coming after her. Omnia felt the icy terror of it once more.

The view Omnia had of the man in the corridor was from high up in the wall, so that she was looking down on him. And yet she wasn't standing so high, which meant that the viewing hole on the other side must be further up, and there must be some system of mirrors or lenses in the wall that reflected the image.

For another moment he stood, slowly looking around the corridor. Then he began to come forward, carefully tapping along the wall, searching for evidence of a door.

Omnia glanced at Winnicott.

'He won't find anything like that,' he said.

'How will he find something?' she whispered.

'He'd have to be very lucky,' said Winnicott. He picked up a huge Bracketball stick that was standing in the corner. 'Or unlucky, to look at it another way.'

The panther-man came closer, tapping as he approached.

He reached the end and tapped across the wall, slowly, methodically. Omnia could see him from above, and yet he must have been passing right in front of her, tapping the wall at just about the height of her face. At some point, she knew, they must have been separated by only a few centimetres, the thickness of the wall.

She held her breath.

He kept tapping. Eventually he tapped his way back to the door. He stood, looking around once more. Omnia watched, hardly blinking. Maybe he was about to take his mask off. Maybe she would see who it was.

Suddenly he looked up, the mask still on his face, and it

was as if he was staring straight at the viewing hole from which she was gazing down at him. As if he knew she was still there and wanted to tell her that her escape today was only temporary and somewhere, somehow, he would finish the job.

Then he turned and went out of the door, slamming it shut behind him.

Winnicott stepped back from the wall and replaced the Bracketball stick in the corner.

'Well,' he said, 'I expect you've come to see Basilica.'

She was in another room. Through a window Omnia could see the top of the Hatted Belfry. Against a wall stood Basilica's fishing net.

'Hello, Omnia,' said Basilica, without the slightest note of surprise in her voice. 'This is an unexpected pleasure.'

'She let herself in,' said Winnicott.

'Really?'

'Someone was after her.'

'Again?' said Basilica, looking at Omnia disapprovingly. 'You shouldn't make a habit of that, you know.'

'A panther,' said Winnicott.

'Nonsense, Winny. You're making a joke of it.'

Winnicott shrugged.

'A panther?' said Basilica to Omnia.

'A man in a panther's mask anyway,' said Omnia.

Basilica frowned. 'How extraordinary. It's not Flip Day, is it?'

Omnia shook her head. 'That was last week.'

'Was it? One loses track.' Basilica paused. 'Well, sit down, Omnia, unless you're in a hurry to leave.'

Omnia wasn't in any kind of a hurry to go anywhere, not after having spent three months trying to find the woman who was sitting in front of her. Basilica looked just as Omnia remembered her, her skin lustrous and her hair, with its strands of grey, twisted in a plait halfway down her back. There were a dozen chairs in the room. Omnia chose one.

'I looked for you,' said Omnia.

'Did you?' said Basilica. 'Well, as you can see, here I am. We've been here . . . How long is it now, Winny?'

'Three months,' said Winnicott. 'It was three days after Omnia dropped in to see us with the young gentleman, I believe, that we left.'

'Three days after the last time I saw you?' said Omnia.

Winnicott nodded.

Omnia calculated. Three days after she last saw Basilica would have been . . . Planque Day. And the morning after Planque Day was the day she had gone back to the Slate Tower and tried to bring herself to jump. The next day she definitely would have done it had the door to the Tower not been barred. And Basilica was already gone!

'Why did you move?' asked Omnia.

'We didn't have much choice in the matter,' replied Basilica. 'If it was up to me, I'd have happily stayed in the

Slate Tower.' She cast a glance at her fishing net and sighed. 'The fishing there was much better.'

'Was it the UnderButlers who made you move?'

'Who else?'

Omnia understood now. Basilica and Winnicott had been removed from the Slate Tower after she told the UnderButlers that she had seen them there. Omnia had blurted it out even though Basilica had told her not to tell anyone. She thought of all the times over the past three months that she had gazed at the Slate Tower and imagined Basilica in her room up there looking out, imagined her putting out her net to fish for a bird. All the time she had been here, closed in behind a wall in the Winter House, where no one ever came.

How many more places were there in Neversuch House, Omnia wondered, where a person could be put without anyone else having the slightest idea that they were there?

'So?' said Basilica. 'Would you like to tell me how you found me?'

'I had no idea that's what I was doing,' said Omnia.

'You must have come through the Snowflake.'

Omnia looked at her blankly.

'The white stairs,' said Basilica. 'It's supposed to look like a giant snowflake, all those white stairs, going off in all directions. Apparently there's a certain pattern to it, like the crystal of a snowflake when you put it under a microscope.'

'It's the Winter House, after all,' explained Winnicott.

'But how you found the right door and knew what to do at the wall . . .'

'I had no idea,' said Omnia.

'I'd have fallen off my chair in surprise if you had,' remarked Basilica. 'And all while being chased by a panther! That's quite impressive.'

Omnia smiled. 'It's quite an extraordinary story.'

Basilica smiled as well. 'But not without logic, I assume.'

'I assume that as well,' said Omnia, becoming serious again. Basilica had told her once before that nothing that happened was without logic, and if you only knew enough about it, you would understand what it was. Omnia didn't know yet what the explanation was for this particular sequence of events – that was why she had gone to Trimbleby to try to find Basilica in the first place – but she was sure there was a logic of some sort behind it.

Omnia recounted the story, starting with the death of Dish, and then of Withers, and her conversation with Trimbleby, and the secret arrangement with Cornelius Slinker to put a stone in the hole of the Captain's Keep whenever she wanted to meet him and how she expected him to be at the Granite Arch, but this time the panther-man was there instead.

At the mention of Slinker's name, Basilica and Winnicott exchanged a glance.

'This Cornelius Slinker,' said Basilica, 'how do you come to know him so well?'

'Don't you remember? He saved me when—' Omnia stopped. Of course! Basilica wouldn't know what had happened on the night that Tobias Hildegrew escaped from the top of the Great Tower, because Omnia had not seen her again after that. Nor would she know that Hildegrew had turned out to be the killer of the Captain and the Older Digby, and that Cornelius Slinker had saved her from him.

So Omnia went back to that night when Tobias Hildegrew flew on the wind from the top of the Great Tower, dropping the keys to the Captain's treasure that he had forged, and back earlier in that same night to the moment when Cornelius Slinker fought Hildegrew on the roof of the Silent Cloister and had been thrown to the ground with a knife wound slashed across his face.

'And now you think it was Cornelius Slinker who was after you today,' said Basilica.

'No!' cried Winnicott.

'Of course she does, Winny. What other explanation is there? Well, Omnia, that's what you think, isn't it?'

Omnia didn't know what to think. She had run when the panther-man appeared under the porch of the Summer House, but until now, until this second, she hadn't consciously told herself why. She hadn't used the words, even in her own mind. But it was obvious, wasn't it? The man in the mask was trying to get her. Probably trying to kill her, like Withers and Dish. If not, why hadn't he uttered a sound? Why hadn't he asked her to stop? Why hadn't he explained what he was doing? He had had plenty of opportunity.

But surely it couldn't be Cornelius.

'If Cornelius wanted to get me,' said Omnia, 'he could have done it before. He's had plenty of chances.'

'Who else knew about the stone?' asked Basilica. 'Whoever was there today was waiting for you. They didn't follow you – they knew you were coming. Who else but Cornelius would have known that?'

Omnia remembered that the last time they spoke, Cornelius had reminded her to use the stone. Why? He didn't need to be so insistent, she had used it before, and yet he had kept telling her as if he wanted to be sure, absolutely certain, that she would use it again.

'Who else?' said Basilica. 'Think, Omnia. Evergrow? Did you ever tell him about the stone?'

Omnia shook her head. 'No one,' she whispered. 'No one else knows.'

'It couldn't be Cornelius!' said Winnicott.

'Of course it could,' said Basilica.

'He's a Slinker!'

'Exactly. Who could be less under suspicion?'

'They could never get to a Slinker!'

'Couldn't they? There's a first time for everything, Winny. They can get to anyone, Slinker or not.'

'I don't believe it,' muttered Winnicott. He shook his head and folded his arms angrily.

'I still don't understand,' said Omnia. 'Cornelius has had

89

chances. Any number of them. Why today? Why not before?'

'We can only guess,' said Basilica. 'Perhaps now's the time. It's started again, hasn't it? Withers and Dish are dead. Trimbleby's likely to be next. Cornelius could have been preparing the ground, making you trust him, and now, when the time has come, you can see why.'

'But why the mask?'

'For precisely this situation,' Basilica replied. 'If he failed, you wouldn't have seen his face. After everything he's done, you wouldn't believe it could be him. You hardly *can* believe it, can you?'

'I still don't understand. Why save me from Tobias Hildegrew three months ago only to kill me today?'

'Perhaps he didn't save you. Perhaps Tobias never intended to kill you. Omnia, nothing in the House is as it seems, remember? Perhaps that whole fight was staged to make you trust Cornelius. After all, Tobias didn't expect to be discovered, did he? He expected to fly away. You just told us yourself, it was only a stray gust of wind that blew the hood off his head that revealed him. If it hadn't, he would have come back undetected, while you would have trusted Cornelius with your life.'

'She can't be sure it was him in the panther's mask,' objected Winnicott, who seemed to be less willing even than Omnia to believe that Cornelius had tried to kill her.

'True,' said Basilica. 'She can't. But if Omnia's told us everything, and unless she has another explanation, that's the assumption she has to make.' Basilica turned to Omnia. '*Have* you told us everything?'

Omnia frowned. She thought she had. There was nothing she could think of that she had forgotten.

'Then if I were you, Omnia, I would work on the assumption that it was Cornelius Slinker until you definitely know otherwise. That's only my advice, of course. You might not wish to take it. But that's the assumption I would make in your shoes – if you want to live, that is.'

Omnia glanced at Winnicott, who shook his head very quickly, very slightly, as if hoping that Basilica wouldn't see him. Omnia shrugged helplessly. She had no desire to believe that Cornelius Slinker had been trying to kill her any more than Winnicott seemed to want to – although Omnia had no idea why he should care one way or the other – but as Basilica said, she didn't see that she had any choice but to assume that he had.

'So Dish and Withers are dead, are they?' said Basilica. 'Tell me again how it happened. Tell me everything you know.'

Omnia told her.

'And everyone's saying they were accidents, I suppose?'

Omnia nodded. 'But Trimbleby knows better. According to him, Digby and Everdean are hidden somewhere safe, so he must be worried.'

'They're in the Hold, I suppose?'

'The Hold?'

'I've never been there myself. I've only heard of it. I

don't even know if it exists or if it's just a legend, this place called the Hold where the Captain and the Butler can go to be safe. What about Trimbleby?'

'He's taking precautions,' Omnia replied. 'He's next on the list.'

'Or you are.'

'Do you really think I'm on the list?'

Basilica looked at her gravely. 'Do you think you're not, Omnia, after what's just happened?'

'I suppose so.' Omnia frowned. 'Do you think it was Slinker who killed Dish and Withers too?'

'Never!' cried Winnicott.

Basilica ignored him. 'That would be the most obvious hypothesis. I never much liked Dish. Too quiet. Withers wasn't so bad. The best of a bad lot. But Trimbleby! Trimbleby . . .' Her voice shook. 'Not that I want anyone to be killed, but if they had to get rid of someone, it's a shame they didn't start with him!'

Basilica took a deep breath. Omnia watched her. It was the first time, Omnia thought, that she could remember Basilica showing what she really felt. She always seemed to be so much in control.

'He said something to me last time I spoke to him,' said Omnia. 'Mr Trimbleby, I mean. He said, what happened to you, he wished it didn't have to happen.'

'Did he just?' Basilica shrugged. 'You should never have told them about seeing me, Omnia. You were never meant to do that. I warned you, didn't I?'

'I'm sorry. I didn't know they'd make you move.'

'Not because of that. It was the worst thing you could do, not only for me, but for you. They'll always doubt you now. They'll always suspect you.'

'Of what?'

'Of anything. Everything. Having had contact with me is enough to put you under suspicion forever.' Basilica paused. 'What did they say when you told them you'd seen me?'

'That you were a ghost.'

'Really? How did I die?'

'In an accident involving a fishing net.'

Basilica laughed.

'Winnicott too.'

'There you are, Winny. You and me both! With a fishing net!'

The servant looked back at her, but he didn't smile. He sat, arms folded, obviously still angry because of what had been said about Cornelius Slinker.

'They told me your food was ghost's food,' said Omnia, 'and I'd turn into a ghost myself if I'd eaten any of it.'

'But you did eat it, didn't you? Perhaps you've turned into a ghost and you don't even realise it.' Basilica chuckled. 'Speaking of food, Winny, shall we have a little something?'

Winnicott didn't reply.

'Come on, Winny. Don't be angry. You know what I said is true. They can get to anyone, Slinker or no Slinker.'

Winnicott shook his head.

'Oh, for heaven's sake, Winny. We're not going to fight about this, are we? Now come on, get us some food. Please. *Please*, Winny.'

Winnicott sat for a moment longer, then got up and left the room.

'Why's Winnicott so angry?' asked Omnia. 'And why do you keep saying that, Slinker or no Slinker?'

'Winnicott's sensitive, that's all. Don't worry about it. Now you talked about Tobias Hildegrew. You said he was the one who was responsible for the murders. Tell me about him.'

'Do you know him?'

Basilica hesitated for a moment. 'Not exactly.'

'He was the Younger Digby's friend,' said Omnia. 'Everyone liked him. We thought he was going to be the OverUnderButler.'

'And now you think Cornelius Slinker was working with him all along.' Basilica thought about it. 'Why not? It's very clever. In case Tobias gets discovered, they wait a few months and then this Slinker – who seems so trustworthy – carries on the work. It's their back-up plan in case the first one goes wrong.'

Omnia frowned. That wasn't what she thought at all – in fact, it was the direct opposite – until today. She still wasn't sure she could believe it.

Winnicott returned carrying an enormous tray with about a dozen different pies and tarts. He put it on a table.

'See, Omnia?' said Basilica. 'I told you the fishing wasn't

as good here. But we'll make do, won't we? What would you like?'

Omnia gazed at the food. She remembered Basilica's response when she told her what the UnderButlers said about eating her food. A chuckle. Perhaps it was true. Perhaps she had turned into a ghost and didn't even realise it. After all, how would you know?

'Just a slice of the pigeon for me,' said Basilica, while they were waiting for Omnia to decide.

Winnicott cut a slice of pigeon pie and silently gave the plate to Basilica.

'What about the red robin tart?' said Basilica to Omnia. 'You liked that last time, didn't you?'

Winnicott looked at Omnia questioningly, knife poised over the tart.

'I'll just . . . I'll have . . .'

Basilica laughed again. 'What have you got to lose, Omnia? You've already eaten with us once.'

'Parrot,' said Winnicott. 'Red, if I remember. That's what she likes.'

He cut a slice of a pie and gave it to Omnia on a plate with a fork. Omnia hesitated a moment longer, then dug in. What *did* she have to lose?

It was delicious, just as she remembered, and got more delicious with each mouthful. The other things she tried were equally tasty and by the time she was finished, she had polished off a starling and herb pasty, a slice of finch pie, rook wings on toast and a goose liver tart.

'Had enough?' asked Basilica, who had finished her slice of pigeon pie long before.

Omnia nodded. She handed Winnicott her plate.

'I have something else to confess,' she said guiltily. 'I told Pedagogia about you as well.'

Basilica's eyebrows rose. 'Pedagogia? I bet that surprised her.'

'It was on the night before Tobias Hildegrew escaped. I found her in the Hall of Leaning and . . . anyway, I told her. I'm sorry. I know I shouldn't have. She said I must have seen you outside the wall.' Omnia paused. 'I've worked out what happened to you, Basilica. You went outside the wall, didn't you? And then you came back and they locked you away. I'm right, aren't I? That's what happened, isn't it?'

Basilica was silent.

'*Isn't it?*'

'Something like that,' said Basilica quietly.

'And is that where you met the Evergones? Outside?'

'I can't tell you about the Evergones.'

'Who are they? I know they're important.'

'I can't tell you,' said Basilica. 'Please don't ask me.'

'Why not?'

'Please, Omnia! Don't!'

Omnia glanced at Winnicott, who was quietly eating a piece of sparrow and spinach pie. He stopped with the fork halfway to his mouth.

Basilica sighed. 'I'm sorry, Omnia. I didn't mean to snap.'

'That's what Trimbleby said to me,' murmured Omnia. 'Don't ask.'

Basilica was silent for a moment, watching her. 'Don't you ever wonder what it's like out there?'

Omnia shrugged. 'Sometimes. Of course I do sometimes.'

'Can you imagine that someone would want to find out?'

'Did you? Is that why you went?'

'Can you imagine what it must be like if they want to find out so much that they go . . . and then they're not allowed back?'

'But *you* came back. You came back and they locked you up. That's the price you paid, isn't it?'

Basilica sighed. 'It's very complicated.'

'Then tell me about it.'

Basilica was silent.

'Why won't you? I promise I won't—'

'None of it matters,' said Basilica. 'It was a long time ago. What matters is what's happening now. Is Everdean still the Captain?'

Omnia nodded.

'Think about it, Omnia. Everdean is too old to learn how to be Captain. The Butler's young and untried. Those who are watching, those who have been waiting, they've see their chance, and now they're trying to take it.'

'But why kill the UnderButlers?'

'Why indeed?'

'Trimbleby says it's a mistake.'

'Does he? One mistake after the other. I rather doubt

that myself. To assume that others are making a mistake may be the biggest mistake you can make.'

'Then why are they after me?'

'Why indeed, Omnia Halibut?'

Omnia frowned.

'It's unfair, isn't it?' said Basilica. 'Is that what you're thinking? Of all the Halibuts, you're the one who gets involved. You're the one who's in danger. But in every generation, Omnia, there's one Halibut—'

'Who can *do* something. I know that. You've said it before, Basilica. It's not me. I'm not the one.'

'How do you know?'

'I don't even know what it means. I don't even know if I believe it.'

Basilica gazed at her. 'There's something about this House, Omnia. You could never realise how much you love it until it's taken away from you. Until you can't walk under its colonnades, can't cross its terraces, can't climb its towers. Until you can't swim in the Pallid Pool or hold a banquet in the Wasps Chamber. Until you can't throw quoits in the Quoitery or swing from the arm of the Stone Trapeze.' Basilica paused, eyes closed, deep in memory. 'Think about it. Try to imagine it, Omnia. Try to imagine what it would be like never, ever, ever to walk in this place again.'

Omnia stared.

Suddenly Basilica opened her eyes and sat forward. 'They're close, Omnia. Closer than they've ever been before. I sense it. They've waited for this. Years. Decades. Centuries.'

'And you think it's Cornelius Slinker who's doing it?'

'Why only one? Perhaps it's more.'

'How many?'

'Who knows?'

'What should I do?'

Basilica clutched Omnia's wrist. 'Trust no one, Omnia. That's the only advice I can give you. Trust no one at all.'

11

To the Warren

The oars splashed. They rose, swung forward and splashed again. The rower bent his back, driving the boat angrily onwards through the water. With each dip of his oars he seemed to be beating his anger out against the river.

He breathed heavily, not breaking pace. The lantern light played over the roof and the walls, lighting up the picture-like cracks and then leaving them behind in darkness again. Finally, where the river took a curve, he came to a place where a ring had been fixed to the wall. Near it was a ladder that hung from the roof, leading to a trapdoor in the rock over the water. He steered the boat across until it bumped into the stone and quickly tied it to the ring. Then he snatched up the panther mask from the floor of the boat, stashed it inside his cloak and climbed the ladder.

A few minutes later, his face hidden deep in the shadow of a hooded cloak, he emerged into the alleys of the Warren.

The Warren was in the north of the estate of Neversuch House, about a mile from the main buildings of the House itself. It stretched over a hill and a valley and another hill, ending at the edge of a cliff that had been formed by the quarrying of stone for the House's construction. Originally, the Warren had been the site of the camp where the workers lived during the five years that it took to build the House in the time of the First Captain, and after that, it was home to the servants who were lured into the House by the first Digby in the years that followed. The structures in the camp weren't built to last, having been thrown up as temporary shelter. Mostly they were made of wood and hastily-dried brick, and within a few years, they were crumbling. But by now the servants in the House included all kinds of skilled workers, masons and carpenters and plumbers, and as the buildings of the old workers' camp fell down, they replaced them with buildings of their own.

The Warren was a kind of opposite version of the House. Every building in the House had been planned by the First Captain, regardless of need, and had been constructed in a single, five-year frenzy of activity after he bought the estate. In the Warren, nothing had been planned and it had been constructed over centuries, bit by bit, as need dictated. The house of a servant family would collapse, or start to crumble, and the Butler would authorise the masons to build another house, and they would clear the one that was collapsing and build afresh.

But this time they built more solidly, with materials that would last, and created bigger and better buildings. Over time, these buildings too became insufficient and were replaced in their turn. Eventually the most important servants lived in houses that were as big as mansions. The High Chef, the Prime Plumber, the Major Pruner, the Grand Glazier and their families lived in luxurious houses with more rooms than they knew what to do with. Most remarkable of all was the mansion of the Chief Mason, Albert Gondolier, as befitted the man who was in charge of all the building repairs in Neversuch House. Over the years, generations of Gondoliers had embellished and enlarged their family house until it resembled a kind of record of every sort of architectural style with every kind of architectural feature, columns, arches, statues, friezes, domes, entablatures, balconies, terraces and even a dozen magnificent flying buttresses, each of which had a beaver, a stork or a crocodile – all animals renowned for the nests they constructed – proudly perching on its point.

Yet space was short in the Warren, and even the greatest mansions stood side by side along its main street with barely a finger's breadth of space to separate them. Elsewhere in the Warren, alleys were narrow and passages were dark. For although there was no planning, there was a rule: the servants' buildings could not extend beyond the area originally occupied by the workers' camp. That was all the First Captain had allowed and so, by tradition, that was all any later Captain would allow as well. The Warren was restricted to the two hillsides and the valley between them, no matter how much the population of servants grew.

In such a case, as any builder will tell you, if you can't add horizontally, you must add vertically. As the number of servants increased yet further, and as more of the valley was taken by the grand buildings of the most important servants, the higher the other buildings went. They piled on top of each other up the hillsides, rising to the crest of the hill on one side and up to the very edge of the quarry on the other, a higgledy-piggledy collection of extensions and elevations and staircases that went nowhere for years until someone decided to build yet another storey and the staircase acquired a destination. Unlike most places, where news spreads along the streets, news in the Warren would spread from window to window, which were so close that people on opposite sides of the alleys could speak to each other without even raising their voices. No one had any idea how many buildings there were or how many rooms they contained or how they connected with one another, because of the way it had all developed, bit by bit, piece by piece, the way rabbits create their warren, which is what it came to be called. But the servants were proud of the name and of the home that they and earlier generations of servants had created. Out they came from the Warren each morning to walk the mile to the House, and back they went each evening to the maze of alleys and stairs and corridors that was their own Halibut-free world. Here, they knew, no Halibut would ever disturb them, because there was another fixed tradition about the Warren that everyone respected: the Warren belonged to the servants and no Halibut but the Captain could ever enter.

But even though space was so limited, there was one area of the Warren that almost everyone avoided. The buildings that had been built in earlier times at the edge of the cliff had been known to suddenly collapse and crash into the quarry below. They should never have been built in the first place, and it was a long time since any had been replaced. People would cram themselves into tiny rooms elsewhere in the Warren or build extensions on top of extensions in order to avoid having to live there. Elsewhere, in the dense buildings of the Warren, there were people everywhere and if you so much as peeped out of a window, a hundred other people would see you. But at the very edge of the cliff, at the top of the long, winding alleys that led from the valley below, there was hardly a soul. If you wanted to hide in the Warren, if you wanted an attic or a cellar where no one would accidentally stumble upon you, this is where you would come.

This was where the man in the hooded cloak was headed. Near the cliff at the edge of the quarry he turned into a narrow alley, paused to look back and see that no one was watching him, then turned into an even narrower alley and pushed on an old wooden door that had come loose from one of its hinges. It opened with a squeak. He closed it behind him and went quickly up the stairs inside.

12

An Idea

The room was bare. The floor, the walls, the ceiling were of rough, unpainted timber. A table was in the middle of the room and on it a lantern gave off a flickering glow. A couple of chairs stood round the table and against one wall was a bed of plain wood covered with an old blanket, and that was all the furniture there was. A window looked out into the darkness over the quarry at the northern edge of the Warren, and if you had been looking up from outside, you would have seen the glow from the lantern as a single light at the very top of a dark jumble of buildings towering high above the edge of the quarry cliff.

Four people were in the room. Two of them sat on the bed, the other two were perched on the chairs.

We know them already, or at least we have glimpsed them. The young Butlery clerk who ran errands for the two Clerks of the Entrance, and who earlier that day had smiled

105

at Omnia as she came and went from the chamber, sat on one of the chairs. His name was William Bell. Owens, the kitchen hand who had answered back to the High Chef, occupied the other chair. On the bed sat a young polisher in a green polisher's smock, Alice Bickerstaff, beside a short youth in the clothes of an apprentice mason. His name was Robert Gondolier and his great-uncle Albert Gondolier was the hereditary Chief Mason of the House.

Robert was the oldest of the four young servants in the room and he was only nineteen. He was also the only one from the high servant families of Neversuch House. The others came from families who had always worked in lower jobs, from which it took exceptional talent and even more luck to rise to one of the higher positions.

They were waiting, and as they waited, they talked.

'I'd chop him up,' said Owens, who was the kind of person who always knows better than everybody else and always finds someone to blame when his ideas fail. 'That'd do the job. Chop old Trimbleby up and boil the pieces, and then I'd feed him to them.' The kitchen hand grinned. 'In a pie with chestnuts and morels. I'd know just how to make it.'

Alice Bickerstaff laughed.

'I don't see how that would look like an accident,' said William Bell.

'Well, no one would know, would they?' retorted Owens. 'He'd be gone. Eaten.'

'But it has to look like an accident.'

'What about his bones?' said Alice Bickerstaff. 'What about his head? What about his feet?'

'His feet are no problem,' said Owens, grinning again. 'I'd feed them his feet in a nice vinegar sauce. Pickled trotters. Pickled Trimbleby trotters, eh! Feed it to the Halibuts. To the gluttons.' He laughed wickedly. 'They'd slurp it up!'

'Still, it wouldn't look like an accident, would it?' said William. 'It would be more of a disappearance.'

'Then it's a disappearance!'

'That's no good. It has to look like an accident.'

'Why?'

'Because that's what he told us.'

'I'm sick of *him* telling us! We could say Trimbleby went outside the wall. Gone outside the wall and never come back.' Owens smirked triumphantly. 'What about that?'

'No one would believe it,' said Alice. 'Not Trimbleby. He'd never do that.'

'Exactly,' said William. 'Now, me, I'd get Trimbleby in the Butlery. Crush him under a big set of shelves or a huge chest of drawers. There are chests of drawers in there so big they'd crush an elephant.'

'An *elephant*?' said Owens sceptically.

'Well, a man anyway. At least it would look like an accident.'

'How would you arrange it?' asked Alice.

'That's the tricky bit.'

'You've got no idea!' said Owens.

'Well,' said William, 'another way is, I could lock him in

107

a room. There are rooms in the Bright Tower, rooms after rooms after rooms in the UnderBasement where the old records are kept and no one ever goes. I know where they are. Lock someone in there and no one would hear them calling out. They'd starve to death before anyone heard.'

'Does he ever go down there?' asked Alice.

William shook his head. 'No one does. Hardly ever. That's the point.'

'How are you going to do it then?' demanded Owens. 'He'd have to go down there and you'd have to know about it.'

'It might happen. He might go down. He might take me if he had to bring some records back. I'd take my chance. I'm always ready, me, if the chance comes.'

'And what if it doesn't?' said Owens cruelly. 'You could wait forever. He could wait forever, couldn't he, Alice?'

Alice smiled. She toyed with a smooth, white stone that she was holding in her hand.

'What about you then?' William asked Alice, noticing the way she was smiling. 'What would you do if you're so clever?'

'Trimbleby crosses the Mounted Bridge every day, doesn't he?' The Mounted Bridge was a steep, peaked bridge, almost triangular in profile, that crossed high above the Court of Palms and was often used by Butlery clerks heading for the Bright Tower. 'I'd loosen the stones.' Alice glanced at the young mason beside her. 'That would work, wouldn't it?'

'Could work,' said Robert Gondolier.

'And it would look like an accident.'

'Yes, but what if someone else crosses it first?' said William. 'You'd kill the wrong person.'

Alice shrugged, turning over the white stone in her palm.

'It's no good if it kills the wrong person! Lots of people use the Bridge. I use the Bridge! How could you time it so it would definitely be Trimbleby?'

'I haven't worked that part out yet.'

'I don't even know why we're doing this,' said Owens. 'Why don't we just poison them all and be done with it?'

'Who?' said William.

'The Halibuts! All of them! Give them all a meal they won't forget. Get them all when they're eating in the Tempered Hall.'

There was silence.

'Could you do that?' asked Alice.

'Why not?'

'You couldn't poison them all with just one dish,' objected William. 'You'd have to poison everything. You'd have to kill the lot of them. If we just got a few, they'd get suspicious.'

'I'd get the other cooks to help me.'

'All the cooks?' said Alice sceptically.

'Why not?'

'What if someone told?'

'I'd make sure no one did.'

'Would you?' said Robert Gondolier. 'Really?'

'If I wanted to.'

Robert rolled his eyes. 'Well, you tell us when all the cooks are prepared to help you, and then we can think about your idea.'

'And you tell us when you can get the masons to help you,' retorted Owens, 'if you think you're so clever.'

'We need to do exactly what we're told,' said William Bell. 'He's got a reason for doing it like this.'

'Who is he?' demanded Alice. 'Why won't you tell us?'

'How do you know I know?' said William.

'You do. I know you do.'

'You've met him too.'

'He never shows his face!'

William shrugged. 'That's his choice. If he doesn't show his face, that's his business. I warn you, he's not the kind of person you want to question.'

The others watched him, but William didn't say anything else. The young clerk was the one who had drawn them into this conspiracy over the past couple of months. Each of them, for their own reasons, was disgruntled, whether it was because of something a Halibut had done to them, or because of something one of the UnderButlers had done, or for some other reason. Not all of them could hide it like William could. He was always able to come up with a smile, no matter how resentful he was feeling, which was the secret of his success. Sitting in the Butlery entrance, he would smile sympathetically as someone was bluntly ordered to sit down by Fellowes and Childes. It was amazing how a friendly glance in that unwelcoming place could unlock someone's tongue. They would lean over and grumble in William's ear, and he would nod understandingly, and then they would whisper some other complaint, and soon they were murmuring about this or muttering about that, revealing all kinds of things about servants and Halibuts and what they were up to. As a result, there was hardly anything going on in the House that William didn't know something about.

Of the other three, Alice had proven the most useful. She was part of the group of thirty-two polishers who burnished the ceiling of the Tempered Hall once a month. For the rest of the time she polished handles, lanterns, railings and the various other fittings that needed polishing all over the House. But no one watched what she was doing – as no one watched what any of the polishers did, so that some things were polished ten times in a week and others were left untouched for months on end. Alice could roam wherever she liked with no one questioning what she was doing there. She could follow anyone.

The other two, Owens and Robert Gondolier, had yet to prove their worth. But William had been told to recruit as many people to join the conspiracy as he could – people so bitter and unhappy that they could really be trusted. It was a slow process, and he had to be completely sure of them before he told them anything. These were the only other two he had found so far.

Owens turned irritably on Alice. 'What's that you keep fiddling with?'

'This?' Alice closed her hand. 'Just a stone.'

'Let me see.'

Alice showed him. 'I don't think we'll be seeing too much more of Omnia Halibut.'

William smirked. 'When he says he'll do something, he never fails.'

There was a creak on the stairs outside.

They listened. The stairs creaked again.

The door opened. In came the man with his face hidden beneath his long, drooping hood.

William Bell jumped up and gave him his chair. The man sat. He took the panther mask from under his cloak and threw it in a corner.

'Did you get her?' asked William.

The man didn't reply.

'She left the stone!' said Alice. 'I promise! Look, here it is. I followed her when she went to leave it and when she had gone I took it, just like you told me!' She jumped up and held it out to him.

The man snatched it from her.

'Didn't she go to the Granite Arch?' said Alice. 'She always goes when she leaves the stone. I've seen her. At five o'clock she's there, every time.'

The man gazed at the stone. He looked at the star incised in its surface.

Suddenly he slammed it down on the table.

Everyone jumped.

'Wasn't she there?' whispered Alice.

'She was there,' growled the man. 'And then she wasn't.'

Alice glanced at William. The clerk shrugged. He had no more idea about what the man meant than she did.

'But what—'

'Enough of that!' snapped the man. 'Who has a plan for Trimbleby? Well? Anyone? Any ideas?'

No one spoke. It was one thing to brag about their plans when the man wasn't in the room. It was more of a game than anything. But not now. Owens's idea to chop up the UnderButler and feed him to the Halibuts didn't seem as clever as it had before, nor did his plan for a mass poisoning of the Halibuts in the Tempered Hall. And Alice didn't think her idea of loosening the Mounted Bridge – which would almost certainly kill someone other than the UnderButler – was going to sound very smart. And William, who claimed that a falling chest in the Butlery might do the trick, had no idea how to make it happen, or how he could get the UnderButler down to one of the rooms full of old files in the Butlery where no one ever went. There really were such rooms, hundreds of them, but the UnderButler was never likely to go down there, much less allow himself to be locked in. It was a shame, thought William, because it really was a clever idea, much cleverer than the other ideas he had heard for getting rid of the UnderButler. But it would work only for someone who didn't know the Butlery, who would follow you wherever you took them, as he sometimes had to take various serv-ants who were sent to talk to various clerks. And of course it would appear to be a disappearance rather than an accident. But apart from that, and if only he could make it happen, it would work. If you could get Trimbleby down to one of those rooms and lock him in, the UnderButler would starve to death long before anyone found him.

The man slammed the table again. 'Have you got *no* ideas?' he demanded from under his hood. 'Choking Dish with a lamb cutlet on Flip Day – my idea. Killing Withers with the chihuahua at the Faunal House – my idea. You've given me nothing! Have you got nothing in your brains?'

'Trimbleby's taking all sorts of precautions,' said William Bell.

'Of course he is. But he's still doing his job, isn't he? He hasn't gone into hiding like Digby and Everdean.'

'Shouldn't we be trying to find *them*?' said William.

'They'll be in the Hold,' growled the man. 'That's obvious. I've told you to try to find out where that is.'

'I'm trying. Really. But I still don't see how killing all these UnderButlers—'

'Do you think I don't know what I'm doing?'

'Sorry,' said William quickly. 'I didn't mean . . . I'm sorry.'

'You're my eyes and ears out there,' said the man. 'Do you see and hear nothing?'

'We're trying.'

'Then try *harder*!'

There was silence.

Robert Gondolier spoke up. 'I have an idea.'

'What?' demanded Alice quickly. 'Not the Mounted Bridge? That was my idea!'

'What about the Mounted Bridge?' said the man.

Alice hesitated. She didn't know how you could possibly be sure of killing the right person by loosening the stones of the Mounted Bridge, so she was reluctant to say anything more. But maybe Robert Gondolier knew, and maybe he was going to steal her idea and pretend it was his own. She watched him suspiciously.

The man turned to the young mason.

'Well, what's your idea?'

13

The Last UnderButler

Horace Trimbleby marched briskly on his way to the Bright Tower. As he did every morning, he went along the side of the West Stable and turned the corner of the Great West Range. Ahead of him, at the top of a broad sweep of stairs, rose the Mounted Bridge.

The UnderButler was accompanied by four young UnderUnderButlers in their plum-coloured coats. There were eight UnderUnderButlers in all, but these four were the ones he most trusted, and ever since the death of Withers, he hadn't taken a step outside without them. One of them walked in front of him, in case any kind of trap was waiting ahead, two others walked alongside him, to protect him if an attack came from the side, and the last followed them, in case something came from behind. They all knew the risks they took and why they were taking them. They also knew that if an attempt was made on the UnderButler's life, it would probably come in a different way from the ones that had accounted for Withers and Dish, and they would only recognise it when it was happening.

The contingent went quickly up the stairs to the foot of the Bridge. They stopped and the first UnderUnderButler, a red-headed young man called Ollendorff, went ahead. The Bridge rose to a peak, from which it was a fifty-metre drop to the Court of Palms below. Trimbleby watched as Ollendorff reached the top and disappeared down the other side. He waited to hear Ollendorff call back that it was safe to cross. If his voice didn't come, there was no telling what waited for him on the other side of the Bridge.

There was silence. Trimbleby glanced at the two UnderUnderButlers who stood beside him.

Then they heard Ollendorff's voice. Trimbleby and the two UnderUnderButlers quickly went up the Bridge and found Ollendorff waiting for them. The last UnderUnder-Butler, a stocky young man called Hazenby, checked that there was no sign of danger behind them and came over as well.

Immediately there were other threats. The route to the Bright Tower led under a pair of ancient trees that stood like a pair of guardians at the entrance to the Grey Promenade. A falling branch was an obvious threat. Ollendorff stopped under the trees and looked up, carefully scrutinising the branches and searching for signs of anyone in the foliage. Then he moved on and the others followed.

At last, they climbed the stairs to the Bright Tower.

Through the entrance chamber they went, past the two Clerks of the Entrance behind their desk and William Bell on his chair beside the door, who turned his freckled face and watched them go.

They arrived at the red door of the Butler's room and went inside. Trimbleby sat behind the desk. Finally he allowed himself a sigh of relief. For the first time that morning, he felt safe.

At just about that moment, Robert Gondolier was climbing the stairs to the Bright Tower.

He came into the entrance chamber, in his clothes of an apprentice mason, carrying a note which he handed to the Clerks of the Entrance behind their high desk. Childes opened the note, read it carefully and handed it to Fellowes, who looked up from his writing, read it and handed it back to him. Childes began to make an entry in the ledger on the desk in front of him, glancing at the note from time to time.

Robert waited. He didn't throw so much as a glance at William Bell. To watch him – as Fellowes did – you wouldn't have had the slightest suspicion that he was acquainted with William, much less that he had sat plotting with him in a room high up in the Warren the night before.

Eventually Childes stopped writing and pushed the ledger towards Fellowes, who read the entry and nodded approvingly. Fellowes looked back at the young mason.

'You can go,' he said. 'Tell the Chief Mason that the note has been delivered.'

'Thank you,' said Gondolier.

Fellowes picked up the note and left the desk to take it to the UnderButler.

The Bridled Mound was a round, thick building that stood not far from the Faunal House. It rose six storeys with stairs on the outside, spiralling round it like a ribbon of stone. The rooms inside were large but dark, and it had never been a particularly popular building with the Halibuts. At the very top, however, lived Eversniff T Halibut, perhaps the most irritable man in the House, with three irritable dogs. He never let them out of his apartment, which may have accounted for their temperament. For years, Eversniff had been demanding that the stairs on the outside of the Mound be fixed. A number of the steps were loose and a few had fallen away, so Eversniff had to step gingerly over holes in the staircase on the way to and from his irritable dogs, or risk plunging to his death. Eventually a step had fallen away directly outside his door, and at that point even the Chief Mason had to agree that repair was urgently required.

Needless to say, once begun, the repair proved difficult to complete. Every part of the staircase that was examined turned out to be in need of work and it was clear that nothing less than complete replacement would be required. It would have been better, in Albert Gondolier's view, and in the view of just about everyone else who was asked – and certainly in the view of those who weren't – simply to strip the staircase off and leave the building uninhabited. But Eversniff refused to move, and since no one had the right to force him to leave, there was no alternative but to replace the entire set of stairs. The first thing Albert Gondolier did was to have the stairs stripped away and then to stop work for a few days to encourage Eversniff to change his mind. But that just made him more determined to stay, and from a window in his apartment, where he had stored a year's supply of food, he shouted down that he wouldn't move out even when the work was being done, much less move out for good.

So the work commenced. A pale spiral of stripped stone marked the line where the stairs had been removed. Scaffolding rose round it and a crane was set up at the top with a long arm like the beak of a stork projecting over the edge of the building with various ropes and pulleys hanging from it. Most of the time the crane was used to raise blocks of stone for the stairs, although it also sent various things up to Eversniff and his three irritable companions. It was also used to raise visitors, but Eversniff had very few of these and his dogs had even fewer.

It was early afternoon by the time Trimbleby arrived, accompanied by the four UnderUnderButlers. They looked up as they approached, scanning the scaffolding round the Bridled Mound. It was an obvious place for something to be dropped on Trimbleby – so obvious that the UnderButler thought it very unlikely that anything would happen here. Nonetheless, he and the UnderUnderButlers stopped well back from the scaffolding.

'Mr Gondolier!' called out Trimbleby, glimpsing the

Chief Mason a couple of storeys up in the thicket of scaffolding.

At the name, most of the men on the scaffolding looked round, all Gondoliers of the Gondolier family.

'Me, Mr Trimbleby?' called down the Chief Mason.

Trimbleby nodded.

The Chief Mason said a word to one of the workers he had been talking to and made his way down.

Albert Gondolier was over sixty, but moved with the agility of a man who has spent his whole life on scaffolding. The Gondoliers taught their children to climb from bar to bar before they taught them to walk. He dropped swiftly through the scaffolding and within a minute he was on the ground.

'Mr Trimbleby,' he said, hands on his hips. 'This is a pleasure. What can I do for you?'

'I'm here,' said the UnderButler. He looked around. 'I see you haven't stopped work yet.'

'Why should we stop work?'

'Because of the problem.'

'And the problem is . . . ?'

Trimbleby stared at the Chief Mason. Albert Gondolier gazed back at him with a pleasant expression, clearly having no idea why the UnderButler had appeared.

In that instant, one part of Horace Trimbleby's brain realised that the Chief Mason hadn't sent for him at all and if only he had let that part of his brain – the instinctive, natural part that knew he was being hunted by a killer who had succeeded in murdering his two colleagues – tell him what to do, he would have turned and run, run from that place as fast as he could. But at the same instant, another part of his brain – the trained, UnderButler part that knew that in Neversuch House mistakes and miscommunications happened all the time, and if you didn't clear them up straight away, you might spend years sorting out the mess – was still trying to work out whether there had been some kind of genuine misunderstanding. And for the next moment, the next crucial split second of Horace Trimbleby's life, it was that part of his brain that won out.

An apprentice mason had dropped down from the scaffolding. 'It's over there,' he said to Albert Gondolier. 'The hole, Great-Uncle, the hole that's appeared in the wall.'

'That? Is that what Mr Trimbleby's here for? He doesn't need to see that.'

'I thought you said he did. Well, he's here now.' Robert Gondolier turned and pointed. 'It's over there, Mr Trimbleby. Over there.' And not only did he point with one hand, but he also gave the UnderButler a slight nudge with the other.

Trimbleby took a couple of steps in the direction he had been shown, and it was only a couple of steps that were needed, because those steps took him under the point of the crane, from which a looped rope – which hadn't been there when the UnderButler first arrived – was now hanging all the way down to the ground.

Unaware of it, the UnderButler put his foot in the loop of the rope, and as he took his next step, the loop tightened and a pulley turned and suddenly Horace Trimbleby flew into the air, jerked up at an astonishing speed by the rope round his foot. The masons on the scaffolding barely saw him as he shot past, and were barely able to look up quickly enough to see what happened next. He hit the point of the crane, feet first, and the power of the impact snapped the arm of the crane all the way back so he went sailing over the top of the Bridled Mound in the other direction. An instant later, the crane snapped back again, and then again, and for about a minute, Horace Trimbleby went snapping back and forth over the top of the Bridled Mound like a ping pong ball over a net until at last he came to rest, dangling by one foot, halfway up the scaffolding.

All over the building, Gondoliers stared.

'Get him down!' shouted Albert Gondolier. 'Get him down now and careful as you do it!'

A dozen Gondoliers swarmed up the scaffolding. They cut him down, but the UnderButler was dead, his neck broken, either from the initial collision with the point of the crane, or from hitting the scaffolding on the other side of the building, or from the force of the snapping in one direction and then another. After being called to inspect the body, Eldred Sturgeon would announce confidently that he would never be able to say.

'What an extraordinary accident,' said Albert Gondolier to his great-nephew, who was still standing beside him. 'I've never seen anything like it.'

Robert Gondolier nodded. 'Freakish, Great-Uncle.'

14

An Unexpected Helper

Omnia came out of the Blue Rotunda, a huge, round building that was open to the sky, at the bottom of which was the Pallid Pool. She hadn't necessarily felt like swimming, but her friends were going, and until she had worked out what to do after her conversations the previous day with the UnderButler and Basilica, she thought she would be safest if she stuck with them. She would have more protection from a would-be assassin if she was with a group than if she was alone. They had played a long game of Pallid Polo, which was something like the game you would recognise as water polo, but at the same time something completely unlike it, as you would expect in Neversuch House.

They all came out together, still arguing about a goal Eversmart claimed to have scored which no one else, apart from Evesia, had seen going into the undernet before supposedly coming out again. It wasn't a particularly important goal, since Eversmart's side had lost anyway, but it *could* have been, which was the point.

'Eversmart,' said Omnia. 'It's eight against two who said they didn't see it go in. That's sixteen eyes against four.'

'Yes, but ten of those eyes were on the other side. Obviously you're not going to agree with me.'

'That still leaves six eyes on your own side who didn't see it. That's six against—'

Omnia stopped.

'Four,' murmured Evergrow, prompting her.

But she wasn't listening. Under the low-hanging roof of the building opposite the Rotunda stood someone in a black cloak.

None of the other children really knew or trusted Cornelius Slinker, and quite a few were scared of him, the more so since his face had mysteriously acquired a long scar a few months earlier. Only Omnia and Evergrow knew how he had come by that scar on the night Tobias Hildegrew flew away – although Evergrow himself didn't know that Hildegrew had survived. After Omnia had been forced by the UnderButlers to promise not to tell anyone what she had seen, Evergrow was left under the impression that Hildegrew had died, as everyone else was told, by falling from the Great Tower.

Slinker came out from under the roof.

'Stay there!' said Omnia.

Evergrow glanced at her in surprise. Omnia hadn't told him about the stone that Cornelius had given her, but he knew that she trusted the messenger as someone who had saved her life and almost lost his own in the process.

Cornelius gave her a confused look.

'Don't come any closer!'

None of the other children had any idea what was going on, but they could sense that there was more to this than the chance appearance of one of the House's messengers. And from the look of it, Omnia wasn't too happy to see him. They were her friends. If she wanted Slinker to stay away, they'd do what they could to make sure he did.

'Omnia,' said Cornelius. He looked at her imploringly.

'If you've got something to tell me, tell me from there!'

Slinker glanced uncomfortably at the children surrounding her. 'Omnia . . .' he said again.

Omnia didn't reply. She still could hardly bring herself to believe that it was Cornelius who had chased her into the Winter House, but Basilica was right – until she knew that it wasn't, she had to assume that it was. Obviously she could ask him, but even if it was true, he would just deny it. She watched him now, and in his place, she saw the panther-man. It would take only a mask to change one into the other.

'All right,' he said. 'I'll tell you. Trimbleby's dead.'

Omnia narrowed her eyes.

'Killed by a crane. Accident. Freakish. I came to let you know.'

The other children glanced at Omnia to see what that meant to her. It meant nothing to them. They barely knew who Trimbleby was, much less cared that he was dead.

'How do I know you're not lying?' demanded Omnia.

Slinker glanced at the children around her again. 'Omnia, can't we—'

'No! Stay there!'

Her mind was racing. If Trimbleby was dead, there were no UnderButlers left. What would happen now? The Master Filer! She remembered the name, even if she had no idea who he was. Trimbleby had said that if he died, she should go to the Master Filer.

'Omnia, it couldn't be an accident. We should—'

'Don't let him come after me!' she called to the others. 'Evergrow, don't let him follow!'

She turned and ran.

Cornelius Slinker took a step after her. But Evergrow stepped forward, arms folded, followed by Eversmart and the others, and before Slinker knew it, he was faced with a dozen Halibut children, all blocking his way.

Cornelius Slinker watched them for a moment. Omnia had disappeared. He turned, stepped back under the roof behind him and slipped away into the shadows.

There was chaos in the entrance chamber. A dozen clerks and servants milled around, waving pieces of paper and demanding to be heard. Behind their desk, Fellowes and Childes struggled to control them. William Bell sat on his chair beside the entrance, waiting to be told where to go, but the Clerks had no instructions for him. The Butler was unavailable and in the absence of even one UnderButler – a situation that was unprecedented in the House, as far as anyone knew – they had no idea how to direct the requests that were coming in. And the less idea they had, it seemed, the more people arrived. It was as if everyone outside had realised, as soon as they heard that the last UnderButler had been killed, that they immediately required an UnderButler's opinion. And so they streamed up the stairs into the entrance chamber – plumbers, pruners, glaziers, gardeners – all waving notes and shouting for attention. The Clerks demanded silence, but didn't get it. They stood up, sat down, smoothed their lapels, cleared their throats, smoothed their whiskers – or Fellowes did, for Childes lacked them – all to no avail. In a word, and perhaps for the first time in their lives, the two Clerks of the Entrance were flustered.

And then Omnia arrived. They saw her come up the stairs at the back of the crowd. 'Go away!' Fellowes shouted at her over the commotion. 'We haven't time for you today.'

'You don't even know what I want!' Omnia shouted back.

'Don't know – don't care!' Fellowes turned to look at a paper someone from the office of the Grand Glazier was shoving at him. Childes was similarly preoccupied.

'Perhaps I can help you,' said a voice beside her.

Omnia turned. The freckle-faced clerk smiled at her from his seat beside the door.

'Will you?' she said.

He jumped up. 'If I can.'

Omnia threw a glance in the direction of the two Clerks

behind the desk who were trying to control a dozen paper-waving servants. 'Won't they be angry with you?'

William grinned. 'Only if they find out. You won't tell, will you?'

Omnia shook her head.

'Come on then. Got to take your chances, don't you? Who do you want to see this time? The UnderButler's dead, you know. It's no good if you want to see him.'

'I want the Master Filer.'

'Do you know how to get to him?'

'No idea,' said Omnia. 'Can you take me?'

The two Clerks of the Entrance were busy with the servants besieging them. The door that led into the Butlery was only a few metres away.

William Bell smiled at her. 'Come with me.'

When Omnia had been through the corridors of the Bright Tower to the Butler's office the previous day, silence had reigned as the clerks in the file-filled rooms hunched over their desks, hard at work. This time there was a hum of anxious conversation, and clerks were leaning back in their chairs or even standing up and talking in groups. News of Trimbleby's death was spreading through the Butlery, leaving uncertainty and consternation in its wake.

'Terrible thing, what happened to poor Mr Trimbleby,' said William Bell over his shoulder as he led Omnia along the corridors. 'Have you heard about it? He's dead, you know.'

'How did it happen?'

'An accident, Omnia.'

'How do you know my name?'

'I heard you say it yesterday. I'm William Bell, by the way.' William laughed. 'Should have done the introductions earlier.'

Omnia smiled.

'Terrible accident, what happened. As I understand it, Omnia, poor Mr Trimbleby got tangled up in a rope at the repairs they're doing at the Bridled Mound, and before anyone could stop it, he was hanged. Hanged by his foot, if you please.'

'You don't die if you're hanged by your foot,' said Omnia.

William stopped and turned to her. 'Mr Trimbleby did. A *freakish* accident, everyone's saying. Getting hanged by your foot. Ain't accidents terrible things?'

Omnia narrowed her eyes. 'Yes,' she said.

William laughed. 'Don't look at me like that. What? Do you think I had something to do with it?'

Omnia shook her head. 'Of course not.'

'Exactly. But I will tell you one thing, Omnia. A person needs to know who she can trust. Don't you think?'

Omnia stared at him. 'What does that mean?'

William shrugged. 'I see things, Omnia. Sitting in the entrance chamber all day, I see all kinds of people that say all kinds of things. You need to know who you can trust, that's all.'

'So, who can I trust?'

William's freckly face creased in a smile. 'I know what you think I'm going to say. Me! I'm right, aren't I? But I won't. I'll tell you why. The person who tells you you can trust him – he's the one you want to be *most* careful of.'

Omnia thought of Cornelius Slinker.

'What about you?' she said.

'Me? I'm just a messenger clerk.'

'A messenger clerk should be trustworthy.'

'That's true.' William appeared to think about it for a moment, then laughed. 'I suppose I must be then. Or I should be anyway.'

They kept going, passing room after room after room. Omnia had no idea where she was. Finally William Bell stopped at a purple door.

'This is it,' he said.

Omnia looked at the door. 'This is the Master Filer?'

'That's right.'

'You're sure?'

William looked at her as if he was offended. 'What are you suggesting? That I've taken you somewhere different?'

Omnia frowned. She was getting suspicious of everyone! 'No. I'm sorry. I don't know why I said that.'

'Don't worry.' William Bell winked at her. Then he knocked at the door and smiled reassuringly. 'In you go.'

15

In the Hold

Inside the room sat a small man. He wore a raisin-coloured coat and on his head he wore a small, round, raisin-coloured hat.

He glanced up, then stared. 'Who are you?' he demanded.

'Omnia Halibut,' said Omnia.

The man peered at her suspiciously. He had milky blue eyes and very smooth, white skin, as if he rarely went outside. He was old, but it was hard to tell how old.

'Don't get many Halibuts in here. Last one I remember was . . .' He frowned, thinking. 'Nineteen years ago, I think. Everplant Z Halibut was his name. Know him, do you?'

Omnia shook her head.

'No, you don't look old enough. How old are you?'

'Twelve and seven-sixteenths.'

'No, I was right. Nowhere near old enough. He would have been dead by the time you were born, I should imagine. Very old, he was, and very frail. Came in here by mistake. Had no idea how he got here or what he wanted.'

Omnia looked around the room. Charts hung all over the walls, showing complicated lists and classification systems. The man himself sat at a desk in front of which was a set of two dozen or more big wooden bins filled to the top with files. Elsewhere in the room was a deep armchair, a large bed with velvet curtains around it and a big wardrobe. There were several chests of drawers as well, and a number of metal safes of various sizes.

'I suppose I don't really need to ask this . . .' said Omnia, glancing at the charts on the walls, 'but you are the Master Filer, aren't you?'

'Indeed I am. Sixth in the line. What did you say your name was again?'

'Omnia Halibut.'

'Ah.' He raised a finger. 'Thought it rang a bell. Just wait a moment, if you will.'

The man adjusted a pair of spectacles on his nose, opened a big ledger, licked his finger and began to turn the pages. Finally he came to the page he wanted and ran his finger down the ledger, peering at it closely as he did.

There was a knock on the door. The Master Filer grunted something unintelligible and Omnia moved away just in time for the door to open. A woman in a raisin-coloured coat came in, pushing a wooden bin on a trolley. The Master Filer glanced at her briefly and turned back to the page. The woman unloaded the bin, replaced it with one of the bins in front of the desk and left.

'Here we are!' said the Master Filer. 'Omnia Halibut.' He looked up at her over the top of his spectacles. 'Mr Trimbleby, apparently, left me a letter to be opened in the event that he died in a freakish accident and you came to see me.'

Omnia stared at him in surprise.

'Mr Trimbleby, you may be aware, was an UnderButler.'

'I'm aware,' said Omnia.

'Are you aware that he's dead?'

Omnia nodded.

'Only today.' The Master Filer sighed. 'Tragic. Third in a row. An unfortunate time to be an UnderButler, don't you think?'

The Master Filer peered at her over the top of his spectacles. Omnia didn't reply. She wondered how much the Master Filer knew or suspected.

'Well, he's dead and you're here,' said the Master Filer at last. 'And the accident that killed him could only be described as freakish.' He looked up at the wall. 'Letters in the event of freakish accidents,' he murmured to himself, scanning the filing charts on the wall. 'Letters in the event of freakish . . . Ah, there we are.'

The Master Filer gazed at the chart on the wall for a moment, then stood up and went to a small, steel safe, got down on one knee, opened the safe and pulled out a sheaf of envelopes of various sizes. He flipped through the envelopes and pulled one out, then put the others back in the safe and closed the door. He brought the envelope back to his desk and opened it.

It contained a single page.

'Hmmm,' he said, raising an eyebrow.

'What does it say?' asked Omnia.

'It says I'm to take you to see the Butler and the Captain.' The Master Filer looked up at her. 'That's if you want to see them, I suppose.'

They left the room by a door in the corner behind the bed. The Master Filer carried an umbrella, even though Omnia told him it wasn't raining. They walked down a corridor with rooms full of clerks on both sides, and the Master Filer kept stopping to peer into the rooms as he went past. He was a tiny man, no taller than Omnia herself, as if all the years locked away in his room had deprived him of his growth, but the effect when he appeared in a doorway was immediate. The clerks in the room sat up ramrod straight in their chairs. Now and again, without any warning, he would go into a room to check the files on the shelves, clambering on to chairs or desks or chests of drawers or anything that was handy with the energy of a raisin-capped chimpanzee. Omnia soon discovered that the umbrella had nothing to do with rain. If he spotted a mistake, the Master Filer swept every file off the shelf with its hook, telling the clerks he'd seen better filing from a monkey. If he found a second mistake, he swept the files off all the shelves in the room, leaving the floor covered in paper.

All this clambering and checking and sweeping of files slowed them down considerably, but finally they left the last of the clerks behind and went into a room and out through a door that led to a long, windowless corridor. Omnia wondered if this was the same closed passage that ran between the Butlery and the Great Tower, through which the three UnderButlers had marched her after Tobias Hildegrew revealed himself as the black condor. But if there was one secret corridor leading from the Butlery, there could just as well be others. Perhaps this was a different one, one that led secretly outside the wall of Neversuch House.

The Master Filer shuffled along quickly. Eventually he opened another door and there were stairs in front of them. Omnia looked up, wondering where the stairs led. The Master Filer nudged her with his umbrella and headed down.

It was very dark down here, almost black, but the Master Filer's pace didn't slow. Down one flight they went and a second. Then they turned and went through a door, and then they began climbing, one flight of stairs after another, until it was light again. They kept climbing. They stopped on a landing with an enormous oak door in front of them. The door frame was carved with sea dragons.

The Master Filer knocked.

There was silence. It went on for what seemed to be a long time, but the Master Filer didn't knock again.

Omnia wondered what was happening.

Eventually a small, plain door, which Omnia hadn't even noticed, opened behind them. In it stood Digby, the Butler, in his green Butler's coat.

He took one look at Omnia. 'Trimbleby's dead, isn't he?' he said to the Master Filer.

The old man nodded.

Digby closed his eyes for a moment and took a deep breath. Then he opened them again and stepped aside.

They went in.

The Butler closed the door behind them and immediately a set of metal bars slid into place.

He led them through a pair of connected rooms. The walls were lined with dark timber and they curved as if within an old, wooden ship. The ceilings were made of wood and the windows were small, made of numerous squares of thick glass set into lead frames. As they walked, a mechanism built into the floors made them tilt, first one way, then another, as if a sea was rolling beneath them. It was enough to make you feel somewhat ill.

Omnia tried to work out where she was. She was still in the House anyway. She caught a glimpse of the top of the Slate Tower through the thick glass of one window. From another she thought she spotted the tip of the roof of the Purple Nave.

They stopped in the third room. In an armchair sat a

man with a bald, egg-shaped head, wearing a blue Captain's coat. It was Everdean, the Captain of the House.

Digby crouched in front of him.

'Trimbleby's dead,' he said loudly.

Everdean nodded slowly.

'Killed in an accident.'

Everdean nodded again. Omnia watched him. He looked as if he would nod at anything. Nothing about him showed that he understood what had been said. He looked so *old*. He looked as if he was in a world of his own.

Omnia remembered him reading the funeral rhyme for the previous Captain, Everwise, three months earlier. It had been almost impossible to hear him, but at least he had stood and read it. Now he didn't look capable of doing even that. He seemed to have gone downhill since he had been forced to become the Captain of the House.

Her heart sank. This was the leader of the House, the person who was supposed to guide them through this emergency. Suddenly Omnia felt there was no hope. Someone else would have to do it or they were lost.

She looked round and saw Digby watching her.

'What is this place?' she asked.

'The Hold,' said the Master Filer. 'Only the Captain, the Butler, the UnderButlers and the Master Filer are allowed to know the way in. The First Captain built it as a place to remind him of his life at sea. Everdew the Third had it strengthened to be used as a place of safety in times of danger.'

Omnia sat down. 'What about the Captain's treasure? Is this where it's kept?'

Digby shook his head. 'We have men guarding it.'

'Do you trust them?'

'Enough. The keys are here,' he said, patting his chest and glancing at Everdean, who didn't show any sign that he had even heard what was being said.

'It's the Evergones who are doing this, isn't it?' said Omnia.

There was silence. Neither the Butler nor the Master Filer replied.

'I know who they are. I've worked it out, so you can stop worrying about telling me. They're Halibuts who have gone outside the wall, aren't they?'

'That's right,' said the Butler quietly. He sat down opposite Omnia.

'Why do they fight us?'

'Because they can't—'

The Master Filer coughed meaningfully.

The Butler glanced at him, then continued. 'Because they can't come back. Some go and we never hear of them again. Others go and then realise what they've left behind. They want to come back, but they're not allowed to. That's their punishment for leaving in the first place.'

'It's a punishment the First Captain created,' said the Master Filer tersely. 'Every Halibut lives with that threat over his head.'

'Why?'

'Do you think the House would have survived without it? People coming and going as they pleased? No, before long it would have ended. It wouldn't have lasted two generations.'

'It doesn't seem fair to punish people for doing that if they don't even know there's a punishment,' said Omnia.

'They know,' said the Master Filer. 'Every Halibut knows.'

'I'm a Halibut and I've never heard of it!'

'You're too young. You'd be told when you turn sixteen.'

'Then why hasn't anyone—'

'And you'd be told it must be kept secret from the children. The punishment for telling them is the same as the punishment for going outside the wall.'

'But you're telling me!'

'Indeed we are,' said the Master Filer, throwing a glance at the Butler.

'There are exceptions,' said Digby. 'But the rule now applies to you, Omnia. Tell this to your friends, tell this to anyone who hasn't turned sixteen, and you'll be punished. You'll be put outside and never allowed back in.' Digby looked at her with a shrug, as if he wished he could change the facts, but he couldn't and he would enforce the rule if he must.

Omnia gazed at the two men in front of her. Then she glanced at Everdean, who sat in his blue Captain's coat, head sunk on his chest, muttering about rocks or sands or some other geological phenomenon of the sort he had spent his whole life studying, apparently unaware of anything around him. *He* had been told, she thought. There had been a day, many years ago, when he must have heard exactly the same thing for the first time in his life, just as she had.

'So everyone is told . . . when?' asked Omnia. 'On their sixteenth birthday?'

The Master Filer nodded.

So her father had been told the day he turned sixteen, and her Aunt Ribelia, and her Uncle Everlook, who had tragically died just a few years later, and every adult who lived in Neversuch House. They all knew! And not one of them had ever told her.

Suddenly it seemed there was a gigantic conspiracy carried out by the people she most trusted. Or at least the people she thought she had trusted. She had always been told that no Halibut left Neversuch House simply because there was no reason for them to want to. But that was a lie. There were Halibuts who did want to, and they did leave. Only no one would admit it. And as a punishment, they were never allowed back.

Omnia struggled to comprehend it. She was twelve years old – twelve and seven-sixteenths – but until that moment she hadn't known what was possibly the most important fact about the world in which she lived.

'What about Basilica?' she said eventually.

At the name, Everdean's head turned, and for a moment, it looked as if he was listening to what was being said.

'What about her?' asked the Master Filer.

'She went outside the wall, I'm sure she did. But she's here.'

The Butler and the Master Filer glanced at one another.

'She died a long time ago,' said the Master Filer.

'I saw her!'

'Then you saw a ghost.'

'I did not! I saw her only—' Omnia stopped herself from saying more. The last time Omnia revealed that she had seen her, Basilica had been moved and it had taken three months, and an extraordinary event, to find her again.

'*When* did you see her?' asked the Master Filer.

'Three months ago,' replied Omnia quietly. 'I saw her twice and she was as alive as you or me. She wasn't a ghost.'

'She must have been.'

'She wasn't!' Omnia appealed to the Butler. 'I know what I saw.'

The Butler opened his mouth to speak.

'There are some exceptions we can make,' said the Master Filer before he could get a word out. 'Others we can't.'

The Butler hesitated for a moment, then closed his mouth.

Omnia crossed her arms in frustration. 'Well, I think it's Cornelius Slinker who's been killing the UnderButlers.'

The two men looked at her in surprise.

'Why?' said Digby.

'I just . . . I have a hunch.'

'You need more than a hunch if you're going to start

making accusations like that,' said the Master Filer. 'Why do you say it's him? What proof have you got?'

Omnia didn't reply. She didn't want to mention anything that had happened the previous day in case she was forced to tell them about Basilica.

'Well?' demanded the Master Filer.

Omnia wanted to get off the subject. 'Why did Trimbleby leave that letter?'

'That's a good question,' said the Master Filer. 'I was going to ask you.'

'I don't know why,' said Omnia. 'He always hated me.'

'He knew who you are,' said the Butler.

'What does that mean?'

'There aren't many Halibuts who can *do* something.'

'That's what Basilica said to me. Once in a generation.'

'That's about right,' muttered the Master Filer.

Omnia ignored him. 'You mean *I'm* it?' she said to the Butler.

'Can you think of anyone else?'

'That's ridiculous! I'm twelve!'

'Twelve and seven-sixteenths,' Digby reminded her.

'Don't tell me seven-sixteenths makes such a difference!'

'It doesn't hurt,' said the Master Filer.

'Omnia,' said the Butler, 'it doesn't really matter whether that person does or doesn't exist, or whether you are or aren't her. You stopped the Evergones last time so this time they'll come after you again.'

'Whoever it is this time,' said the Master Filer, 'they'll know who you are. Tobias Hildegrew will have told them.'

143

'So you know he survived, do you?' said Omnia.

'I see all the files,' replied the Master Filer. 'The secret as well as the known.'

'And I'm the bait again, is that it?'

'No. You're a target. Like Mr Digby is. It's not your choice, it's theirs. Have they tried to get you? Tell us the truth.'

Omnia bit her lip.

'Something's happened, hasn't it?'

'I'm not saying.'

'Omnia,' said the Butler, 'you should tell us.'

'I'm not saying!'

Digby glanced at the Master Filer, who shrugged, as if to say, if you actually found a Halibut who could do something, they were bound to be difficult.

'What are they trying to do?' asked Omnia. 'What's the point of all this? I thought they wanted to get the treasure.'

'I'm sure they do.'

'Then what's the point of killing the UnderButlers?'

'Who knows?' said the Master Filer. 'Whatever good they thought it was going to do, they're mistaken. They've given us warning. The Captain and the Butler are both in here, where they're safe.'

'But if they're in here, and the UnderButlers are dead, who's going to look after things?'

'The UnderUnderButlers.'

Omnia looked at the Butler doubtfully. She didn't know the UnderUnderButlers, but she had seen them. They all looked very young.

'I'll send them orders,' said the Butler.

'The first thing is that the Captain and the Butler have to stay alive,' said the Master Filer. 'As long as they're safe, the House is safe. They'll stay here in the Hold until it's all right to come out. That's how it's always been done.'

'Omnia, you should stay here with us,' said the Butler.

The Master Filer frowned.

'She's under threat,' the Butler said to him, noticing the expression on his face.

'That's not what the Hold's for,' replied the Master Filer.

'There's no reason why it shouldn't be.'

'That's something for the Captain.'

'Do you expect him to decide?'

They both turned to look at Everdean. He was snoring now, his chin sunk on his chest.

'He's still the Captain,' said the Master Filer.

'She can stay in the Hold. We can make an exception.'

'That's up to the Cap—'

'It doesn't matter!' said Omnia.

The two men looked at her.

'I'm not staying here. Maybe it's true that you have to be kept alive, Mr Digby, so maybe you do have to stay here in this place. But I don't matter, do I? And I don't see what I can do if I'm locked up in here.'

'Quite right,' agreed the Master Filer.

'Omnia, what will you do?'

'I don't know.' Omnia had no idea, but she did know one thing – if she stayed here, she wouldn't be able to do anything at all. And right now, she couldn't see who else would.

'What about protection?' said Digby. 'Some of the UnderUnderButlers perhaps?'

'They didn't help Trimbleby.'

'That doesn't mean they won't help you.'

Omnia shook her head. Who knew if they could be trusted? She had trusted Cornelius and look where that had got her.

And who knew if Cornelius was acting alone? Why did it have to be only one person? It could be more. Perhaps one of the UnderUnderButlers was helping him. Perhaps it was one of them who had arranged Trimbleby's death, one of the UnderUnderButlers who was supposed to be guarding him.

Trust no one, that was what Basilica had said.

'I'll take my chances, Mr Digby.'

She went back with the Master Filer. He said very little along the way, and by the time they got back to the Bright Tower, he seemed to have lost his appetite for wielding his umbrella. They went past the clerks' rooms and into his office by the door in the corner through which they had left. He took her across the room to the other door where Omnia had first entered.

He paused before opening it. 'I knew you wouldn't want to stay in the Hold,' he said.

Omnia looked at him doubtfully. He didn't sound as if

he knew, she thought, when he was arguing with the Butler about letting her stay there.

'Every so often, there does come along a Halibut who *can* do something.'

'I've heard that already,' said Omnia.

'I know.' He peered at her. He was so short that they were eye to eye. 'Understand something, Omnia Halibut. This is our House. Not just yours, ours as well.' He paused. 'Each must do what he or she can. Servant or Halibut, it makes no difference.' He opened the door. 'I hope we'll see each other again soon.'

Omnia nodded. She knew what that meant. He hoped they'd live to see each other again – at all.

Outside, William Bell was waiting.

'Have you been here all this time?' asked Omnia in surprise. She must have been gone for a couple of hours.

'Of course I have. I said I'd wait. I wouldn't be much of a servant if I didn't.'

Omnia smiled. She was beginning to like William Bell. Everyone else in the Butlery seemed at best to be indifferent and at worst they were downright rude. 'Thank you,' she said.

William smiled back at her. 'Not at all. Shall we go back or do you want to go somewhere else?'

'No. Let's go back.'

William led her along the corridor. 'You were in that office an awfully long time.'

'We went somewhere else.'

'Where to?'

'To the—' Omnia stopped. 'Somewhere. It doesn't matter.'

William turned and smiled. 'Quite right, Omnia. Best not to say. Times like these, you don't know who you can trust. Say nothing to anyone, that's my advice.'

He brought her to the entrance chamber. The crowd was bigger and noisier than before.

'Here you are,' said William. 'If you ever need me, Omnia, you know where to find me.'

16

Decision

She sat bolt upright. It was pitch-dark. Her heart was thumping.

The dream had come back. She was falling from the Slate Tower with a black cloak fluttering above her, and then the cloak turned into the black condor and she knew she was looking up at the face of the person who had thrown her off the Tower, the person who had tried to kill her, and if only she could see who it was she would be saved, but the face was a blank and as hard as she looked she couldn't make out a single feature. So she continued to fall, overcome by panic and desperation until an instant before she hit the ground – which was always the moment she woke up, pulse racing, in a cold sweat, with an icy terror in her heart.

She hadn't had the dream for weeks. At first, after the night Tobias Hildegrew escaped, Omnia had had it almost every night, and then every couple of nights, and eventually it stopped. She thought it had gone forever, but now it was back.

Omnia turned on a light and waited for the terror to subside. The light helped. But the terror, as always, took its time. It couldn't be rushed, as if it was a visitor that would leave when it was ready, and not before. She tried to think of something else. Nice things. But her mind kept coming back to the dream, and not only the dream, but the events that had been happening in reality.

She looked round the room, her own room in the Long South Range. Was she safe here? She shouldn't have come back! If Slinker wanted to find her, wasn't this the first place he'd look? She should have gone somewhere to hide. Where? Evergrow's? She had hidden there three months ago when she was in danger, in the big wardrobe in Evergrow's room. She could even stay in the secret room she'd discovered behind it. What was she *doing* coming back here—

She heard a noise. Quickly, Omnia turned off the light and listened. Cornelius wouldn't know exactly which room she was in, but he would know the general whereabouts. Maybe that was him now, going from room to room, searching for her . . .

Her eyes narrowed as she listened in the darkness. Quietly, Omnia went to the door and opened it a fraction. There was a dim light from a lamp that glowed further down the corridor. Cautiously, she put her head out. No one.

Another noise. Now Omnia knew where the sounds were coming from. Her brother's room. Suddenly she was aware of the sweet, cloying smell of one of his experiments, most of which he carried out at night. With each week that passed, Eversmooth seemed more detached from the real world and more lost in a world of hair waxes, oils and gels, which he concocted himself. Nowadays, he hardly seemed to leave his room except to roam the House – its lodges, its towers, its galleries and halls – looking for the space that he would turn into the great laboratory he had in mind. He was only seventeen and yet the obsessional nature of the Halibut genes, or the Halibut air, or whatever it was had taken him over.

Omnia wondered whether that would happen to her as well, and when the obsession would start, and what it would be. And whether she would even recognise it as an obsession when it started. None of the adult Halibuts seemed to. That was the scariest thought of all – that you would be obsessed like everybody else, but you would think you were still normal.

Digby and the Master Filer had said to her yesterday that perhaps she was a Halibut who could *do* something. Basilica had said it too, or something similar. Omnia didn't know if it was true. If it was, she didn't know what to think of it, whether it was a good thing or a bad. Wasn't it better to be like everyone else? It was less scary. What good had being different done her? It had turned her into a target, a name on a list of people to be killed.

She had guessed some of what Digby and the Master Filer had told her about the Evergones, but not all of it. Certainly not the fact that at sixteen everyone was told the truth and sworn to secrecy. Secrecy! There were so many secrets in this House that she had begun to wonder if *anything* she had *ever* been told was true. Maybe that was why everyone seemed to end up lost in some kind of private obsession, because that was the only way of avoiding the lies that everyone else was telling, of finding some kind of truth you could rely on. And this? This secret was the worst of all, one that was known by every adult and withheld from every child. As if there was some kind of vast conspiracy against the children in the House, and everyone over sixteen was part of it.

Everyone over sixteen . . .

Everyone . . .

Omnia marched out of her room, down the corridor and thumped on Eversmooth's door. She wasn't worried about waking her parents, who were asleep two rooms further along. They went to bed early and were up with the dawn, and were renowned for their ability to sleep in between. They often said that the Long South Range could collapse around their ears, and as long as it happened before five in the morning, it wouldn't disturb them in the slightest. Omnia wasn't sure if it was meant as a joke.

She thumped again. And again.

The door swung back fractionally.

Omnia pushed it open. In front of her stood Eversmooth

in a white coat with a pair of goggles on his face and a huge glass dropper in his hand. The hair on his head was waxed into a helmet of points.

Omnia hadn't been in his room for months. She barely recognised it. Eversmooth had pushed his bed into a corner, his clothes were piled in another corner and everywhere else were pots, beakers, test tubes and retorts bubbling over burners, line after line of them, with pipes, tubes, dials, gauges and spiralling connectors carrying liquids between them. A pair of large vats bubbled over bigger burners under the window. The sweet, cloying smell was overpowering.

'What do you want?' demanded Eversmooth. 'I'm in the middle of something!'

'Who cares?' retorted Omnia and she closed the door behind her. 'I've got something to tell you. I know about the Evergones! I know what the punishment is for leaving the House!'

Eversmooth stared at her.

'I know about them, I said. Do you understand me, Eversmooth? I know.'

'You didn't hear it from me,' said Eversmooth quickly.

'That's the point! You know too, don't you? You've known for over a year. You were told when you turned sixteen.'

Eversmooth sat down on a stool in front of a bench of bubbling beakers and test tubes. He took his goggles off and gazed at Omnia silently.

'How could you not have told me? Eversmooth, how could you not have said a word?'

'You said you know what the punishment is for leaving,' replied Eversmooth quietly. 'Do you know what it is for telling?'

'Yes.'

'Then . . . ?'

'But I'm your sister, Eversmooth! Your own sister! Do you think I would have told anyone?'

'You were going to find out in a few years anyway. What difference did it make?'

Omnia shook her head. 'Who was it who told you?'

'Digby and the Captain.'

'On your sixteenth birthday?'

Eversmooth nodded.

'Are they always the ones?'

'I suppose so,' said Eversmooth. 'Who told you?'

'Digby.'

'Why?'

'He just . . . It's very complicated. They make exceptions.'

Eversmooth frowned. Omnia watched him, waiting for her brother to ask more. But he didn't. She could see his eye wandering back to the vessels that were boiling and bubbling around the room. He didn't really care why she had been told, she realised. It didn't interest him. Nothing seemed to interest him any more but this.

'I miss you, Eversmooth. We never do anything any more. Do you remember when we used to climb down the

154

ladder to the meadow? I was too small and you'd carry me on your back.'

Eversmooth looked back at her and nodded.

'And we used to laugh about all the silly Halibuts with their silly obsessions. Don't you remember?'

Eversmooth smiled. 'Aren't they ridiculous?'

Omnia stared at him. How could he say that, sitting here in this room with all these vessels boiling and bubbling around him? Couldn't he see that he was turning into one of those Halibuts himself?

'What's happening to you?' she murmured.

Eversmooth gazed at her, not understanding. Then he noticed something out of the corner of his eye, and suddenly he jumped up, put his goggles over his eyes and rushed across to adjust a flame that was overheating one of his beakers. The beaker was part of a complicated array of vessels all connected by tubes and in another few seconds he was running up and down along the line checking dials, fiddling with flames and adjusting valves to get everything under control.

Omnia watched him. He had forgotten about her. Eventually she got up and went back to her room.

It was still dark outside. Omnia got back into bed. But she left the light on and sat up with her pillows against the wall. The residue of the terror from the dream was still in her.

Why tell no one the secret until they turned sixteen? Why didn't they want anyone younger than that to know the punishment for going outside the wall?

Omnia thought about the things she *had* been told. *Each Halibut is like a prince or princess in their realm.* She had heard that from the day she could remember hearing anything. *Life in the world outside is hard, dirty, nasty and tough.* She had heard that just as often. *Outside, you have to work all day just to earn the money to have enough to eat so you can work again tomorrow.* That was another one. *No true Halibut would ever want to go outside the wall. If someone does, they're not a Halibut at all.* She nodded to herself. It's better to teach a child to do something because they want to do it rather than because they'll be punished if they don't. Anyone knows that. Better to teach them to do it out of pride than out of fear. By the time they reached the age of sixteen, and were told the truth, each Halibut would have learned the lessons so well, believed them so deeply, that the punishment would hardly be needed. Except for a few, the ones who hadn't learned the lessons well enough. The ones, perhaps, who were so difficult and rebellious that they were tempted to go outside the wall *because* the punishment was there.

Omnia wondered, if she had not been told the secret now, whether she would have become one of those ones when she turned sixteen.

So many secrets, thought Omnia. So many lies to keep the House intact and the life of the Halibuts protected. A House of lies. For two hundred years it had stood up. How much longer could it go on? Perhaps now it was about to come down.

The Master Filer had said that each must do what they could. Omnia knew what he meant by that. He was telling her that she had to do something, she had to join in the fight. She frowned. Who gave him the right to say that? What was *he* doing anyway? Sitting in his room with his tubs of files all day. What was *anyone* doing? This had nothing to do with her! Why *should* she get involved? As Basilica had said, it was unfair. It really was. Omnia hadn't started this thing – why should she be expected to help finish it?

Well, she wouldn't! There! She would pretend she knew nothing about it. Someone else could deal with it. She would be just like Eversmart and Artesia and her other friends, doing whatever they wanted without any worries at all.

She folded her arms and nodded to herself. That was it. Done! She had decided.

For about two minutes. She sat pretending she knew nothing about it, but she knew she wouldn't be able to. She did know about it. What if the Evergones got their way? What if the House did fall?

So what if it did? Omnia didn't know if she even wanted to stop it. Maybe a place built on so many lies deserved to fall.

But not like this. She had never liked Trimbleby – and she doubted that he had ever liked her – but he didn't deserve to be murdered by being hung by his foot. Or in any other way, for that matter. And Withers didn't deserve to be crushed by a chihuahua, nor Dish to drown in a bowl of gravy, nor the Older Digby and the previous Captain to be killed three months before, nor the other Butlers and Captains and the other servants and Halibuts whom she suspected had been killed down the years in this never-ending feud.

And what about the things Basilica had said to her? Try to imagine what it would be like if there was no House, Basilica had said, if all the places Omnia had known since she was a little girl were no longer there. It must be a torture for Basilica, being locked up within the House yet unable even to walk through it. What if it was gone forever? What if she, Omnia, could never walk there again either?

Omnia is only twelve and seven-sixteenths, and at twelve and seven-sixteenths, if you have always lived in one place, it isn't necessarily so easy to imagine what life would be like if that place was gone. It's not necessarily that easy when you are twice that age either, or even older. Yet Omnia began to feel it, the sense of loss, the memories of something you could never recover. She began to have a sense of what Basilica meant.

What if she *was* someone who could make a difference? What if she was the Halibut who *could* do something? If she was, whether it was fair or not, did she have the right not to do it? Did she – after the others in their generations had done their share – have the right to refuse?

Even if she was scared? Even if the thought made her

shudder with the memory of falling from the top of the Slate Tower, of being chased by the man in the grey panther mask?

Omnia sighed. She would never be able to pretend that she didn't know. And she couldn't be the one who refused when it was her turn. Which meant that, in reality, she had no choice; she would do whatever she had to do. Whatever she could, as the Master Filer said.

That was her decision. There had never really been another that she could make.

But what was it that she should do?

She frowned. Trap Cornelius Slinker? She still found it almost impossible to believe that he had turned on her. And yet with the three UnderButlers dead, and someone obviously trying to add her to the list, she had to make that assumption, and she had to act on it until she had another explanation.

And it was possible that there might be others as well. If Cornelius really was involved, could he be doing all this alone? Or did he have helpers?

Omnia didn't like the idea of the Butler staying in the Hold. She understood that he had to be safe, but there was something in the thought of him being hidden while the House was reeling from the deaths of three UnderButlers that made her uneasy. It wasn't long until Rinque Day, the next big feast, when teams of Halibuts competed in an ancient dance on stilts. Everyone would expect to see the Captain and the Butler as they did at every feast. What would happen if the killer – or killers – were still on the loose? Would the Captain and Butler stay hidden then? If they didn't appear on Rinque Day, there would be panic in the House.

The only way to prevent that would be to make sure they did appear. Which meant making sure the killers were no longer at large.

How? Omnia didn't know. But she knew that to come back here again, to her room, was too dangerous. She had to leave. That was the first thing she had to do.

Omnia didn't know what she was going to do after that, but she knew where she was going to start. It was still dark outside. Omnia lay back, thinking. She was certain that Basilica had been outside the wall, which meant she should never have been allowed back – yet here she was, inside the House, locked away. Was it possible the Butler and the Master Filer had lied, and that whoever went out wasn't kept out, but was actually brought back and locked up? That meant there might be tens of people, or hundreds, hidden away behind sliding walls and moving floors and false ceilings in secret rooms all over the House. Before she went any further, Omnia needed to know the truth. She needed to know exactly what had happened to Basilica, why Basilica was locked up and if there was anyone else like her. Maybe if she knew that, at least – something solid, something she knew wasn't a lie – she would know what to do next.

And she would free Basilica. If that was the reason

Basilica was locked away, for having gone outside the wall, she had been locked away long enough, and Omnia would bring her out. That was another decision Omnia made that night. She didn't know how, but she promised herself that she would.

She lay there, wondering how to do it.

After a while, Omnia fell asleep again. When she woke up, it was light outside. Quickly, she got dressed and opened the door to leave.

A small package wrapped in brown paper was on the floor outside her door. Omnia brought it in and opened it. A jar of hair wax. She smiled. A gift from Eversmooth. He hadn't forgotten her entirely.

She opened the jar and smelled the wax. It was rich with fragrance, spicy and woody. The scent of it made her happy and sad at the same time. So much time and thought had gone into making it. So much experimentation and effort. And yet now, having perfected one wax, Eversmooth was almost certainly starting on another.

She put the wax down. She would thank Evergrow, but it would have to wait. Across the House now, she knew, the day had begun. Servants had arrived from the Warren, Halibuts were rising. Each must do what he or she could. It was time for her to go.

In the corridor, the door to her father's library was open. Omnia could see that the window was open as well, and the rope ladder had been lowered. He must already be out in the meadow behind the Long South Range, collecting butterflies. Further along the corridor, the door to her mother's study was ajar. Omnia glimpsed her in her night gown, reading at her desk.

Omnia kept going, down the stairs and out of the Long South Range, not knowing when she would be back.

17

Burnt Toast and Dry Muffins

Evergrow stepped outside and headed for the Tempered Hall. The morning was bright and warm. He crossed the court in front of the Middle Range and walked along, hands in his pockets, thinking about what he was going to have for breakfast. Porridge, perhaps, with apricot compote. And milk. And lots of honey. Or possibly pancakes with strawberries. And banana. And maple syrup. Difficult choice – and that was without thinking about everything else he could have!

As he left the Middle Range, someone emerged from a doorway and followed him.

Evergrow went down the Middle Stairs, still deep in thought about the complicated choice ahead of him, and round a corner into the Alley of Arches. Only then did he hear footsteps. He looked around, but it was too late.

'*Shhhhhh!*' hissed Cornelius Slinker, grabbing Evergrow by the arm and pulling him behind one of the arches.

'What do you want?' demanded Evergrow.

'Where's Omnia?'

'I don't know. What was going on yesterday anyway?'

'Is she hiding with you?'

'No.'

Slinker peered at him disbelievingly. 'She's with you, isn't she? Like last time.'

Evergrow shook his head.

'I waited outside all night.'

'Well, you waited in the wrong place! She isn't with me, I'm telling you. Maybe she went home.'

'She wouldn't have. Too dangerous.'

'Why?' demanded Evergrow. 'What's going on? Why was she so scared of you yesterday, Cornelius?'

'No idea.'

'What did you do?'

'Nothing!' The messenger, who hardly ever raised his voice above a murmur, looked around quickly. 'Nothing, Evergrow.'

Evergrow looked at him doubtfully.

'Do you know where she is?' Slinker grabbed him again. 'It's important! Do you know or not?'

'I don't know, I told you.' Evergrow shook his arm loose. 'I wouldn't tell you if I did! That would be up to Omnia.'

He began to walk away.

'Evergrow!'

Evergrow walked faster.

'Evergrow, stop! Listen!'

Evergrow felt Slinker's hand on his shoulder. He turned. 'What?'

'I don't know what she thinks I've done, but if you find her, tell her I didn't do anything. Tell her she needs protection.'

'And you'll provide it, I suppose?'

'Listen to me. Tell Omnia to let me know where she is. Tell her to use the stone. I'll meet her at the place where we meet at the usual time.'

'What stone? What place where you meet?'

'She'll know. Tell her.'

Evergrow stared at him.

Slinker looked up at the clock in the Hatted Belfry. 'Got to go. Tell her what I said. She'll know what to do.'

Evergrow watched him doubtfully.

'One more thing.'

'What?' said Evergrow impatiently.

'Stay with her, Evergrow. Until she lets me protect her, it's up to you. Don't let her be out in the House by herself.'

In the Tempered Hall, the children giggled. Every minute or two came a shout of outrage from the table where Everfull V Halibut, his wife Insatia, his friend Everround Y Halibut and a number of other gluttons of the House had gathered for breakfast. Stalks in the ice cream were one thing – you could even imagine they were a delicacy – but this was something else. The food was terrible. Even the simple things were wrong. Toast was burnt, porridge was

165

salty, eggs were overcooked, sausages were raw. No one could remember a morning like it.

Halibuts at the other tables ate gingerly, picking out the edible food and discarding the rest. They didn't shout with outrage at each new discovery, but no one could fail to notice the problems. The cooks, they thought, must be having a bad day, or perhaps the High Chef was carrying out some kind of experiment which obviously wasn't working. Either way, they found it disturbing. Coming hard on the heels of the death of a third UnderButler, any change in the routine of the House – not to mention a breakfast as awful as this – was unsettling. If losing one UnderButler was unfortunate, and losing two was careless, what was losing three? Evertell G Halibut didn't know, largely because none of the writers whose works he secretly copied had ever said. But it was something, that was for sure, and whatever it was, it wasn't something to be admired.

If the Halibuts in the Hall that morning had known the truth of what was happening in the kitchen beneath their feet, they would have been even more disturbed. The huge vats of oversalted porridge that came up in the dumb waiters, the trays of burnt eggs, omelettes, pancakes and muffins, the barrels of soggy cereals and tubs of spoiled yoghurts, were coming from a kitchen that was in a state of disorder. Cooks and kitchen hands wanted to know where the Butler was now that all the UnderButlers were dead. The High Chef told them to mind their own business and get back to work. As soon as his back was turned, Owens egged them on, saying they had a right to know, joined by half a dozen other kitchen hands who followed his lead and were always eager to make trouble. Owens ran gleefully around the benches, ducking to hide whenever the High Chef turned in his direction, popping up again when the High Chef turned away and whispering questions. Where *was* the Butler? Wasn't it true that if there were no UnderButlers, and the Butler didn't appear, they didn't need to listen to the High Chef? Soon the other kitchen hands were running around asking the same questions, spreading confusion. Owens was right, said some of the cooks, who wanted to have a day off. He was talking nonsense, said others, and told them to keep working. They didn't, or they worked slowly, purposely botching the work they did. The others kept going, struggling to make up for the ones who were resisting, and becoming more and more angry. Arguments broke out while food burned. The kitchen hands ran riot. The High Chef and his assistants marched constantly through the kitchens, shouting, forcing people back to their work, but as soon as they turned away, the arguments recurred and the troublemakers dropped their implements. Fights erupted and the High Chef himself was forced to wade in, fists flying. He pulled out the loudest kitchen hands, Owens among them, and locked them in a larder with twenty brace of dead pheasants. But the arguments went on. The fires of discontent that Owens had lit continued to smoulder.

Upstairs, Omnia arrived and went quickly to a table where her friends were eating. They moved up to make room for her.

'This is *disgraceful*!' cried Everfull from the gluttons' table. 'I'd rather eat my blue boots. This lark's egg is *barely* cooked!'

Eversmart glanced at the twins. Evesia started giggling.

'What's going on?' asked Omnia.

'The food's funny,' replied Sororia.

'Want some toast?' Eversmart turned over the pieces in a big pile of toast he had brought to the table. 'If you like it burnt, you can take your pick.'

Omnia took a piece of toast that wasn't too badly burnt and nibbled on it. Her main reason for coming here wasn't to eat. She glanced at Evergrow.

'What was all that yesterday with Cornelius Slinker?' asked Artesia.

'Omnia's in love with him,' whispered Evesia, sitting beside her in a matching red sunhat.

Omnia rolled her eyes.

'Why did he want to tell you the UnderButler was dead?' asked Artesia.

'I don't know. He just did.'

'I can't believe we've lost three UnderButlers,' said Eversmart. 'In barely more than a week! Honestly! If it's not unfortunate, and it's not careless, it's just ridiculous!'

It was worse than that, thought Omnia.

'For *heaven's sake*,' came a cry from the gluttons. '*I can't believe this!*'

Omnia glanced at Evergrow again. 'Are you finished?'

Evergrow hadn't even started on the bowl of porridge that was in front of him, nor on the pancakes that were ready on a plate. He had picked out the pancakes carefully and one or two looked almost normal. He had found a couple of muffins as well that looked as if they could possibly be edible, in case nothing else was. But he could see the way Omnia was looking at him. And he needed to tell her about Cornelius Slinker, although he didn't see why that couldn't wait until he had finished his breakfast . . .

Omnia grabbed another piece of toast and got up.

Evergrow sighed. He put the muffins in his pocket.

'Are you coming to the Hall of Leaning this morning?' called out Eversmart as they headed off. 'Everhale's going to be there. There'll be lots of jokes.'

Omnia looked back at him. 'No,' she said. 'Maybe tomorrow.'

They walked quickly away from the Tempered Hall. Omnia stopped when they reached the Minor Terrace. They stepped behind a column.

'What is it?' said Evergrow. 'Are you going to tell me?'

Omnia nodded.

'By the way, I saw Cornelius Slinker this morning. He was looking for you.'

Omnia stared at him. 'What did he want?'

'He said you're in danger. He said you need protection.'

'And he's going to provide it, I suppose?'

'That's exactly what I said.'

'Let me tell you about Cornelius Slinker! I'll tell you exactly what—'

Omnia stopped. A couple of elderly Halibuts were crossing the Terrace on their way to the Tempered Hall. She waited until they were gone.

'Two days ago, Evergrow, someone came after me and almost got me.'

'Not Cornelius? Is that who you mean?'

'I didn't see his face. But if it wasn't Cornelius himself, he must have been involved.'

'How do you know if you didn't see his face?'

'There's a place where I meet him when I need to talk to him.'

'You use a stone, don't you?'

Omnia's eyes narrowed. 'How do you know about that?'

'And there's a particular time you always meet him, isn't there?'

'How do you know?' she whispered.

'He told me this morning. He said to tell you to leave the stone and he'd meet you in the usual place at the usual time.' Evergrow paused. 'Where is that exactly?'

'What else did he say?'

'He wanted to know where you were.'

'Did you tell him?'

'Of course not! Anyway, I didn't know. He said he'd waited outside the Middle Range because he thought you must have been hiding with me. He thought you wouldn't have gone home.'

Lucky escape, thought Omnia.

'Why not? Why wouldn't you have gone home? Is Cornelius right? Are you in danger?'

'I think I am – from him.'

'You couldn't be. He saved your life, Omnia.'

'Maybe it just looked like that. Maybe that was part of the plan.'

'What plan?'

'The plan to make me trust him.'

Evergrow looked at Omnia as if he doubted that everything was right inside her head. 'Omnia, that was three months ago!'

'This has been going on a lot longer than three months, Evergrow. Three months is nothing compared to how long this has been going on.'

Evergrow was still looking at her in the same way.

'What did he tell you about the stone?' she asked.

'He just said you'd know what he meant. Omnia, what's this about?'

She told him. And she told him about the last time she had left the stone, and what had happened when she arrived to find the panther-man waiting for her. 'Now do you understand why he must have been involved? Apart from me, Cornelius was the only person who knew I would be in that place at that time. I never told anyone else.'

'Where's the stone now?'

'I don't know. I don't have it. Normally, after I left it at the Captain's Keep, Cornelius would give it back to me when we met so I'd have it in case I needed to use it again. This time, obviously, he didn't do that.'

'But he told me to tell you to leave it. That must mean he thinks you still have it. But if you left it, *he* should have it. Omnia if he doesn't have it, it means someone else took it.'

'Who? How would they know I'd left it, and even if they did, how would they know where I was going to meet him?' Omnia considered for a moment. 'It just shows how cunning he is. It's obvious, Evergrow. He said that to make me think it wasn't him. If you ask me, that just shows it was.'

A group of Halibuts crossed the Minor Terrace on their way back from the Tempered Hall. They were grumbling about the food.

'It's hard to believe it could have been Cornelius,' murmured Evergrow when they had gone.

Omnia shrugged. There were a lot of things she had learned recently that were hard to believe. This wasn't the hardest.

'He told me to tell you he hadn't done anything,' said Evergrow. 'He said I should stay with you until you let him protect you.'

'He probably thinks he'll get both of us that way. Listen, Evergrow. Cornelius is right about one thing: I'm in danger. But you don't have to help me.'

'Do you want me to?'

Omnia frowned. Last time, she had decided to try to

do everything alone, and if not for the help of Cornelius Slinker – which now seemed not to have been help at all – she might have paid for that decision with her life. This time, she didn't want to make that mistake. If the grey panther came after her again, she would stand a better chance if someone else was with her. Last time, Evergrow had shown not only that he was trustworthy – which she had never doubted – but that he had more courage than she had given him credit for. He had told her that if anything ever happened again, he wanted her to let him help.

But could she really ask him for that? She remembered the grey panther coming after her, the sense of terror and panic she had felt. Could she really ask Evergrow to put himself in such danger?

'If I say yes, that's my decision,' said Evergrow, watching her. 'Just tell me, Omnia, do you want me to help or not?'

Still Omnia was silent.

'If you didn't want me to help, why did you come and find me in the Tempered Hall?'

He was right about that. That was the reason Omnia had gone there, but now she didn't know if she should have. She was the one who was involved. Did she have the right to drag someone else into it just so that she could feel safer?

'I don't know if it's fair to ask you, Evergrow.'

'You'd ask Everlook, wouldn't you, if he was still alive? Whatever Everlook would do, I'd do too!'

Omnia hesitated. Evergrow always measured himself against what he thought their dead uncle would have done. But Evergrow was just a boy, and small for his age, and Everlook had been a grown man of twenty when he tragically died, having fallen from a stair that crumbled under him in the High North Lodge.

'If you want me to help, you only have to ask, Omnia.'

She still didn't know if it was right. But she could feel danger all around her; she could literally *feel* it creeping over her skin.

'Will you help me?' she blurted out.

Evergrow smiled. 'Why not? I wasn't planning to do anything else today.'

'This isn't a joke. Think about it.'

'I already have.' Evergrow was serious. 'Every day for the last three months. I almost wished something would happen so I could show you how I could really help if you needed me.'

'Be careful what you wish for,' said Omnia.

'What's next?' asked Evergrow eagerly. 'Where are we going?'

Omnia watched him. Whether she had the right to ask him to put himself in danger, she still didn't know. But it felt good to have her cousin by her side.

'I didn't tell you how I managed to get away when Cornelius chased me,' said Omnia. 'I found someone.'

Evergrow looked at her, not understanding.

'Guess who.'

Evergrow's eyes narrowed for a moment, then they widened in surprise.

'You'll never believe how I found her.'

'It couldn't be as unbelievable as last time.'

'You can make up your own mind about that,' said Omnia. 'Come on, I need to talk to her again.'

'He was over there,' said Omnia, pointing to the grape-encrusted porch that ran along the length of the Summer Lodge. 'He must have been hiding there while he waited for me.'

Evergrow looked at the porch and at the shimmering green wall of the Summer Lodge above it. He took a nibble from one of the muffins he had brought from the Tempered Hall. The muffin was so overcooked that it was too dry to eat. He put it back in his pocket and tried the second one. It was no better.

They went to the Granite Arch and Omnia led Evergrow up the stairs. At the top they turned into the Winter House.

'I've never been in here before,' said Evergrow.

'Neither had I.'

They went down the corridor. Omnia opened the door to the Snowflake, as Basilica had called it.

'*Look at this . . .*' murmured Evergrow in amazement.

The whiteness was dazzling. Omnia didn't remember the impression being so intense, but that was because the last time she saw it she had been running for her life. Now she felt the full effect. Everything was white, the stairs, the walls, the floor. The roof was a vast layer of frosted white glass, letting in an even, white light. The very air of the space seemed to be white.

Within it, the shape was extraordinary. At first, it was hard to pick out the stairs from the whiteness of the walls around them. As you did, you saw that they were like an explosion in space, a big, frozen bang that sent an unendingness of arms shooting out through the air in every direction.

'Where's the door to Basilica?' asked Evergrow.

Omnia looked around. She realised that she had no idea.

They went out on the stairs. Up they went, down, sideways, far out into the space. They came to a staircase that led to the wall and saw a door in the whiteness. Omnia opened it and found herself looking into a cupboard containing a few bricks. They turned around.

They found more doors. One led to a long stone corridor with bright blue doors. Another led to a small green room. A third opened on a balcony in dazzling sunlight that looked down over a huge drop with a blank, white wall on the other side, far away. At the bottom of the drop was what seemed to be a lake with tiny islands dotted across it. Omnia wondered if it was some kind of illusion. They could hear bird calls coming from somewhere below. They closed that door and opened others. The constant whiteness and the geometry of the forms was disorientating. It was impossible to keep in mind which direction you were looking at, and after a while, they opened a couple of doors they had already opened before. Wherever you looked, however you turned, the stairs seemed to have the same arrangement, like something out of a dream.

Omnia was almost beginning to wonder whether the whole thing had been a dream. Or a nightmare. The red space with a wall that opened was the kind of thing you'd find in a dream. So was the panther mask on Cornelius's head. Maybe it really had been a dream, and seeing the mask in Evermay's painting had set it off.

'Where now?' asked Evergrow.

Omnia looked around. They could keep going here for hours and even then, if they were unlucky, they'd keep opening the wrong doors and continue to miss the right one. If it even existed. She had no idea how many doors there were.

'Have you got a pencil?' she asked suddenly.

Evergrow shook his head.

'Chalk? Charcoal? Anything?'

He shook his head again.

'Crumbs!'

Evergrow nodded. 'Sorry.'

'No. *Crumbs!* Have you got any muffin left?'

'As much as you like.' He pulled the muffins out of his pockets. 'They really overcooked them.'

'Lucky for us!' Omnia took the muffins and crumbled part of one in her hand.

Now they went from door to door, and at each one they

tried, and which proved not to be the one they needed, Omnia left a fragment of the muffin at the bottom of the stairs that led to it. The whiteness was so stark that even a tiny pile of crumbs was enough to mark it. There were so many doors that Omnia soon began to worry she would run out, and the fragments she left became smaller and smaller. But all the time the number of doors remaining to be opened was growing smaller as well. Now they found themselves turning back from staircases they had already marked, and they began to see which parts of the Snowflake they hadn't yet investigated.

And at this point, some readers might be wondering whether this could possibly be true. Leaving crumbs? You might doubt it, and think that I don't know what really happened at this point and am filling in the gap with an idea from a fairy story I once read or some such thing. And if that's the case, you might decide to put this book down and stop reading right now, because this isn't supposed to be a fairy story, and if it is a fairy story, it isn't something you should be wasting your time on. And I'd agree. I'd be the first to tell you to stop reading – *if* that was the case.

But it isn't. The truth of the events that befell Omnia Halibut at the age of twelve and a quarter – and twelve and seven-sixteenths, because time marches on, as we saw at the beginning – are much stranger than anything you're likely to read in a fairy story, as you have already probably worked out. And that, after all, proves they must be true, because it's often said that truth is stranger than fiction.

And if fairy stories are fiction – which they are – and Omnia's story is stranger – which it is – then simple logic tells us that it must be true.

So imagine, if you can, that you're standing in something as unique as the Snowflake, which is like a perfectly symmetrical maze in three dimensions, suspended in space, with any number of doors – perhaps a hundred, perhaps a thousand – but every one of which looks the same. How would you know which doors you have already tried if you couldn't mark them in some way? And if you had nothing else to mark them with, you would mark them with whatever you could. Wouldn't you? Even muffin crumbs, for instance, if that was all you had.

So that was what Omnia and Evergrow did. And eventually Omnia opened a door and saw a red space in front of her with no obvious exit.

At last! She walked to the other end. 'Watch this,' she said to Evergrow and she thumped on the wall.

Nothing.

Omnia thumped again.

Evergrow looked at her sceptically. After all of this looking for doors, he was beginning to wonder if Omnia had any idea where she was actually going. Seeing her thumping on what appeared to be a solid wall didn't give him much more confidence.

She thumped again. This time, a flurry of thumps.

'You sure there isn't a fishing net involved?' asked Evergrow.

'Very funny.' Omnia looked around the small, blind-ended space. It had to be the same one. Unless, of course, there were two that were identical. Which meant she would have to go back out into the Snowflake and keep looking.

She thumped again. 'Winnicott!' she cried as she hit the wall with her fists. 'It's me! Omnia! *Winnicott!*'

Still nothing. Omnia thumped the door one last time, and then turned around, folded her arms and leaned against the wall in frustration.

At once she tumbled backwards.

18

To the River

'Hello, Omnia,' said Winnicott, looking down at her. Then he glanced up. 'And it's Evergrow, isn't it? Are you coming in?'

'Of course he's coming in,' said Omnia irritably, getting to her feet.

Evergrow grinned at her and stepped in. The wall closed behind them.

'Do I really have to fall over like that every time I come here?' asked Omnia.

Winnicott shrugged, raising his heavy, owl-like eyebrows. 'Is Basilica in?'

'I can't remember the last time she was out,' replied Winnicott and turned to lead them into the apartment.

Basilica was sitting with a net over her knees, mending it with fishing line.

She glanced up at the two children. 'Hello, Omnia,'

she said. She turned to Evergrow. 'I've seen you before, haven't I?'

'I'm Evergrow.'

'That's right, Ribelia's son. What's she been knitting recently?'

Evergrow shrugged.

'A kettle. A saucepan?'

'She doesn't knit things like that.'

'She used to. Just ask her. Well, anyway, it's nice to see you again.' Basilica glanced at Omnia. 'I have to say it's rather odd, Omnia, the way you do things. I don't see you for three months and then twice in three days! Are you like this with everyone, hot and cold?'

Omnia smiled. 'No.'

'I should hope not. You wouldn't be very popular and rightly so.' Basilica turned back to her net-mending. 'What can I do for you today?'

Omnia sat down. Evergrow took a chair beside her.

'I need to know the truth,' said Omnia.

'What truth is that?' replied Basilica, as if there might be more than one. Her eyes stayed focused on the net, her head tilted slightly as her fingers dexterously looped and tied the fishing line to close up the tears in the mesh.

'The truth about what happened to you.'

Basilica was silent.

'I need to know. Basilica, please! I need to start some-where. I need something I know I can believe.'

'Perhaps you do,' replied Basilica, 'but that doesn't mean

I'm obliged to tell you.' She looked up at Omnia. 'One person's need isn't necessarily another person's obligation. You must have heard Pedagogia say that before.'

'I don't think so.'

'Really? When we were younger, it used to be one of her favourite sayings. She said it all the time, whenever anyone asked her a favour.'

'It makes sense,' said Evergrow thoughtfully.

'Yes, but it gets tedious after a while if you hear it all the time.'

'I suppose anything does,' remarked Evergrow.

Basilica nodded. 'That's true. Perhaps that's why she stopped using it. But honestly, when she was younger, whenever—'

'Why won't you *tell* me?' demanded Omnia, who couldn't care less about Pedagogia's sayings. 'Will they punish you if you tell? Like they will if you tell about the Evergones? See, I know that secret already, Basilica. They told me.'

'What secret is this?' asked Evergrow.

Omnia ignored him. 'The Butler told me.'

'Well, that's very unusual at your age,' murmured Basilica.

'I know. We're not supposed to know until we're sixteen, are we?'

'What?' said Evergrow. 'What aren't we supposed to know until we're sixteen?'

'Is that what you're frightened of, Basilica? Is that why you won't tell me the truth, because they'll punish you again?'

'*What are we talking about?*' demanded Evergrow.

Omnia and Basilica both looked at him.

'I'm just asking,' he said.

Neither of them replied. Evergrow glanced at Winnicott, who merely raised his owl-like eyebrows and shrugged.

Omnia turned back to Basilica. 'Trimbleby's dead. All three of the UnderButlers are gone.'

'What about Digby?'

'He's in the Hold.'

'Did you see him?' asked Basilica quickly. 'Did you go there?'

Omnia nodded.

'So the Hold does exist. Well, eventually he'll come out.'

'Basilica, I need to know the truth!'

Basilica turned to her servant. 'Winnicott, shall we have something to eat?'

'Yes,' said Evergrow. 'I'm starv—'

'No!' said Omnia. 'No food!' She jumped up and took the fishing net out of Basilica's hands and tossed it away. 'How can you sit here like this, day after day, locked up? You are locked up, aren't you? I know you are! How can you bear it? You're the best one of all, the only honest one, the only one who's ever told me anything.' Omnia paused, breathing heavily. She fell to her knees, clutching Basilica's hand. 'Basilica, I don't know what to do. Please, tell me the truth. Give me somewhere to start.'

Basilica gazed at her. 'Get up, Omnia,' she said quietly. 'Please, get up.' She lifted Omnia's hand. 'Now sit down.'

184

Basilica watched as Omnia sat. She threw a long glance at Winnicott, who stood in the doorway, watching. Then she turned back to Omnia.

'You say Trimbleby's dead?' said Basilica.

Omnia nodded.

'An accident?'

'Of course.'

'And you still think Cornelius Slinker is responsible?'

'I don't know. And I don't know if he's acting alone.'

Basilica looked at Evergrow. 'What do you think?'

Evergrow didn't know what to think. There was a lot more going on here, he knew, than he understood. The secret that Omnia had been talking about – he was determined to find out what it was.

'Has anyone seen anything suspicious?' asked Basilica, turning back to Omnia. 'Anyone where they shouldn't be, doing things they shouldn't be doing?'

Omnia shrugged. She was beginning to think no one in Neversuch House would know something suspicious even if it walked up to them with a big sign saying SOMETHING SUSPICIOUS stuck on its forehead.

'You told me Dish was killed on Flip Day. That was on the Long Terrace, I suppose?'

Omnia nodded.

'And Withers was killed at the Faunal House?'

'That's right.'

'And Trimbleby?'

'The Bridled Mound. Hung by his foot.'

Basilica raised an eyebrow.

'From a crane.'

'That hardly excuses it,' murmured Basilica. She was silent for a moment, thinking. 'And no one saw anyone coming or going?'

Omnia shrugged.

'Three deaths? And no one saw anyone?'

'Not that I've heard,' said Omnia. Rumour travelled fast in the House, growing as it did. If someone had been seen coming or going from the scenes of the murders, someone who wasn't expected to be there, surely she would have heard something about it.

'No,' murmured Basilica to herself. 'It couldn't be.'

'What?' asked Omnia quickly.

'They're all quite close to each other, have you noticed, the places where the UnderButlers were killed?'

'So?'

'There's a river underground. Did I ever tell you about that?'

Omnia nodded. 'Your father used to take you there and you'd ride in a gondola while he sang opera.'

'That's right. I did tell you. Well, the entrance . . . I don't remember exactly where it was, but I remember we used to go past the Bridled Mound, and I can remember always being frightened because of the statues nearby on the Faunal House. Sometimes my father would tease me, you see, by saying we had to come home along the alley next to Midges Mansion. We never did, of course.'

'Where does this river go?'

'I don't know,' said Basilica. 'At some point it must leave the House and presumably at another point it enters it. In between, it runs under us. It's perfectly possible that it runs under the Warren as well.' She paused. 'If one of the servants knows that it exists, and how to get there, and if they want to move between the Warren and the House at certain times without anyone knowing they're doing it – which might be very convenient if you just happen to be killing people at those times – that would be a way. From what I remember, it would bring them out near the places where the UnderButlers were killed.'

'I bet Cornelius Slinker would know about it,' said Omnia. 'He knows everywhere there is to go in the House.'

Winnicott folded his arms and frowned. He let out a kind of low growl, as if unable to completely bottle up his anger.

'Don't start, Winny,' said Basilica. 'If it's not him, let him prove it.'

The servant shook his head and clenched his jaw in an effort to stay silent.

Basilica turned back to Omnia. 'They'd need a boat, of course.'

'We have to find this river,' said Omnia.

'It's underground. I couldn't tell you how to get to the entrance.'

'But you went there.'

'When I was small.'

'Maybe you'd recognise it if you saw it again.'

Basilica shook her head.

'Why not?'

'I wouldn't.'

'Basilica, you have to show us.'

'I can't,' she said. 'I can't go out.'

'You have to.'

'I mustn't.'

'I know you mustn't – but you must.'

Basilica shook her head.

Omnia got up again and crouched in front of her. 'Basilica, now's the time. You said to me once in every generation there's a Halibut who can *do* something. You were the one in your generation, weren't you?'

'I don't know if I was. I did what I could, Omnia. And look what happened. It only made things worse.'

'Tell me. Why won't you tell me? What happened?'

'I've had my time, Omnia. I did what I could, I told you.'

'There's more to be done. Show me where it is, this entrance to the river. I need you to show me.'

'I don't know where it is. I couldn't tell you how to get there.'

'But if we go there together, you'll recognise it, won't you? I know you will. Basilica, there's more to be done – for those who can *do* things. This is the time. I don't know how long you've been locked up. I don't know why because you won't tell me. But this is the time, Basilica. Take us there. Take us to the river.'

188

Basilica was silent. Omnia watched her. She hardly knew what must be going through Basilica's mind – what memories, what fears, what tragedy and disappointment. And yet there was still a spark inside Basilica, she knew that. A spark of energy, a spark of courage. When she was younger, Omnia imagined, before whatever it was that had happened to her – Basilica must have been unstoppable. All that had to happen now was for the spark to flare into flame once more.

Omnia watched her intently, unwaveringly, putting all her will into her gaze.

Basilica closed her eyes. Finally she took a deep breath and looked back at Omnia.

'I can't promise I'll recognise it.'

They left the apartment through a door in another room. The wall through which they had come couldn't be opened from the inside – it was only a way in, not out. The door in the other room led to a chute. They slid down the chute in turn, Omnia, Evergrow and Basilica, leaving Winnicott, who had given Omnia and Evergrow each a pigeon pasty to eat on the way, wishing them luck. At the bottom, they found a set of stairs. Down they went, flight after flight, until the stairs ended in a tunnel.

'Where does this go?' asked Omnia.

Basilica shrugged. 'I've no idea. I've never been here before.'

'But it's the way out of your apartment.'

'And do you know what the punishment is if I use it?'

Omnia frowned. She could guess. Only now that Basilica had left the apartment did it seem real, the risk that she was taking, the enormity of the thing that Omnia had asked her to do.

'Thank you,' said Omnia quietly.

They moved quickly along the tunnel until they found a set of stairs that led upwards. Omnia went to look where the stairs came out and found that they led to an opening behind a statue in the court at the top of the second arm of the Splitted Stairs. She went back down to Basilica and Evergrow and told them where they were.

'Do you know how to get to the Bridled Mound from here?' asked Basilica.

Omnia and Evergrow nodded.

'Good. I'm not sure if I can remember.'

Basilica pulled her cloak over her shoulders and a hood over her head,

'Are you ready?' asked Omnia.

Suddenly Basilica reached for Omnia's hand and held it tight. She took a deep breath and then let it go. 'I'm ready.'

Up they went. Omnia stepped out first, looked around to make sure nobody was there and called them out.

They set off briskly down the Splitted Stairs, but soon Basilica was slowing them down. She glanced from side to side, her pace falling to a walk. Then to a shuffle. She gazed at the long iron balcony of the Railed Deck that stood on their left at the bottom of the Stairs, at the carvings that covered the walls of the Frog House on their right. It was here, in an empty niche, that Omnia had hidden from Tobias Hildegrew three months earlier after he had chased her out of the Ribbled Lodge. Basilica came to a complete stop.

'It's like a dream . . .' she murmured.

Omnia glanced at Evergrow. They watched her, hoping that no one was about to come around the corner.

'How long has it been?' asked Omnia.

'Seventeen years,' murmured Basilica. 'Seventeen years, three months, a week and six days. I've counted every one. I don't know why, it's not as if I thought it would ever end.' She shook her head, glancing at Omnia and Evergrow with a look of disbelief. 'And here it is. It's like a dream. All those years . . .' She clicked her fingers. 'Gone, as if they never existed.'

They heard footsteps.

'Quick,' said Omnia. She pulled on Basilica's arm.

They hurried away, round the corner of the Railed Deck, down the steps beyond it, then under the overhanging roof of the Capped Porch. They moved quickly through the House, avoiding the busiest courtyards and terraces, diverting when someone came towards them into an alley or a doorway where Basilica would avert her head and raise a cloaked arm to shield her face until the person had gone. At last, the Bridled Mound came in sight, clad in the scaffolding of Albert Gondolier's construction works.

'That's where Trimbleby died,' said Omnia.

Basilica gazed at the Mound. 'They're repairing it. I never thought anyone would bother.'

'Eversniff T Halibut lives there.'

Basilica smiled. 'Really?'

'Do you know him?'

'Oh, yes, I knew him. Not exactly the easiest person to get along with.'

'He refused to leave his apartment even when they took down the stairs,' said Evergrow.

'Sounds like he hasn't changed,' said Basilica.

Omnia and Evergrow grinned.

They moved on in the direction of the Faunal House and came into a series of alleys that twisted around tall buildings with conical tops. At various points between the roofs they could see the leaning statues of the Faunal House not far away.

'It's somewhere around here,' said Basilica. 'I remember these alleys. I can remember my father taking me round corners like these . . .' Suddenly she stopped. 'Oh, yes. I'd forgotten! The clown.'

Omnia and Evergrow looked up. High on the wall was a carving of a dancing clown.

Basilica's voice dropped almost to a whisper. 'It's close. We used to go . . .' She took a few steps around a corner and looked down the next alley. 'It was somewhere—' She stared. 'That's it!'

Omnia and Evergrow looked. All they could see was an alley stretching ahead of them.

192

'That door.' Basilica pointed to a small wooden door a short way down the alley. There was nothing that would have made you take notice of it. Its hinges were rusted and some of the timber had broken away at the top and bottom, leaving a jagged, gap-toothed appearance.

'That's it?' said Omnia. 'Are you sure?'

'That's it.'

Evergrow and Omnia glanced at one another doubtfully.

Basilica went to the door and pulled it open.

'What's happened to the lock?' asked Omnia.

'There never was a lock.' Basilica smiled. 'Put a lock on a door and someone will want to open it. Make a door interesting and someone will want to find out what's behind it.'

Evergrow nodded to himself. 'Clever.'

Omnia wondered about all the other doors she had walked past in the House, ordinary doors standing half ajar that she had never bothered to look beyond. She wondered what marvels might wait behind them.

Basilica bent her head and went in. Omnia and Evergrow followed.

There was a lantern inside. It stood on the floor near the top of a set of stairs. A tiny flame glowed in the glass.

'Someone's here,' whispered Omnia.

'Or *was* here,' said Basilica. 'If they were here, they'd be using this lantern, don't you think?'

She picked it up and turned up the light. Then she

headed down the stairs. It was as if she had forgotten all her caution and become bold and reckless, the unstoppable Basilica she had once been.

Omnia and Evergrow glanced at each other. Basilica was probably right. Whoever had used that lantern had left it while they went outside – *probably*.

The glow of the lantern came up faintly now from the bottom of the stairs. Either they followed it down or they would be left in darkness.

They looked at each other again. Then Omnia shrugged and they headed down.

Basilica was waiting for them at the bottom. They went around a corner and came to a passage half filled with rubble.

'It's collapsed here,' said Omnia.

'No,' said Basilica. 'It was always like this, to make people think it wasn't worth going further.'

She clambered over the rubble. Omnia and Evergrow went after her.

They went further in and eventually came to a set of spiral steps. Basilica led them down, their shadows looming on the walls. The stone of the steps was damp. They came to the bottom. Now they were on uneven, uncut stone, the raw rock beneath Neversuch House. Basilica disappeared into a narrow opening that led into the rock. Omnia and Evergrow followed the glow of the lantern. They went through a twisting passage where the rock was close on either side, then suddenly it opened out and the roof soared and in front of them, beyond an area of bare, flat stone, ran a dark river.

Basilica raised the lantern and the glow lit up the roof. Cracks in the rock were like the lines of pictures. Here there seemed to be horses, there a horde of butterflies.

'It's just as I remember it,' she murmured.

'What about those?' asked Evergrow.

On the stone beside the river rested two vessels.

'This is my father's gondola,' said Basilica. She shook her head in amazement. 'Still here.' She knelt beside a long, narrow boat with peeling paint. 'This is where it would always be when we came down here. It was beautiful then, black, with red trim.' She ran a hand gently over the bleached wood and a flake of paint came away under her fingers. 'It must be forty years since we used it.'

Omnia went to the other boat, which was wider but shorter.

'What about this one?'

Basilica shrugged. 'Never seen it before in my life.'

A pair of paddles lay in the bottom of the boat. Omnia felt them. They were wet. The hull of the boat was damp. Suddenly she knew what had happened. Someone had used the boat to come here. They had left the lantern and were outside in the House right now.

'Who else would know how to get to this place?' asked Omnia.

Basilica shrugged. 'My father's dead now. He never told anyone. He always said it was our secret.'

'Yours and his?'

Basilica was silent.

'You have a brother! I remember, you told me. Your father used to bring both of you down here. He'd know as well, wouldn't he?'

Still Basilica didn't speak.

'Could *he* have—'

'What do you want to do now?' asked Basilica suddenly. 'If someone's up there, they'll be coming back. They could be here any minute.'

Omnia knew Basilica was changing the subject. But she was right. If someone had come here by the boat and gone out into the House, sooner or later they'd be coming back.

Omnia looked around. There was nowhere to hide down here. Nor had she seen anywhere on the stairs or in the passage.

'We could jump on them when they come through the rock,' said Evergrow.

'How do we know how many there'll be?' replied Omnia.

Evergrow frowned. 'We could push the boat into the water before we leave. At least they wouldn't be able to use it.'

'And they'd know someone had discovered it.' Omnia felt the skin prickling at the back of her neck. They were up there and might return at any moment. 'We've learned what we wanted to learn. Let's go.'

'Are you sure?' said Basilica.

Omnia nodded. If they waited, it would be a direct confrontation between them and the person – or people – who had already killed the three UnderButlers. There was no way of knowing how many would be coming back. It might not only be Cornelius. The boat could hold five or six. If it came to a fight, they would have the river at their back, without a single weapon at their disposal.

Omnia told herself the sensible thing was to leave, but even as she did, she knew that something else was impelling her. Dread of the grey panther rose inside her. Her skin prickled. Even if he was by himself, even if it was Cornelius against the three of them, the thought of facing him again made her blood run cold.

She took the lantern out of Basilica's hand. 'Let's go.' She headed back through the opening in the rock towards the steps.

With each turn of the spiral Omnia imagined the panther-man suddenly appearing on the steps above her, his face hidden in the mask, his hands reaching for her. She moved faster. Her heart was pounding. Suddenly the walls and the roof of the steps seemed to press close and she just wanted to be out of there. She got to the top and held the lantern up, waiting impatiently for Evergrow and Basilica to catch up. She led them back up the passage, then climbed over the rubble. As she held the lantern up to give them light and waited for them to come through, she kept glancing at the corridor ahead, expecting to see a shadow coming towards them.

On they went. At last, the final set of stairs was in front of them. Omnia put the lantern down at the top and went quickly to the door.

Out they came and then away, away from that place as quickly as they could go.

But they needn't have been in such a rush. Hours passed, and dusk fell, and still no one had come back. The shadows in the alleys turned inky black. Only now did someone appear, his face deep in a hood, the panther mask clutched in his hand. He stooped and slipped quickly through the door.

But he didn't immediately pick the lantern up. He listened, put his head out of the door again to see if anyone had followed him, then turned back to the lantern once more. Cautiously, he lifted it.

As soon as he had come in, he knew the lantern wasn't standing exactly where he had left it.

19

Truth

Basilica walked between them. She feared being discovered, but wanted to walk and walk through the House that she knew so well, but had seen for so many years only from the high windows of her places of imprisonment. She kept looking around and stopping, as if each building she saw was an old friend she had imagined she would never see again, and now, on her way back, she feared that this would be her last chance. And yet she feared being seen by people who had truly been her friends, or her enemies, or by anyone who could recognise her, and each time someone came near the three of them, they hurried into a doorway, and each time they came out of a doorway, she could barely bring herself to walk away, and so she hurried, and stopped, and hurried, and stopped, unable to draw herself away, yet unable to linger.

Basilica gazed at the huge, intricately punctured wall of

the Rose Lattice. 'I have to get back,' she murmured, making no sign of moving on. 'If anyone recognises me out here . . .'

'There's something else I want to show you,' said Omnia.

'What is it?'

'It won't take long.'

'I have to get back.'

'You'll want to see it.'

Basilica hesitated for a moment, then nodded, unable to resist the temptation to stay out a little longer.

They headed around the corner of the Lattice, along the Line of Grinning Mugs – and straight into the path of someone coming towards them.

Basilica's hand shot up before the other person could see her face. She stood, head turned down in her hood, arm raised.

It was Pedagogia in their path. She came closer and looked suspiciously at the hidden figure.

'Who's that?' she said to Omnia.

'It's no one, Pedagogia.' Omnia said the name loudly to make sure Basilica heard.

'I don't think it's *no one*.' Pedagogia took a step closer. 'Who are you? Show me your face.'

Omnia stepped between them.

'I need to see her face,' said Pedagogia.

'That doesn't mean she needs to show it,' replied Evergrow. 'One person's need isn't necessarily another person's obligation.'

Pedagogia stared at him. 'Where did you hear that?'

Evergrow didn't reply.

'From *her?*'

Evergrow was silent.

Pedagogia looked at the hooded, hidden figure of the woman who stood beyond Omnia. 'Show me your face,' she said slowly.

Basilica stayed still, as if frozen.

Omnia and Evergrow stood resolutely in front of her, keeping Pedagogia away. Pedagogia took a couple of steps to her left – they took a couple to their right.

'You'll come to a bad end, Omnia Halibut,' said Pedagogia. 'I can see it now.'

Omnia smiled.

'It's nothing to laugh about. And you, Evergrow. Getting mixed up in something like this! I'd have thought you'd know better.'

'If I ever learned anything in the Hall of Leaning, maybe I would!'

Pedagogia gasped. Her hand went to her mouth. 'I always thought you were such a good boy. Your cousin's leading you astray, Evergrow D Halibut. Be warned!'

'All right, he's warned,' said Omnia impatiently. 'We're going. And I wouldn't try to follow us!'

Pedagogia stared at her in affront. Omnia put her hand on Basilica's arm and led her away. Evergrow stayed behind, keeping his eye on Pedagogia in case she tried to follow, and then hurried after them.

'Pedagogia was always officious,' said Basilica after they had gone around a corner. 'Even when she was young. From the sounds of it, she's got worse.'

'She hates you,' said Omnia.

Basilica glanced at Omnia as they walked. 'Does she?'

'Yes. We talked about you once, when I told her that I'd seen you. She really hates you.'

'I'm very sorry to hear that.' Basilica walked silently for a moment. The encounter seemed to have shaken her. 'I have to go back.' This time she said it as if she meant it.

'There's something you have to see.'

'I can't.'

'You *have* to.' Omnia pulled on Basilica's arm. 'You can't go back until you do.'

Basilica stopped and stared at Omnia. *She knows*, thought Omnia. Basilica knew where she was taking her. And she wanted to go. Omnia could see it in her eyes.

'The quicker we do it, the quicker you can go back.'

'All right,' said Basilica. 'Quickly!'

They headed for the Middle Range and managed to get there without being stopped again. They climbed the stairs to Evergrow's apartment and went straight to his room. Just before they could all disappear inside, one of Evergrow's younger brothers came running down the corridor.

'Who's that?' he said, staring at Basilica.

'No one,' replied Evergrow, 'and if you tell that anyone's here, if you *tell*, you'll be sorrier than you've ever been in your life!'

The boy stared at him, eyes wide.

'Now go away!' said Evergrow, and they all went inside and he locked the door behind them.

'He's going to tell, isn't he?' said Omnia.

Evergrow nodded. 'Probably.'

But Basilica wasn't listening. She knew where she was.

'It's through there,' said Omnia, pointing at Evergrow's wardrobe.

They went inside. Evergrow removed a pile of blankets covering the hole in the plaster at the back of the wall.

'Can you get through?' asked Omnia.

Basilica nodded. She knelt and crawled through the hole.

The light on the other side came dimly through the ivy pressed against the windows. Basilica stood looking around, her eyes adjusting, as Omnia and Evergrow followed her in.

'It's nearly twenty-six years since I last stood here,' mummered Basilica.

'Was the door open then?' Omnia asked.

'No, it was closed off. That was the whole point.'

'Then how did you get in?'

Basilica turned to Omnia and smiled. 'Haven't you worked that out?'

Omnia shook her head.

Basilica chuckled. She went to the wall where two paintings hung. One of them showed a young, smiling woman. The other showed the same woman with a man against the background of the House. Between the two paintings stood the huge chest of drawers that Omnia had opened the last time she was here, only to find the drawers almost empty.

'It's you in those paintings, isn't it?' said Omnia.

'Yes. Evermay painted them.'

Evergrow looked at her in surprise. 'But he always paints enormous pictures!'

'Not in those days. Back then, he used to paint portraits, often quite small ones.'

'How old were you?' asked Omnia.

'In the paintings? Eighteen.' Basilica peered closer and shook her head, as if she could barely believe the young, smiling woman in the paintings was her. 'Eighteen and four-sevenths, as I recall.'

'That's your brother, isn't it?'

Basilica gazed at the man in the second painting.

'What's his name?'

'Evernow G Halibut,' whispered Basilica.

'I've never heard of him.'

Basilica smiled sadly. 'I'd fall off my chair in surprise if you had.'

'Where is he?'

'Dead. An accident.'

'Freakish?'

'You could say that.'

Omnia was silent.

Basilica continued to stare at the painting of her and her brother.

'Will you tell me the truth?' asked Omnia.

'The truth,' said Basilica quietly. She turned and leaned against the chest of drawers. 'Whose truth is that, Omnia?'

'The truth. Your truth. What actually happened to you.'

'You mean what I've been told I may never say? You mean what I'll be punished for if certain people ever discover that I've said it?'

'You'll be punished if certain people ever discover that you came out of your apartment, won't you? But you came out today when you had to. You came out when the House needed you to. When I needed you to.'

Basilica dropped her head and was silent. At last, she looked up. 'He doesn't know about the Evergones, does he?' she asked, glancing at Evergrow.

'No,' said Evergrow. 'He doesn't.' Evergrow folded his arms. 'If that's the secret you're not meant to know until you're sixteen, I think it's about time he did!'

Basilica looked at Omnia searchingly. 'Are you going to tell him, Omnia?'

Omnia understood. If Basilica was going to risk everything by telling the truth about what had happened to her, Omnia would have to take a risk as well. A risk for a risk.

Omnia nodded. 'I'll tell him.'

So she told Evergrow about the Evergones, and about the punishment for going outside the wall, and about the fact that every Halibut was told about it when they turned sixteen and were sworn to secrecy in their turn. 'And if you ever tell anyone that I told you, Evergrow, then they'll throw me out and I'll be an Evergone too.'

'And what will they say happened to you?' demanded Evergrow incredulously.

'That she's dead,' said Basilica. 'And they'll make a false grave in the Field of Dreams, and there'll be a funeral and they'll bury an empty coffin. And even people who suspect, will never know for sure whether Omnia Halibut really did die or whether she went outside the wall.'

Omnia stared at Basilica in astonishment. She hadn't known about that part, although now that she thought about it, it was obvious. She had never heard of anyone having gone outside the wall, so there had to be another way to account for people disappearing from the House. If you couldn't talk about them being Evergones, the only other way to do it was to say that they had died.

And perhaps they really had died, in a way. Or at least a part of them had.

But empty coffins and false graves? More secrets, more lies. Omnia wondered how many times she had sat in the trees around the Field of Dreams and watched an empty coffin being buried. She wondered how many of the grassy mounds covered no one at all.

Omnia glanced at Evergrow. She knew what must be going through his mind, the same thing that had gone through her mind, the almost inconceivable sense of betrayal that everyone in the House knew this secret except for him and his friends and the other children who were under sixteen.

'When did you find out?' Evergrow asked her.

'Only two days ago. I'm sorry, Evergrow. I couldn't tell you.' Omnia felt terrible about it. Even now she had a horrible sense of guilt that she knew this secret and that her friends – Artesia, Eversmart, Sororia, Everright and so many others – had no idea. It was as if they were still living in some kind of artificial world, and she had become part of the conspiracy that was keeping them there. 'The Butler told me. He said there are exceptions to waiting until people are sixteen. But there's no exception to the punishment if I tell.'

'You can trust me,' said Evergrow.

'I know. But it's the same for you now. If you tell, they'll make you an Evergone too.'

Evergrow frowned. 'That would almost make me *want* to go out. If someone told me I couldn't, I'd just about want to do it.'

'That does happen,' said Basilica. 'And yet people must be told. At some point, they must learn that you can choose to leave Neversuch House – but if that's the choice you make, you can never unmake it. That's why they leave it as late as they can. By the time you're sixteen, they hope, the punishment won't be as important as the fact that you've been told that life outside is hard, dirty, smelly and tough so often that you'll truly believe it'.

'Is life outside really like that?' asked Omnia.

'Be careful what you ask, Omnia. Once you start to be curious about life outside, that's the first step on the path.'

Basilica paused. Omnia had completed her part of the bargain. Now, she knew, it was her turn. 'You want the truth.' Basilica nodded to herself, then sighed. 'Where do I start? Let me tell you about my brother.' She gazed at the painting, shaking her head sadly. 'The man in that painting was the finest man I ever knew. He was strong and happy and I thought there was no one better in the whole world. People said one day he'd be the Captain, but . . .' she shrugged, 'he went outside the wall. I don't know why. He knew he shouldn't have. Tempted, I suppose, as some of us are. Just as you said, Evergrow.'

'So you never saw him again?' said Omnia.

'I wish that was the case. I wish he had gone away and lived happily and never come back – although that was the last thing I wished for at the time. But no, he did come back. He was twenty years old when he left – just a few days after that painting was painted – and he was twenty-two when he came back. And this is where he lived when he returned. This room. He must have been thinking of leaving for a while before he went, because he prepared it before he left, and when he came back, he had this place to hide in. This was the main place. Usually he kept a parrot with him for company. He had other places too.'

'Like the room in the Ribbled Lodge?'

Basilica smiled.

'How did he get food?' asked Evergrow.

'People helped him.'

'You mean you did?'

'He was my brother.' Basilica paused. 'He had other ways of getting food, of moving around the House. Evernow was clever enough to do anything he wanted. He had a dream that a Halibut could live on both sides of the wall and he wanted to make that dream come true. For a while, he did. For a while, he went in and out whenever he wanted, but when he was here, he wasn't really *here* like you or me, he was always hiding in one of these places. If he left his hiding place, it was in the dark, at night. Then, during one of the times he was in the city, he met a lady and they fell in love, but she wouldn't come in with him, not even for a few hours, not even at night just to see the place. Not into Neversuch House.' Basilica smiled, seeing the looks of incomprehension on the faces of Omnia and Evergrow. 'They hate us in the city. I don't suppose you know that, do you?'

The two children shook their heads. How could they know?

'Oh, yes, they hate us. They really hate us. You can't imagine how much.'

'Why?' asked Omnia.

'Who knows? They never even meet us. But they tell terrible stories about us, terrible lies. So this lady wouldn't come in with him, but Evernow couldn't tear himself away from this place, the place where he was born, so whenever he came back, he would come by himself.' Basilica paused. 'And then he was seen. It had to happen eventually, I suppose. It was Pedagogia, of all people, who spotted him. She had been rather in love with him, I think, and had been told that he was dead.' Basilica shook her head. 'I don't know if she ever really recovered from that.'

'Is that why she hates you?' asked Omnia.

'Maybe. Partly. We were friends when we were young, even though Pedagogia was always a little too officious, even as a child.' Basilica smiled for a moment at some memory. 'What's her obsession, by the way?'

'She's the unofficial headmistress,' said Omnia.

'And poet,' added Evergrow.

Basilica chuckled. 'I should have guessed. Well, Pedagogia must have realised that someone was helping Evernow and it had to be me. She was always a great one for the rules. I suppose she felt betrayed, then doubly betrayed later on when I went outside the wall. Or when they told everyone I had died in a freakish accident, of course, which amounted to the same thing.'

'So you *did* go outside the wall!' cried Omnia. 'I knew it! I knew you did. Why did they let you back in?'

'Patience, Omnia. You asked for the truth – let me tell you the story.' Basilica frowned for a moment. 'Once my brother had been seen, the Butler ordered his men to keep watch for him, and then he was seen again, and they tried to follow him. He told me they'd never catch him, but I knew they'd never give up. One by one they found his places. Trimbleby was the worst. He was a young UnderUnderButler back then, very ambitious, and he tracked him like a bloodhound. Evernow tried to reason with them, tried to find a compromise. He left them notes. But the old Captain wouldn't hear of it. That was Everdew the Fourth, who was the Captain before Everwise. He simply wouldn't hear of it. There could be no compromise. Evernow had gone outside the wall so an Evergone he must be. Trimbleby tracked him and tracked him, until eventually there was only this one place left, and they found it and came for him. Through there, the same way we just came in, through the door he had closed up. They broke it down. Evernow got away just in time and left the House again. He had no time to take anything, had barely enough time to get out of this room. He often wondered what happened to the parrot he kept here. He had no time to take it with him.'

Omnia nodded towards the bird cage that stood beside the table in the room. Basilica peered into it. 'Ah,' she said to herself when she saw the tiny skeleton lying at the bottom of the cage.

'And he never came back, I suppose?' said Omnia.

Basilica turned back from the cage. 'Not exactly. That's the worst of it.' She paused, frowning hard, as if the next part was almost too difficult to tell. 'Something happened to him after that. He changed. He wasn't the Evernow I had known, he wasn't the happy young man in that painting any more. He became bitter. I got letters from him, smuggled in by I-don't-know-who, and they were filled with hate. Then Everdew, the Captain, died in a freakish accident – as so many Captains seem to do. And soon after that, the Butler, Digby – the same Digby you knew, who was murdered three months ago – narrowly escaped with his life from another accident, and then another and another. The accidents seemed to keep happening. So suspicion fell on Evernow, that he was directing this from outside, paying servants to try to destroy the House. 'It went on for years, accidents happening. UnderButlers, clerks, they all got caught up in it. When it was especially bad, Digby and the new Captain, Everwise, would disappear into the Hold. I don't know how they survived. It was like a war, it really was, only it was being fought by the small number of people who were involved and everyone else, the vast majority, was completely unaware that it was happening. That's how it's always been in Neversuch House. Then Everwise and Digby came to me one day. Somehow they had learned that I still received letters from Evernow. They told me that if he agreed to stop, they would let him come back. That they would make an exception for him, and let him go in and out of the House, as long as he kept it secret from everybody else. But, they said they didn't think he would believe their promise if they sent him a letter, but that he might believe it if he heard it directly from someone he trusted, and so they asked me to go out and find him, and tell him, and bring him back so they could talk to him.'

'They *sent* you outside the wall?' asked Omnia incredulously.

'More or less. I didn't have to do it. But they made it clear they thought there was no other way to bring the bloodshed to an end.'

'But then . . .'

'Exactly. So Digby and Everwise promised me that I'd be allowed to come back and live in the House as well. As long as I never told anyone that I had been outside, I would be an exception too. And they said that because Evernow trusted me, only I could do it, and that in every generation, when destruction threatened the House, there had always been a Halibut who could *do* something, and I was that Halibut. So I thought, maybe I am. I didn't seem to have any obsession like all my friends had developed. And they said to me, at such a time, each must do what he or she can. So I thought, if it's up to me to do what I can to save the House, then I had to do it.'

Omnia frowned. The Master Filer had said the exact same thing to her. And as a result, she had made exactly the same decision as Basilica.

Basilica smiled ruefully. 'I was young. I thought nothing could stop me.'

'Why didn't they go and find him themselves?' asked Evergrow. 'Or why didn't they tell someone out there he'd been killing people? Surely even if life outside the wall is hard, dirty, smelly and tough, it's not all right to go around killing people!'

'It isn't,' said Basilica. 'There are authorities outside who catch murderers and punish them. And wouldn't they just love to get into Neversuch House! The city would love to take us over. I told you, Evergrow, they hate us out there. All they need is an excuse. If someone came out and said there were murders happening in here, that's all they'd need. In they'd come and Neversuch House would be finished.'

'Then why don't the Evergones tell them?'

'That would defeat their purpose as well. They don't want to destroy the House, Evergrow, they want to be able to come back. They want it for themselves.'

Evergrow nodded thoughtfully. It was a strange balance in which the House and the Evergones seemed to find themselves, each unable to fully destroy the other for fear of destroying themselves.

'So you went outside the wall?' said Omnia, eager to hear the rest.

'I did. Seventeen years, eight months, two weeks and four days ago. It took me weeks to find my brother, but I finally did. He had changed. He didn't only want to come back to the House now, he wanted to control it. More than that, he wanted revenge for what he saw as the wrong that had been done to him by driving him out. Around him were people I had known before, people I thought were dead, other Evergones. They welcomed me as an Evergone too, and I pretended to join them, not telling them the truth. Evernow was their leader. They were drawn by his energy, by his strength. He was the one who would gain revenge for all of them. I saw servants as well, people who came out of the House on errands. Two of them especially would come to him whenever they were in the city to get their instructions. Secretly, I told Evernow what the Captain and Digby had said and why I had come out. At

214

first, he didn't believe me. It took months to convince him. In fact, I don't know if I ever did. By this time, he was just as bad as the rest of them. Much as I loved him – or loved the Evernow I had known – that's the truth. For all I know, when he finally told me he believed me, and would come with me, he was only planning to come back so he could do for himself what the servants had failed to do on his orders.'

'You mean kill Everwise and Digby?' said Omnia.

Basilica nodded. 'And get the keys to the treasure.'

'So he went back with you?'

Basilica nodded again. 'Before he did, he told his wife that he was going. Her name was Elisabeth. Elisabeth Felt. She begged him not to go, fearing that he would never return. They had a baby, a little boy. He was just over a year old. On the night that we left, Elisabeth turned to me and pointed at the sleeping baby and she said, "Basilica Halibut, if my husband doesn't come back, if something happens to him in that cursed House, this boy of his will take his revenge, on you and on every Halibut there is. Neversuch House will pay, and this baby you see in front of you, when he's grown, will be the one to make them do it. I swear to you, Basilica, this will happen. If Evernow doesn't come back, every day of my child's life I'll remind him what he must do."'

Omnia and Evergrow stared at her, eyes wide, standing in the room where Evernow had hidden, where Basilica had visited him so often and where Trimbleby had tracked him down.

'So my brother came back with me.' Basilica shuddered and her voice dropped, and there was a blank gaze in her eyes, as if she was seeing again the events of that night unfolding before her. 'Everwise and Digby met us at the gate. It was midnight, because they didn't want anyone in the House to know. They had brought two carriages to the gate and we rode back to the House, me in a carriage with Digby and Everwise with my brother and two of the UnderButlers. On the way, Digby asked about everything I had seen, and I told him about the other Evergones I had met, and the two servants who frequently came to see my brother. By the time I had finished we had arrived at the West Stable. My brother's carriage was ahead of us, and it drew up very close to a post that held up part of the roof. I remember thinking, that's odd, how close the driver had drawn up to that post, and then the door opened and Evernow got out and just as he did . . .' Basilica paused and took a deep breath. 'Just as he did, a freakish accident occurred. The post fell and with it two of the beams from the roof. In my horror I looked up to see what had happened and I swear I saw a figure in the moonlight on the roof, just for an instant, and I could swear it was Trimbleby. And then he was gone.'

'And Evernow?'

'Dead. Instantly. Crushed by the post before my eyes. They had used me to lure him back. I was nothing but a piece of bait for my own brother.' Basilica stopped and shrugged. 'It was too late to take back any of the things I had said to Digby in the carriage. The two servants I had named soon died in freakish accidents as well. One was called Roberto Rivers. The other's name was Andreas Hildegrew.'

Omnia stared at her.

'I believe Hildegrew had a young son, who would have been ten or eleven at the time.'

'Tobias?' said Evergrow.

'I never knew his name.'

Evergrow glanced at Omnia, his eyes wide.

'And what about you?' asked Omnia.

'Me?' Basilica smiled painfully. 'They did what they said, didn't they? They kept their promise. Here I am. They let me back in, they let me live here. Only it turns out I hadn't been careful enough. I hadn't asked exactly how I was going to be allowed to live.'

'So that's not what they do with the other Evergones?' said Omnia. 'Let them back in, but keep them locked away?'

'No. Just me. The others all get left outside. Apparently, I'm the lucky one.' Basilica smiled bitterly. 'I don't know what's harder, to be far away, or to be in the middle of it and see what you can't have every day. Seventeen years. Seventeen years, three months, a week and six days, to be exact, I've lived in captivity, with no one but Winnicott for company. I shouldn't complain, I suppose. Winny's not so bad, although a touch morose at times. He hasn't got much of a sense of humour. Well, I imagine he didn't bargain on spending his life in captivity either. Seventeen years. This is my reward for doing what I *could* do, what the Butler and the

Captain asked – seeing my own brother killed and then being locked away. Now, Omnia, do you understand why I tell you not to trust anyone in Neversuch House?'

Omnia nodded.

'Still, there's been peace in the House, hasn't there? Seventeen years of peace.' Basilica leaned forward. 'Evernow's boy would be eighteen years old now. The vow that Elisabeth made, it's coming true. That boy is trying to finish the job his father started. Every day of his life, just like she said she would, Elisabeth will have told him that's his destiny.'

'And Tobias Hildegrew was avenging his father as well,' said Omnia.

'Maybe. Maybe he had other motivations. There are always servants the Evergones can tempt. They give them money, they promise them riches. I've seen it. Just ask yourself, who are the ones who go into the city? Any one of them could be involved.'

Cornelius Slinker, thought Omnia. As a messenger, he often went into the city.

'How do we stop it?' she asked.

'I don't know. Ever since the House was founded, there has been this fight. Let me ask you a question. Can you name the children of the First Captain?'

'Evergreen, Evertrue, Ribonia, Estonia, Yvonnia and Everwell,' replied Evergrow, reciting the list that every child in Neversuch House learned.

'Six children?'

Evergrow nodded.

'What about the seventh?'

'The seventh?'

'Everlet T Halibut. You haven't heard of him? Of course you haven't. The very first Evergone.'

'The First Captain had another son?' asked Omnia in disbelief.

'So they say, those who know. Those who have seen the secret files. They say Everlet went out. Some even say he came back and killed his father, and was killed by his brother Evertrue in turn. This House lives in blood, Omnia. Blood that's hidden from all except the few who choose to be involved. How to bring it to an end? I don't know. I only know that another round is beginning, and just when we need a strong Captain, Everdean wears the Captain's coat.'

'And I'm one of those involved'.

'You are. You made your choice without realising it. That doesn't matter, I'm afraid. It seems that you're involved now too, Evergrow. It seems you've made your choice as well.'

'I'd make it again,' said Evergrow with a frown of determination.

Basilica shrugged. 'Once you're involved, there's no way out. Only death.'

'There has to be a way to stop this,' said Omnia.

'If there is, no one's found it in two hundred years. Defeat one of them and another comes up. And if—'

Basilica stopped. There was a noise. It was coming from

beyond the wardrobe, from the direction of Evergrow's room.

Evergrow scrambled back into the wardrobe, was gone for a moment and then put his head back through the hole in the wall.

'It's my mother!' he whispered. 'She wants to know who's in here.'

'Your brother told, didn't he?' said Omnia.

'She said if I don't unlock the door, she'll break it down.'

'Would she do that?'

'You never know.'

The banging on Evergrow's door continued.

'If your mother finds Basilica . . .' said Omnia.

'She won't,' said Basilica.

'How do we get out?'

'I told you, that hole isn't the entrance.'

Omnia looked around. The window! She began pulling on the handle of one of the windows, trying to get it open so they could climb down the ivy against the wall – although how they would get through the leaves and branches that were pressed up against it she didn't know.

'No.' Basilica pushed one of the paintings aside and touched something in the wood panelling behind it. Suddenly a section of the panelling slid away and the huge chest of drawers swung backwards and down into the opening that had appeared in the wall, revealing a staircase. 'Still works,' she said with satisfaction, and stepped into the opening. 'Quite an engineer, my brother.'

220

The banging from Evergrow's room was louder. Omnia's mind raced. After what Basilica had told her, she needed to talk to the Butler again. In the morning she would go to the Hold. She would need the Master Filer to take her. Well, if the Clerks of the Entrance wouldn't take her to the Master Filer, she knew who would.

She threw a glance at Evergrow. 'I'll see you tomorrow.' She paused for an instant. 'I'll meet you at the Hall of Leaning. At midday.'

'But wouldn't it be safer if I meet you earlier and—'

'I'll see you then!' Omnia stepped through the opening and on to the stairs. Basilica pulled her further in, touched something in the wall and the chest swung up behind them.

They were in pitch-darkness.

'Don't worry,' said Basilica. She reached for Omnia's hand and took it firmly. 'I've been this way many times before.'

20

One New Plan – and a Second One

William Bell climbed the flights of stairs, hearing the creak of his own feet on the wood. He walked along the gallery at the top and paused for a moment, listening, to hear if anyone was following him. Then he climbed yet another set of stairs to the attic in the Warren.

The man inside had thrown his hood over his head. 'Anyone else with you?' he demanded.

William shook his head.

The man let his hood fall.

William put a bag on the table. The man looked inside and took out a hunk of bread, cheese and a couple of pieces of pickled fish wrapped in paper. He took a knife out of his pocket and cut a thick slice of bread from the loaf that William had brought. He cut himself some cheese and began to eat.

William watched him.

The man chewed hungrily. He unwrapped the paper and took some of the fish on his knife.

'So?' he said, pausing for a moment before he put the fish in his mouth.

William smiled. 'It's going exactly as you said. No one knows what they're doing. The UnderUnderButlers are making things up for themselves. Some people listen to them, others don't.'

'What about the Butler?'

'Still hasn't been seen.'

'Is he going to come out?'

'No one knows.'

'And are you all doing what you're supposed to?'

William nodded. 'I keep telling whoever will listen that there's no one in charge. The others are making as much trouble as they can.'

The man chewed his bread thoughtfully. He took another piece of fish. He had taken a risk today and had used the underground river to row to the House, where he crept from one secret place he knew to another, trying to see for himself what was happening. He had taken the panther mask with him. Originally he had intended to use it only on Flip Day, in order to be able to attend the feast, but he had decided to keep it afterwards. Halibuts were prone to all kinds of fears and fancies, he knew. They were easily scared or confused. Today, he had intentionally let a few people glimpse him in the mask. Rumours would start. Fear and uncertainty could only help him.

'Anyone saying the Butler's dead?' he asked.

'Not yet.'

'Start a rumour.'

William Bell grinned.

The man didn't smile. Everything was going as he had planned. It needed to keep going. Time was on his side – but only if no one discovered what he was doing.

The lantern today had been moved. Someone had picked it up and put it down in a slightly different place, he was sure of it. And if they had done that, it was best to assume that they had used it between the moment they had picked it up and the moment they put it down. And what else could they have used it for but to go down to the river, where they would have seen the boat he was using to move between the Warren and the House? As far as he had been aware, no one else knew about the river at all. He only knew about it himself because he had been told by the one person – he had thought the only person – who was aware of it. Surely someone else wouldn't have stumbled on it by mistake? Not now. That would be too great a coincidence.

A name came into his mind. Was it her? It would be just like her to start interfering, although how she could have found the river, he had no idea. Yet who else could it be? No other Halibut, that was certain.

'Have you seen her again?' he said to William.

'Who?'

'Who do you think? Omnia Halibut.'

'No.'

'What about Alice? Has she seen her?'

William shrugged.

'Has Alice been looking?'

'We think she's hiding. You'd expect it after you . . .' William paused, hesitating to remind the man of his failure, '. . . tried to get her.'

The man stabbed a piece of fish with his knife and raised it to his mouth. He could barely believe that Omnia had escaped from him at the Granite Arch. Omnia Halibut may have been a child, but she was capable of spoiling a perfectly good plan. She had shown that three months earlier.

'Maybe someone else might have better luck getting rid of her,' he muttered.

William frowned.

'Well, William? Let's see what you're made of.'

'We'd have to arrange an accident.'

'I don't care any more! She can disappear. Just kill her.'

'How?'

'You tell me.'

William thought about it. He began to smile.

'What?' demanded the man, cutting off a chunk of bread and chewing on it.

'Let's say she comes back to the Butlery and asks me to take her somewhere, like she did yesterday. Of course I'll say yes. But this time, I'll take her somewhere else.'

'Where?'

'You know the Butlery. There are all those rooms in the

UnderBasements full of old files no one ever looks at. Rooms within rooms, with thick doors between them. All I have to do is lock her in.'

'And then?'

'She starves. No one will hear her screams. Maybe in ten years someone will have a reason to go down there and find a skeleton and wonder who it was.'

The man considered it. 'Why didn't you do that yesterday?' he demanded suddenly. 'You had your chance.'

'You didn't tell me to.'

'Do you need to be told? You knew I've been trying to get rid of her!'

The young clerk's face crumpled. He looked as if he was about to cry. 'I thought everything had to look like an accident!'

'That's changed.'

'It hadn't changed yesterday!'

'All right, all right. Don't be such a baby.'

'I'm only trying to do what you want.'

'All right, I said!'

William wiped his nose with the back of his hand. 'I was trying to find out where the Hold is. You said that's what you want to know.'

'How do you know she went there?'

'She must have. She was away so long, I peeked inside after a while and there was no one there. And when I asked her where she went, she wouldn't say.'

The man was silent. He thought about the young clerk's

226

idea for getting rid of Omnia. It appealed to him. The thought of Omnia Halibut starving to death, all alone, unheard, abandoned, was something to savour. It would serve her right for all the trouble she had caused.

'What if she doesn't come back to the Butlery?'

William shrugged.

'That's not good enough! I'm not going to let her ruin things again. We need a second plan. If she doesn't come back to the Butlery, we'll need to winkle her out.'

William was silent. He had no idea what that was supposed to mean.

'You know her cousin Evergrow?' said the man. 'They're close. Say we got hold of Evergrow. All we'd have to do is let it be known and she'd come running.' The man's eyes narrowed. 'Who would Evergrow trust? Would he trust Alice?'

'Why not?' said William. 'He doesn't know her.'

'What if she told him Omnia was in trouble? What if Alice told him she could take him to her?'

William grinned.

'Go and get Alice.'

'She wants to know who you are. She keeps asking.'

'She'll find out soon enough. Go and get her.'

William got up. He stopped at the door. 'What if Omnia does come to the Butlery?'

'Then do what you said, if you really think you can.'

'I can.'

The man looked at him doubtfully. 'She's clever. I know

227

what those rooms in the UnderBasement are like. They're cold. No one's down there. How do you know she'll believe you when you say you're taking her where she asked to go?'

William Bell smiled smugly. 'She trusts me.'

21

Knock Out

Midday. That was when Omnia had told him to meet her. Evergrow had the whole morning to kill.

The food at breakfast was even worse than the day before. All over the hall, Halibuts grumbled and complained. What was happening to the servants? It wasn't just the food in the Tempered Hall. Everyone had a story of a task that had gone undone or a servant who had failed to appear. Laundry workers were failing to launder, polishers to polish, pruners to prune, messengers to messenge. It was simply incomprehensible. There was a rumour going around about a man with the head of a panther who had been glimpsed in various places – under the roof of the Silent Cloister, in a window of the Hatted Belfry, round the corner of the Captain's Keep – and had then disappeared. The Halibuts peered at each other with anxious eyes. What did it mean? Was it a sign? No one knew, but it filled them with unease. Pedagogia said darkly that she wouldn't be surprised if Omnia Halibut was involved, but when she was asked what she meant by that, she wouldn't say.

Evergrow joined Eversmart, Sororia and some of the other children. After picking at burnt eggs and charred sausages, they headed for the Hall of Leaning.

Outside, Evergrow thought he caught a glimpse of Cornelius Slinker loitering on the other side of the Great Kitchen Court, but if it was Cornelius, he disappeared, deciding not to approach him, Evergrow imagined, with so many people around.

At the Hall of Leaning, a polisher in a green smock was rubbing at the handles on the doors.

'At least *someone's* working,' said Eversmart.

The polisher opened one of the doors for them. She kept polishing the other.

As Evergrow went past, she suddenly stepped back and knocked him over.

'Sorry!' she cried. She bent down, as if to help him up. 'I have a message from Omnia,' she whispered.

Evergrow stared up at her.

'Evergrow, are you all right?' asked Sororia, who hadn't gone in yet.

He nodded and got to his feet.

Sororia was waiting for him to go in. Evergrow glanced at the polisher. 'Wait,' he whispered, and he went inside.

Everbox D Halibut was at the front of the Hall. He had just started a lecture about the design and manufacture of the packing materials in which various items were delivered to the House, complete with samples of brown paper, string, cardboard, assorted packing cases and wooden chests. A couple of minutes later, Evergrow glanced at Sororia, rolled his eyes as if he hadn't realised how boring this was going to be and slipped out.

Everbox didn't even pause. Departures during his lessons were hardly a rarity. Most of the seats were usually empty by the time he finished.

The polisher was waiting outside.

'Did you say you had a message from Omnia?' asked Evergrow.

She nodded.

'What is it?'

'She asked me to bring you to her.'

'Where is she?'

'I told you, she wants me to bring you.'

'But I was supposed to meet her at—'

'Evergrow, she's in trouble. I can't tell you more than that. Every minute counts. You can come with me right now or you can stand here asking questions.'

Evergrow nodded quickly. 'Let's go.'

They set off. The polisher moved fast, always half a step ahead of Evergrow. Evergrow asked her again, but she refused to say where they were going. She refused to say what kind of trouble Omnia was in either, or how it was that she knew about it. Evergrow tried to imagine what it could be as they hurried along. Omnia had said there was something she had to do that morning, but hadn't said what. Was she going after Slinker? Not by herself, surely. And he had seen Cornelius only a little while before. Surely Slinker wouldn't have had the time to catch her since then. But perhaps he had got her earlier. The last Evergrow had seen of Omnia was when she left the secret room behind his wardrobe with Basilica. Where had she gone after that? Maybe Cornelius had got her during the night.

The polisher had slowed down, as if unsure of her way. Evergrow looked around. Behind him was the Bridled Mound. Ahead, over the conical roofs, was the gap-toothed outline of the top of the Faunal House. They weren't far from the entrance to the underground river. They came to a corner and he recognised the carving of the dancing clown high up on the wall.

'She's around there,' said the polisher loudly and pointed around the corner.

Evergrow looked at her questioningly. Had Omnia come back to the river by herself? Had she got into some kind of trouble using the boat?

'Go on,' said the polisher.

Evergrow hesitated, then went around the corner.

He had gone only a few steps when someone stepped out of a doorway.

Evergrow stared, then he started to laugh. The man in front of him was wearing a grey panther's mask. For some reason, the mask didn't strike Evergrow as scary, but absurd.

'Funny, is it?' said a voice through the mask. The man

stepped forward and the last thing Evergrow saw was the mask suddenly jerking forward and coming at him at a tremendous speed.

The man's masked head smashed into Evergrow's, instantly knocking him to the ground.

His eyelids fluttered. He was aware of a throbbing pain in his head. The light was dim. He was on his back and could see some kind of a roof above him, rough rock, with cracks in it. The cracks were moving. He became aware of a rhythmic sound.

Splash . . . splash . . .

Evergrow turned his head. He was in a boat. A giant panther was rowing.

No, that made no sense. It was a man. Yes. A *man* in a panther's mask.

He tried to remember how he had got there. The polisher had been taking him to find Omnia, and he had gone around a corner and seen a man in a panther mask – but that was where his memory ended. He had no recollection of the way the man had knocked him out, picked him up, thrown him over his shoulder and then carried him down to the river.

The panther was watching him.

'You're awake,' said a voice from inside the mask.

Evergrow didn't reply.

'Had a nice little sleep?'

'Where's Omnia?'

'Omnia? Wouldn't we all like to know?' The panther-man stopped rowing for a moment and let the boat drift. 'I don't suppose you can tell me.'

Evergrow was silent, trying to work out what was going on.

'Well, if we can't find her, she'll come looking for you, I'm sure.'

Suddenly Evergrow understood. 'No, she won't!'

The panther-man laughed. 'No? *You* came looking for her.'

Evergrow watched him rowing. 'Take off your mask, Cornelius.'

'Cornelius?' said the man.

'And you can stop talking in that voice.'

'So you think I'm Cornelius, do you? Cornelius Slinker?' The man laughed. 'Good. I suppose that means Omnia thinks I'm Cornelius as well.'

Evergrow was silent, trying to give no sign of his dismay. If this man wasn't Cornelius . . . then Cornelius really was trying to protect Omnia! But she had no idea.

The man steered the boat towards a ring that was fixed in the wall and tied it up. A ladder rose to a trapdoor above the water.

'Get up,' he said.

Evergrow shook his head.

The man stood in the boat, which rocked, and grabbed Evergrow by the collar. 'Get up! Get up unless you want me to knock you out again!'

Evergrow stood. The man pulled something out of the boat, another panther mask, a blue one.

'Put this on. We wouldn't want anyone recognising you, would we? Especially here. Halibuts aren't meant to be here, you know.'

'Where's here?'

'Don't you worry. Put it on.'

Evergrow stared at the mask.

'Put it on!'

The man began to force it on, holding Evergrow with one hand while trying to get the mask over his head with the other. Evergrow struggled and the boat rocked violently. The man hissed, trying to get the mask on to Evergrow's moving head. Evergrow hit out at him. The man bent closer and suddenly Evergrow felt the man's mask under his hand and he clutched at it. His fingers closed around one of the panther ears. Instinctively, he pulled.

Off came the mask.

The man jerked upright.

Evergrow stared. His eyes went wide. His mouth dropped open.

'You . . . ?' he whispered. 'But you're dead!'

22

Locked Away

Omnia had spent the night in Basilica's apartment. She and Basilica had made their way from Evergrow's room back to the Winter House and through the Snowflake. In the morning, Winnicott served a breakfast of the usual pies and pasties. There was a yellow parrot pie that was absolutely delicious. Later, Omnia left by the chute and followed the tunnel to the exit near the Splitted Stairs. From there she headed for the Bright Tower.

In the Long Palisade she passed a group of servants who were arguing about something. They fell silent as she approached. Omnia could feel them watching her as she walked by, and she was certain the argument would flare up again as soon as she was gone. In front of her rose the Chequered Wall, but the huge banners that were normally unfurled by a pair of servants each morning from the windows – red and pink if it was a sunny morning, green and yellow if it was cloudy – and rolled up each night were nowhere to be seen. Omnia couldn't remember them ever being missing before. On the Minor Terrace, she found a pair of Halibut ladies seated on a porpoise-shaped bench talking in great agitation.

'What's wrong?' asked Omnia.

'The servants have all gone quite peculiar,' replied one of the ladies. 'One of them said the most extraordinary thing to me this morning.'

'Just listen to this!' exclaimed the second lady.

'He said: "This time next year, I won't be doing this." ' The first lady threw up her hands, as if she had never heard anything so amazing.

'What do you make of that?' asked the second. 'Have you ever heard anything like it?'

Omnia shook her head.

The two ladies stared at her, utterly nonplussed at the story they had just told. Behind them, over the edge of the Terrace, Omnia could see the Pitted Court. Two servants were down there, one walking quickly away while the second was staggering along with a washing basket that the other should have been helping to carry.

Omnia kept going. At the Hatted Belfry, she heard a voice calling out. She looked up. Evertwitch Halibut was high in his cage with no sign of the rope ladder that normally dangled from it.

'Help me, Omnia,' he called to her faintly.

'What's wrong?' she called back.

'They've taken the ladder and no one's come back. I've been here since yesterday. I'm starving.'

'I'll try to do something.'

'Quickly, please!'

All over the House she found bewildered Halibuts. In the Court of the Spouted Fountain she came across Evermay who was standing in his paint-smeared smock, looking around with an expression of utter confusion.

'I've run out of black paint,' he told her, shaking his head in confusion. 'They were supposed to bring me some this morning, but they didn't. Black! What can I do without black? It's impossible. I'm working on a great picture of the grey panther. It's been seen, you know.'

'What?' asked Omnia quickly. 'The panther? Someone's seen it? Where?'

'I don't know. What does it matter? Where are my paints? It's not only black. Cerulean blue. Cadmium yellow. Viridian green. I've run out of all of them!' Evermay's face crumpled in anguish. 'What am I going to do?'

Omnia gazed at him. Evermay had no idea where his paints came from or how he could find the servants who always brought them. They simply appeared, as if out of thin air, and now that they hadn't, he had no idea where to start looking.

'Go back to your studio, Evermay,' said Omnia. 'I'll see what I can do.'

She hurried on to the Bright Tower. As she approached it, a figure stepped out from behind a column.

Cornelius Slinker.

Omnia froze.

The messenger came closer.

'What do you want?' demanded Omnia.

'Why are you running from me?'

'Why are you after me?'

'Why do you think?' said Cornelius. 'These are dangerous times, Omnia. You need protection.'

'And you're going to provide it, are you? I trusted you, Cornelius.'

'What did I do? If you'd at least tell me what—'

'Stay away from me!'

'But you need—'

Suddenly Omnia dashed past him and ran for the Bright Tower. She raced up the stairs and didn't stop until she was at the door to the entrance chamber.

She glanced down. Slinker was at the bottom. He hesitated for a moment and then began to come up.

Omnia turned round – and came face to face with William Bell.

He smiled. 'Hello, Omnia.'

The chamber was full, as it had been for the past two days. People were waving papers and shouting to be heard. Hazenby, Ollendorff and the other UnderUnderButlers shouted back. Behind the desk, the two Clerks of the Entrance, normally so imperious, helplessly watched the chaos. Now and again, Childes poked a finger at someone or Fellowes shouted, but mostly they just sat and looked, and would even have considered leaving their posts and going home except for the fact that the entrance chamber was as much of a home as either of them had.

'I need to see the Master Filer,' said Omnia quickly to William Bell. 'Can you take me?'

'Of course.'

Omnia threw another glance down the stairs. Cornelius Slinker was halfway up.

William looked down as well. 'Is he worrying you?'

'Let's just go!'

William nodded. He grabbed Omnia's hand and made way for them amongst the crowd to the door on the other side of the room. He ushered her through. Omnia looked over her shoulder and glimpsed Slinker arriving up the stairs just as William shut the door behind them.

In the entrance chamber, Cornelius Slinker saw the door close. He went straight for it, pushing his way through the crowd. The sight of a messenger heading into the Butlery without so much as a do-you-mind would normally have had Fellowes up on his feet in a rage and Childes scribbling furiously in his ledger. Instead, the two Clerks merely glanced at each other and shrugged.

By the time Slinker got to the door and ran after them, William and Omnia were far down the corridor. He saw them turn down a flight of stairs and disappear.

Down they went, one flight, and another, and another.

Omnia stopped. 'This isn't the way we went last time.'

'The Master Filer's in a different room today,' said William.

'Are you sure?'

William nodded.

'Why?'

'He changes rooms every day. That's what he's like.'

Omnia hesitated. The Master Filer hadn't seemed like a man who changed rooms every day – he looked like someone who had occupied the same room for years.

'Listen!' said William. They could hear Slinker's footsteps coming down the stairs above them. 'He's close! Come on!'

They ran down a corridor. It was cold down here and there were no clerks in the rooms that came off the corridor. The rooms were all stacked high with shelves and shelves of files. William took her round one corner, and another, and down another flight of stairs. It was even colder.

Omnia threw a glance at William as they ran. 'You're sure he's down here?'

'Of course. He's a filer. He loves files. Here. Turn here. And here. Down there. All right. In here. And here. This is it.'

They were in a room off a room full of ancient, yellowed files. There was another door in front of them.

William pushed her towards it. He knocked. 'Master Filer, are you in?' William listened for a second, then nodded and opened it. 'In you go.'

Omnia took a step closer, peering into the gloom. 'Why's it so dark—'

She felt a shove and stumbled forward and by the time she turned around, the door had slammed behind her. She heard a key turn.

241

It was pitch-black.

'Hello?' she said.

There was no reply.

She put her hands in front of her and took a small step forward in the darkness. Immediately her hands hit a pile of papers and suddenly the air was full of dust. Omnia coughed. She felt around the papers, but couldn't find the top of the pile or either side. A wall of papers was apparently in front of her.

'Master Filer, are you here?' She waited a few seconds, coughing, trying to clear her throat of the dust. 'You're not here, are you?'

Silence.

Omnia turned back towards where she knew the door was and felt for the handle. She turned it. The door was locked. She pulled on the handle, then pulled harder. The handle broke loose in her hand and she fell back against the pile of papers behind her.

She could feel dust and cobwebs all over her. She brushed at them, coughing, sneezing.

Omnia got up and beat on the door.

'William?'

She kept beating. 'William? *William! William!*'

She stepped back and leaned against the papers. The darkness was complete. She tried to remember when she had last seen a clerk on the way to this room. They had gone down and down and down. There was no one to hear her.

Suddenly an image flashed into Omnia's mind: the

skeleton of the dead bird in the room behind Evergrow's wardrobe.

What had William done to her?

She jumped up and hammered on the door.

'William! William! William! Will—'

She stopped. She had heard the key turn in the lock.

Suddenly she felt like a fool. What had she been imagining! It was ridiculous. William hadn't left her down here. Of course he was coming back.

The door opened. William stood in front of her, with Cornelius Slinker holding him by the collar of his walnut-coloured coat. A big, red bruise was coming up on William's face.

'I knew you were behind this!' yelled Omnia at Cornelius.

'Me? But I—'

'He hit me!' yelled William quickly. 'I told him I was only helping you.'

'You're not going to get me, Cornelius!'

'I don't want to—!'

'That's why I left you there!' cried William. 'To be safe until he was gone!'

Omnia threw herself at Cornelius, trying to get past him. William kicked and thrashed in his grip. Cornelius struggled to explain himself as he fought to keep his grip on William's coat with one hand and to keep Omnia back with the other,

'I was helping you, Omnia!' yelled William.

Omnia launched a kick at Cornelius's shin.

'Omnia, trust me,' he pleaded.

'Trust *you?*'

'Yes, *you?*' yelled William, turning and squirming in his grip. 'Where were you the other day when she needed your help?'

'Exactly!' cried Omnia, aiming another kick at Cornelius's shin.

'Where were you when she gave you the sign to meet? Well? Where were you when she left the stone?'

'Yes, where were you when I—' Omnia stopped. She looked at William. 'How do you know about that?'

The clerk stopped struggling as well. He frowned for an instant. 'You told me.'

'No, I didn't.'

'Yes, you did.'

Omnia stared at him. Slowly, she shook her head. 'I never told you that.'

'You forget.'

'No,' said Omnia. 'I'd remember if I did.'

Cornelius Slinker watched her, wondering what was going on.

'Cornelius, did you find the stone?' asked Omnia. 'Three days ago. I left it for you.'

Cornelius shook his head.

'Did you check?'

'I always check. It wasn't there.'

'But I—'

Suddenly, forgotten for a moment, William slipped free

and ran. In a flash, he was out the other door and around the corner, having pulled a pile of files down on the floor behind him to slow them down. Cornelius and Omnia kicked the files away and ran after him. He was far down the corridor. He stopped and turned for a second.

'Of course he didn't find the stone!' cried William. 'We took it. We know everything. You're dead, Omnia Halibut! You too, Cornelius Slinker! Dead! Dead! You're both as good as dead already.' Then he disappeared into another room and was gone.

Cornelius ran after him. He got to the room and stopped. In front of him were three doors.

Omnia arrived behind him. Three doors. Which one? And what then? William Bell knew all the rooms and corridors in this vast anthill of a place.

Omnia looked at Cornelius. Was *he* the trustworthy one, after all? Or was this just another trick to make her think so? Perhaps he and the young clerk were working together.

But why another trick? She had been locked in that room and no one would ever have found her. She would have ended up like the bird in the cage. If they wanted to get rid of her, they had already found a way.

'Did you really not find the stone?' she asked. 'Three days ago, Cornelius.'

Cornelius shook his head.

'I left it for you.'

'They must have seen.'

'Someone was there. In a mask. I thought it was you.'

'They must have followed you.'

'He was waiting for me.'

'Maybe they followed you another time. Maybe they knew that's where you'd go.'

Omnia was silent. The polisher! She must have been the one. Trimbleby had been telling the truth. She wasn't working for him. Was she working for the Evergones too? How many of them were there? How long had they been preparing this?

'You can trust me, Omnia. I told you a long time ago. Have you forgotten?'

Omnia shrugged ruefully. 'He said you should never trust someone who says that.'

'Who?'

'*Him*. William.'

'Look what he did to you.'

'Where did you find him?'

'He was leaving,' said Slinker.

'Leaving . . .' Omnia nodded. Leaving. Leaving her to die.

'He was going back to the entrance a different way. Probably thought he'd avoid me.'

'How did you find him then?'

'I took a wrong turn.'

Omnia smiled in disbelief. If not for that wrong turn, she would still have been in that room.

'I had to hit him to make him take me to you.' Slinker paused. 'I'd have killed him if I had to.'

Omnia watched him. She was beginning to understand

that behind Cornelius Slinker's quiet, shy exterior was a fierce loyalty and determination – fiercer than she had realised even after he saved her from Tobias Hildegrew – and for some reason, that loyalty and determination were devoted to her. She didn't know why. She didn't know what she had done to deserve it. But she would be dead now, twice, if it hadn't been for Cornelius.

'You saved my life again.'

Cornelius shrugged.

'You're making a habit of it.'

'Rather not need to,' murmured the messenger.

'Thank you, Cornelius.'

Cornelius nodded.

'I came to find the Master Filer. I don't know the way.'

'Nor do I.' Slinker shrugged. 'Thing like that shouldn't be a problem.'

They went back the way they had come. They found the stairs and went up and came out into a corridor, and went up another flight of stairs, and through more corridors, and up more stairs. Eventually they found a room with a clerk and Cornelius walked in and said they needed to know how to get to the Master Filer.

The clerk ignored them.

Cornelius went around the back of his desk and dragged the startled clerk off his chair.

'The Master Filer,' he growled. 'Take us!'

23

Back to the Hold

Omnia knocked and then opened the door. She had asked
Cornelius if he could go and rescue Evertwitch, who was
probably still stuck in his cage on the Hatted Belfry, and
then come back to her in the Bright Tower. Evermay and
his paints, unfortunately, would have to wait.

Inside, the Master Filer sat behind his desk. The big
wooden chests in front of him were empty.

'Nothing's coming in,' he said, looking at her with his
milky blue eyes. 'Everything's stopped.'

'Are you surprised?' said Omnia. 'I need to speak to the
Butler.'

'Your need isn't my obligation,' said the Master Filer.

'The letter still holds,' replied Omnia. 'Trimbleby's dead
in a freakish accident and I've come to see the Butler. You
have to take me.'

The Master Filer sighed. After a moment, he got up,

settled his raisin-coloured hat on his head, picked up his umbrella and led her to the door in the corner.

Clerks sat idly in the rooms that they passed, desks lacking the huge piles of papers that usually sat there. Omnia glimpsed one throwing a paper dart. In another room a group were playing mini-Bracketball. The Master Filer went in, flailing at them with his umbrella.

At the door to the Hold, Digby greeted them in his green Butler's coat. 'Glad to see you're still alive, Omnia,' he said, as if he had half expected her to have been killed by now.

'One of your clerks tried to make sure I wasn't,' replied Omnia, as the door closed behind her. 'William Bell.'

'William Bell?' Digby glanced at the Master Filer. 'Do you know him?'

The Master Filer shook his head. 'What colour is his coat?'

'Walnut,' said Omnia.

'Not one of mine then,' said the Master Filer.

'What difference does it make whose he is?' demanded Omnia.

'It may not make much difference to you,' replied the Master Filer. 'But it makes quite a difference to me.'

They went in. Everdean was sitting in his chair, his bald, egg-shaped head gleaming in the light, apparently unaware of anything that was happening around him.

Omnia turned back to the Butler. 'Mr Digby, you have to do something.'

'He has done something,' snapped the Master Filer. 'He sent instructions to the UnderUnderButlers.'

'I told them they have to take charge while I'm in here,' said the Butler. 'Especially Hazenby and Ollendorff. I've made them OverUnderUnderButlers. If they do a good job, I'll make them UnderButlers when I come out.'

Omnia told them about the scene of chaos she had witnessed in the entrance chamber to the Bright Tower.

'They're learning,' said the Master Filer, who didn't appear to be perturbed.

'Not very fast,' said Omnia.

'Give them time.'

'We don't have time!' Omnia could have screamed in exasperation. 'Mr Digby, things aren't good out there. Things aren't being done properly.'

'Like what?' demanded the Master Filer.

'Like anything. Things aren't being delivered. Things aren't being done. The banners on the Chequered Wall weren't there.'

'The banners on the Chequered Wall,' said the Master Filer dismissively.

Omnia could have given him another hundred examples. 'Look, someone has to do something!'

'We have done something. The UnderUnderButlers have been told to take control.'

'It's not working!'

'Omnia,' said the Butler. 'Give it a chance. Not

250

everything happens at once. Sometimes we have to be patient. If you're patient, everything will be all right.'

Omnia gazed at him, wondering if he really believed what he was saying. It seemed to her that the Butler had spent so long hidden away in this place that he really had convinced himself that as long as he stayed safe, everything would turn out well.

She looked at Everdean. The Captain of the House lay slumped in his chair. 'Is he even awake?' she demanded.

'Everdean?' said Digby loudly. 'Are you awake?'

Everdean gave a start. His eyes opened and he looked around the room.

'Look who's here,' said Digby. 'It's Omnia. Omnia Halibut.'

Everdean stared at her for a moment, then rested his head back and closed his eyes again.

'Listen, Omnia,' said the Butler. 'The situation isn't good, that's clear. But the important thing is, we have the keys. I have one, Everdean has the other. Without them, there's no way to get to the Captain's treasure.'

'You can't just break the door down,' added the Master Filer. 'Even if you could, there's a mechanism. If the door isn't opened with the keys, the entrance will collapse on whoever's standing there and a second set of doors will shut behind them.'

'What if that's not what the Evergones want this time?' said Omnia.

'What else could they want?' replied the Butler. 'That's what they always try to get.'

The Master Filer shook his head. 'They're idiots! Killing the UnderButlers was a stupid thing to do. It gave us warning.'

Omnia frowned. All along, everyone seemed to have assumed that killing the UnderButlers was a mistake. Trimbleby himself had assumed it before he became the third victim. But why make that assumption? It was the biggest mistake you could make simply to assume that others had made a mistake. That was what Basilica had told her.

Assume it wasn't. Then the question was: what would the plan be if killing the UnderButlers *wasn't* a mistake? According to what Omnia had been told, previous attempts had failed because the Evergones wanted to get the Butler and the Captain, who had the keys to the treasure, but the Butler and the Captain found safety in the Hold. So surely the Evergones would know they would go to the Hold this time as well. Which meant – if they had planned this, if killing the UnderButlers wasn't a mistake – that they *wanted* them to go there.

Why would the Evergones want that?

Omnia thought about what she had seen happening outside. Halibuts wandering around in confusion, servants arguing with each other about whether they were going to work. With the Captain and the Butler in the Hold, and the UnderButlers dead, the House was falling into chaos. What if that was what the Evergones wanted this time? What if that was what they were trying to achieve?

The Butler and the Master Filer couldn't see it. They

hadn't been outside. Even if they had, they might not have understood the enemy's plan. Like generals who have read about too many battles in the past, they wouldn't realise when they had a new kind of battle in front of them.

'What if their plan is to do exactly this,' she said, 'to make you hide in the Hold and get rid of the UnderButlers so it seems no one's in control?'

'Nonsense!' retorted the Master Filer. 'What good would that do them?'

Omnia was wondering exactly that. She thought about what she had seen – Evermay, Evertwitch, the two Halibut ladies on the dolphin seat, others she had passed in court-yards and squares. All utterly helpless. Suddenly she realised that the House's vulnerability wasn't the treasure beyond the locked door to which Digby and Everdean had the keys – it was the servants who lived here. What if they decided to stop doing what they were meant to be doing? What if they all stayed in the Warren and refused to come out? What if they all left? There wasn't a single Halibut who knew how things ran, except for the Captain, perhaps. And look at him!

In fact, now that she thought about it, she didn't under-stand why any of the servants stayed. What were they doing here? Why hadn't they gone, all of them, years ago?

'Omnia, you don't understand,' the Master Filer was saying. 'We're not going to fall apart just because a few UnderButlers have been killed. You Halibuts, you always think this place is all for you. No. I told you, it's not just your House, it's ours too. The traditions are as much for us as for you. For the Digbys, the Gondoliers, the Coffiers, the Sturgeons. For all of us. My father was the Master Filer, and before him, his uncle, and before him, my grandfather, and so on. We're not going to let—'

'You have to come out!' said Omnia suddenly, ignoring the Master Filer and speaking to the Butler. 'Today. Now. You have to show yourself.'

'He'll do no such thing!' retorted the Master Filer.

'Mr Digby, they need to see you. Halibuts, servants. They need to see that you're still in charge.'

'They need him to stay alive! And he stays alive if he stays here!'

'And what about the Rinque?' demanded Omnia.

'What about the Rinque?' retorted the Master Filer.

'It's in two days' time. Is he still going to be hiding here then? Is that your plan? What about Everdean? Is he?'

'They don't need to be at the Rinque,' said the Master Filer.

'But everyone will expect—'

'They don't *need* to be there! I can give you twenty examples. I know all the files, the secret as well as the known. Evertrue the Second missed it twice. And Everdew the Fourth hardly ever turned up to the Rinque at all.'

Omnia was silent. The Master Filer could say what he liked, he could go back into history as far as he wanted, but if Everdean and Digby weren't seen on Rinque Day in two days' time, there would be panic. The disturbance she had seen in the House would be just the beginning.

She looked at Digby. 'Why don't you answer me? Why do you let him do the talking?'

The Butler was silent. He dug his hands into the pockets of his green velvet coat and gazed at the floor, frowning. Eventually he looked up at her.

'The House goes on, Omnia. Today, yesterday, tomorrow. It goes on because we do what we've always done. That's what my father taught me. That's all I can do.'

'Today, yesterday . . .' said Omnia. 'Yes. But the way things are going, I'm not sure about tomorrow.'

The Master Filer shook his head. 'Omnia, you need to have faith. You need to have patience. Neversuch House has stood for two centuries. Why? Because we do as Mr Digby just said. We always have. Two centuries. Do you think something that happens in two weeks can bring it down? You're young, it's natural you should want everything to happen quickly. But the keys are safe. The servants are good. One or two will turn, but there are always a couple of bad apples in any barrel, like William Bell. We'll deal with him. We'll put him out of the House and he'll never be allowed back. The others will stay true. Whoever's doing this, if their plan is to make the servants rebel, if that's what you're thinking, they'll soon find that the servants in Neversuch House are made of different stuff! It's our House too. That's what I keep telling you. The servants will carry on the traditions.'

'But already they aren't,' said Omnia, wondering what more she could possibly say to make these two men understand that things really were changing outside.

'A few banners missing, is that what you said?'

'That's only a part of it!' Omnia shook her head in exasperation. The Butler hiding here in the Hold, the Master Filer locked away in his room, they would talk themselves into doing nothing for so long that they would lose the chance to act. Well, she wouldn't! She regretted not having done more when she found the boat. She should have stayed to fight. It was fear that had impelled her, she knew. Pure fear. A fear that went back to the day Tobias Hildegrew had thrown her off the Slate Tower, to the night he had hunted her under the roof of the Ribbled Lodge. The same fear she had felt when she had seen the man in the grey panther's mask.

She would simply have to overcome that fear. There was no room for it now.

'Omnia,' said the Butler, 'you should stay here this time.'

She shook her head.

'I'm serious. You'll be safe.'

'I'll take my chances.'

'If you go out, we can't promise to protect you.'

Promise to protect her? Omnia almost laughed at that. No one could promise her anything, she thought, except that if she stayed in here, there would be nothing left to fight for when she came out.

Cornelius had returned and was waiting for her outside the Master Filer's room when she got back. He persuaded another clerk to show them the way back to the entrance chamber and they went quickly through the milling, shouting crowd. By the time they were outside, it was almost midday.

'I said I'd meet Evergrow,' said Omnia.

They hurried to the Hall of Leaning. There was no sign of her cousin outside the building.

Omnia went in and looked around. She couldn't see him. The headmistress marched towards her. Omnia ran out before Pedagogia reached her.

'Did you find him?' asked Cornelius.

Omnia shook her head. 'We were only a few minutes late.' She frowned and looked around again. 'It's not like Evergrow not to wait.'

'Omnia, we shouldn't wait here either. It's not safe. That's probably why Evergrow left when you weren't here on time.'

'Should we look for him?'

'Let's get you to safety first.'

Omnia thought for a moment. 'All right. Let's go. I know somewhere safe.'

'Does Evergrow know about it too?'

Omnia nodded. 'That's probably where he's gone.'

24

Axes

'*Where is she?*' demanded Tobias Hildegrew.

His hand came swinging at Evergrow's face and stopped just a centimetre short, leaving Evergrow in no doubt what would happen if he refused to tell.

'*Well? Where?*'

Evergrow shook his head. He still found it barely possible to believe that the man in front of him – the man whose face he had revealed when he pulled off the panther mask – was the supposedly dead servant who had murdered the old Captain and Butler.

'*Well?*' demanded Hildegrew again. He jerked Evergrow to his feet, bending down to look him in the eyes. 'You know, don't you? Of course you know.'

'I don't know.'

'You do!' He pushed Evergrow away. 'Sit down! There! On the floor.'

Evergrow sat.

'Do you want me to hurt you? Is that what you want?'

Hildegrew already had hurt him. Evergrow's head ached from the blow that had knocked him out. The pain ran all the way down into his teeth. He didn't know what else Hildegrew might do. He hoped he could bear it. He thought of Everlook, as he always did when he needed courage. His uncle would have been able to bear it, he thought. Everlook would have been able to hold on.

Hildegrew stood over him. 'Where's Omnia? Where *is* she?'

'I don't know.'

'She's hiding.'

Evergrow shrugged.

'You know where she's hiding.'

'I don't.'

'Where is she?'

'She didn't *tell* me.'

'You knew last time. Under the roof of the Ribbled Lodge.' Hildegrew smirked cruelly. 'I followed you.'

'That's why she didn't tell me this time.'

Hildegrew stood back. Evergrow could see him considering what he had just said. It was smart, Evergrow realised after he had said it. It had just come out – but it could just be true.

He tried to think straight. It wasn't easy with his aching head.

'She said the less I know, the safer we'd both be.'

Hildegrew raised an eyebrow. Suddenly he pulled Evergrow up by collar, then sent him stumbling across the floor. 'Get over there,' he snapped, pointing to a corner of the room.

Evergrow went to the corner and sat on the bare floorboards, watching Hildegrew. He was still asking himself how it was possible that this terrible man, this cold-blooded killer, was back. Omnia had told him that he had fallen from the top of the Great Tower. How could he have survived?

Hildegrew caught sight of him watching and growled. Evergrow looked away. A moment later, he stole a glance at him again.

Evergrow didn't know exactly where Omnia was hiding, but he could guess. Basilica's apartment in the Winter House was the safest place he could think of, and he would have bet anything that Omnia was there. But as far as he was aware, there was no reason for Hildegrew to know that such a place existed, so there was no reason for him to suspect that he, Evergrow, would know about it either.

The stairs outside creaked.

'Stay there!' Hildegrew jumped up and stood behind the door. 'We'll continue this later.'

'You can do what you like to me,' muttered Evergrow. 'I've got nothing to tell you.'

Hildegrew glared at him, then pulled his hood over his head.

In came William Bell, panting. His face was red and he had a big bruise on one cheek.

Hildegrew came out from behind the door and threw off his hood. 'What are you doing here?' he demanded. 'Did you get her? Is that what you've come to tell me?'

'Why are you letting him see your face?' said William, throwing a glance at Evergrow.

'Who are you to ask?' snapped back Hildegrew, embarrassed to admit that Evergrow had managed to get the mask off him. 'What's happened? Why are you here? Did you get Omnia or not?'

William shook his head. He told Hildegrew what had happened, or a version of it anyway. He had run all the way to the Warren and up the stairs to the attic and was still pausing to catch his breath as he spoke. 'It wasn't my fault,' he whined. 'I had her locked in . . . and then . . . there were four of them who came after me . . . and I beat one of them off, and I beat another one off, and I beat another one off, and then the fourth one . . . the fourth one . . .'

'What?'

'He got me. He got me while I was fighting the others. I couldn't do anything, Tobias. Honestly, I couldn't.'

'Who were they?' asked Hildegrew sceptically.

'I didn't see. They were huge.' He paused, trying to think of something else to say. He saw Hildegrew's pather mask lying on the ground. 'And they wore masks!'

'What kind of masks?'

'Masks . . . I don't know. Masks! I saw who one of them was though, the fourth one. I fought him and fought him and pulled off his mask and it was Cornelius Slinker.'

Tobias Hildegrew sighed. 'So, what you're saying is that Cornelius Slinker caught you and gave you that bruise on your face and made you open the door. Is that right? Is that the truth?'

'After I fought off the other three.'

'Of course. I forgot about them.' Hildegrew rolled his eyes. 'Where did Omnia go then? Do you know?'

'She wanted to see the Master Filer.'

'And did she see him?'

William shrugged. 'I didn't wait to find out.'

Hildegrew glared at him. Then he glanced at Evergrow. 'What are you smiling at?' he demanded.

'Nothing,' said Evergrow quickly.

Hildegrew turned back to William. He shook his head in disgust. He could hardly blame the young clerk for failing to kill Omnia – he himself had failed more times than he cared to admit – but after this, it was certain that William would be identified as part of the conspiracy. He had been Hildegrew's most important assistant. William Bell had been part of the original plot three months earlier and had stayed in place ever since, undetected, after Hildegrew had escaped. He was the one who had found this place to hide when Hildegrew came back, the one who had recruited the other three young servants to their conspiracy. He was an indispensable source of information, hearing and seeing all kinds of things as people came and went in the entrance chamber to the Butlery. Now he wouldn't be able to show his face there. He wouldn't be able to show it anywhere.

Hildegrew would have to smuggle him out of the House – or get rid of him some other way.

Tobias Hildegrew shook his head in annoyance once more. The young clerk was no use to him now that he had been exposed as a member of the conspiracy, no use at all.

Soon the others arrived. First, Robert Gondolier, then Owens, then Alice Bickerstaff. Hildegrew left his hood off. They stared at him in amazement.

'Yes, yes, yes,' he said impatiently when Alice Bickerstaff told him he was supposed to be dead. The other two had said it already. 'Don't you think I know that?'

'Then why aren't you?'

'It's a miracle,' he snapped.

Alice glanced at Evergrow and smirked. 'Hello.'

Evergrow didn't reply.

Alice laughed cruelly. 'Don't want to talk to me now? You had no end of questions before! No need to sulk, Evergrow. No one made you come with me, did they?'

'You lied. You said Omnia was in trouble.'

'And isn't she?'

They laughed at him. Evergrow clenched his jaw. Words couldn't hurt him, nor could laughter. That's what his Uncle Everlook would say in this situation, he thought.

'All right,' said Hildegrew suddenly. 'What have you all been doing? What's happening in the House? Tell me.'

'I've been stirring things up in the kitchen like you told me,' said Owens.

'And?'

'Old Tom Coffier doesn't know what to do. The more he shouts and hits people, the more they hate him. You should see the food we're sending up. I swear to you, the Halibuts will panic if this goes on much longer.'

'Good. What about the cooks?'

'Everyone's wondering what's happened. I keep telling them the Butler's left the House.'

'And Coffier?'

'When he hears that, he says it's nonsense. He says the Butler and the Captain will be at the Rinque as always. Just wait and see. They'll be there. Everyone will see them then.'

Hildegrew allowed himself a smile. 'What about you?' he said to Robert Gondolier.

'I keep telling everyone there's no point working when no one knows what's going to happen. I tell them the Butler's gone, but my great-uncle keeps saying we'll see the Butler on Rinque Day and we'll know who our new UnderButlers are, and everything will be back to normal. Most people are carrying on. A few are starting to grumble.'

'Keep working at them,' said Hildegrew. The masons, he knew, would be a tougher nut to crack than the kitchen staff, where Thomas Coffier's way of treating them always had half the cooks and kitchen hands on the verge of rebellion. 'Alice? What about you?'

'It's starting,' said Alice. 'Everywhere I go I see things that should have been done that aren't. And I hear people saying that things aren't right, things aren't balanced any more.'

'You mean Halibuts?'

'Not only them. Servants too.'

'And what do you say to them?'

'I say things *aren't* right, and in my opinion, Neversuch House is coming to an end. Just like you told us. I say we should start thinking about what will happen after the House is finished. We should start thinking about ourselves.'

'And what do they say?'

'Some of them agree. Some of them are scared when I say it. But some of them who were scared yesterday, I heard them saying it themselves today.'

'Excellent,' said Tobias. 'I want to know the names of the people who are saying it. I need to know who are the willing ones.' He glanced around at the young servants. 'I need to know who are the ones who'll join us. Then, when the time comes, I'll come out and the fun will really begin!'

'Why don't you come out now?' asked William Bell.

'Because things aren't ready,' retorted Hildegrew. 'Every day we wait makes us stronger; every day of uncertainty and confusion brings more people to our side. It gives you all the chance to talk, to put ideas into people's heads, to let those ideas spread. Continue what you're doing. The longer we can wait, the stronger we'll be.'

'But what if the Butler appears on Rinque Day?'

'What if he doesn't? There's only one fly in the oint-ment. William tried to deal with her today, but didn't quite succeed, did you, William?'

William shook his head, dropping his gaze to avoid the others' eyes.

'It's time we dealt with Omnia Halibut once and for all.'

'Another accident?' asked Robert Gondolier.

'I don't care. The time for accidents is past. Perhaps a really bloody murder is just what we need to push things along. Give everyone a fright, make them think this whole place and all its traditions is coming to an end.' Tobias Hildegrew glanced at Evergrow. 'Cut off her head and leave it in the middle of the Great Kitchen Court where all the Halibuts can see it on their way to breakfast. What would they do then, eh?'

'Spoil their breakfast,' said Alice maliciously.

'The gluttons would keep eating,' muttered Owens. 'Nothing could stop them.'

'I'm serious!' said Hildegrew. 'You don't think I am?'

There was silence.

'Are we going to use *him*?' said Robert Gondolier, nodding towards Evergrow.

'If we have to. We can use him as the bait if necessary. I'd rather keep that as a last resort.'

'Do you know where she is?'

'I have an idea.' Hildegrew turned and looked at Evergrow. 'What would you say if I said she was in the Winter House. Eh, Evergrow? What would you say to that?'

Evergrow didn't reply. He tried to make sure that nothing moved in his face, not a muscle, not a blink, to betray that he knew what Hildegrew was talking about.

Hildegrew got up and stood over him. The others watched.

'Eh?' said Hildegrew. He nudged Evergrow with his foot. 'What do you say to that, Evergrow D Halibut? The Winter House. Think your cousin might be there, do you?'

Hildegrew squatted in front of him. He grabbed Evergrow's chin in his fist, turned his head forcibly towards him.

'I think she's in the Winter House. What do *you* think, Evergrow?'

He thought Omnia was there as well. In fact, he was sure of it. But how did Hildegrew know? Of course! He was the one who had chased her on to the Snowflake!

'Well, Evergrow? You're not saying very much.'

Evergrow's mind raced. His first instinct was to deny it. But if he did that, if he tried to persuade Hildegrew that Omnia wasn't at the Winter House, Hildegrew would probably conclude that she was. And he would probably conclude that Evergrow would know how to find her. Which meant Hildegrew would do whatever he could to make him tell.

But if he could make Hildegrew believe that he knew nothing about it – really knew nothing – there might still be an element of doubt in Hildegrew's mind. And if he remembered correctly what Omnia had told him, even if Hildegrew could find his way past the Snowflake, he still didn't know how to get into Basilica's apartment.

As long as Hildegrew didn't know that, thought

Evergrow, Omnia might still be safe, at least for long enough for him to get away – if he could – and tell her who the man in the panther mask really was.

Hildegrew's hand squeezed tighter around Evergrow's chin. 'Well, Evergrow?'

'I told you,' said Evergrow, forcing the words out between his clamped jaws. 'I don't know where she is. Maybe she is in the Winter House. I've got no idea.'

Hildegrew pushed him aside and stood up. He glanced at the four servants. 'We can just about fit you all in the boat.'

'You want us to come?' said Owens.

'Yes, I want you to come. I don't think she'll be alone.'

'How many will be there?'

'I don't know! That's why I want you to come.'

There was silence in the room. In the past few weeks they had all talked about killing this person or that person as if they did it every day, but in truth, they weren't as brave as their words suggested. Only Owens, the most malicious of the four, was excited at the thought. Alice had never killed anybody, and her idea about loosening the stones of the Mounted Bridge was one that she knew was never really going to be used. William Bell had tried and failed, and the fear he felt as Cornelius Slinker had dragged him back to the room where he had imprisoned Omnia gave him no desire to repeat the experience. Robert Gondolier, it was true, had come up with the idea about how to kill Trimbleby and had helped by delivering the note that had lured the UnderButler to his death. But it was Hildegrew himself, dressed as a mason with a mason's cap on his head and a bandage over his face to disguise himself – as if he was recovering from an injury – who had rowed to the House and climbed the Bridled Mound in the dead of night and then had hidden all day at the top beside the crane until the UnderButler appeared below him, when he dropped the rope and swung the crane to set the trap that killed him.

'When will we do it?' asked Owens.

'Tonight. Midnight.'

Owens grinned. The others were silent. They were being faced with taking part in an actual murder, and not even one that was going to look like an accident.

'If you're in this, you're in it,' said Hildegrew. 'Understand? Words are words. Actions are actions.' He held up his hands. 'Don't ask how many lives these hands have taken. I doubt Omnia Halibut's will be the last either. Better get used to it.'

There was silence.

'I need all of you. I'm warning you, don't try to back out.' He held up his hands again. 'If you're not with me, you're against me. Believe me, that's not something you want to be. You don't want Tobias Hildegrew as your enemy.'

They stared at him.

'There's something we'll need.'

They waited to hear what it was, the blood already freezing in their veins.

'Axes.'

25

Not One Slinker . . . But Two

Omnia watched as Cornelius Slinker looked slowly around at the dazzling shape of the Snowflake.

'Have you ever been here before?'

Slinker shook his head. 'Never been asked to.'

Omnia smiled. The more she saw of Neversuch House, the more it amazed her. So many things seemed to have been built as a form of entertainment, or in order to surprise, or just because they could. The more she saw of it, she realised, the more she loved this amazing, complicated creation that the First Captain had constructed and which had become populated by his descendants, the buildings and spaces and grounds that had surrounded her from the moment she was born. The extraordinary events that were happening made her realise that she had taken it for granted. She thought that perhaps she was beginning to have some small sense of what it must be like to be an

Evergone – the desire to come back, the anguish at knowing you never could.

'Come on,' she said.

She stepped on to the stairs and led Cornelius into the Snowflake, and then headed for the doors. She still didn't know her way perfectly through this place and looked for the crumbs on the ground for guidance. They were still there, undisturbed since she and Evergrow had deposited them.

Slinker followed behind her.

She tried a couple of doors that were unmarked by crumbs and eventually found the one that led to the short red corridor to Basilica's apartment.

They went in. Cornelius closed the door behind him.

Omnia hesitated before showing him the last secret, the way to get into the apartment. Cornelius had saved her life. Twice. She believed that William Bell really had intended to leave her locked in that forgotten room to starve to death. That episode couldn't have been staged, could it? And yet she didn't *know*. She couldn't be absolutely certain that she could trust Cornelius.

'Something wrong?' he asked.

Omnia didn't reply for a moment. Then she shook her head. Basilica, she decided, who seemed to be right about so much, was wrong about one thing. You couldn't distrust *everyone*. There have to be some people you can trust.

How much more proof could Omnia ask for? Cornelius had given her everything she could expect. More.

'I'll show you how to get in.'

Omnia went to the blind end of the corridor. She thumped on the wall a couple of times, then turned and leaned back hard against it. This time, she knew what to expect and managed to avoid tumbling over as it opened.

'Hello, Winnicott,' she said to the servant who was standing inside.

Winnicott nodded. 'Hello, Omnia. I see you've brought another—'

He stopped, staring at Cornelius as if he was seeing a ghost.

Omnia looked at Cornelius to see if something horrible had happened to him in the last two seconds. But he looked perfectly normal – except for the fact that he was staring at Winnicott in exactly the same way.

'This is Cornelius Slin—'

'I know who this is,' said Winnicott quickly. 'Come in. Come in.'

Cornelius stepped inside. The door closed behind him.

Suddenly Winnicott opened his arms and gave Cornelius a hug. Then he stood back and looked at him again, gripping his shoulders.

'Cornelius! Oh, Cornelius! It's you, isn't it? Of course it is! The last time I saw you, you were only seven, but still I'd know you. Look how you've grown! What a fine boy! What a fine lad!'

Omnia stared at the servant in amazement. His thick, owl-like eyebrows were jerking up and down as if in a wild dance of joy. There were tears in his eyes.

'They told you I was dead, I suppose,' said Winnicott. 'But I'm not. You see, I'm not! Never was! Never!' He paused. 'You don't remember me, do you, Cornelius?'

'I do, Uncle.'

Omnia's mouth dropped open. 'Uncle?'

The two men turned to face her.

She looked at the servant, and at Cornelius, and back at the servant. 'Your name's Winnicott, isn't it?'

The servant nodded, his arm around his nephew's shoulder, beaming with pride. 'Winnicott Slinker.'

'Ah, you've brought us another visitor,' said Basilica. 'You're turning our lives into quite a social whirl, Omnia.'

'This is Cornelius Slinker.'

'Yes, I guessed as much.' Basilica smiled at Winnicott, who was standing with his arm still around Cornelius's shoulder. She turned back to Omnia. 'I take it this is the same Cornelius Slinker who tried to kill you the other day.'

'No.'

'A different one?'

'No, I mean he didn't try to kill me. In fact, this morning he saved my life.'

'How kind of you, Mr Slinker. I'm Basilica Halibut. Do sit down.'

Winnicott pushed Cornelius towards a chair and then stood back, hands on his hips, and looked at him with a big smile on his face.

'Oh, Winnicott, stop being such a ninny,' muttered Basilica. 'You'll embarrass the boy.'

'I will not,' said Winnicott. 'You're not embarrassed, are you, Cornelius? You're not embarrassed by your old uncle?'

Cornelius muttered something in confusion.

'There! You see, Winny? Leave him alone.' Basilica looked back at Omnia. 'What about Evergrow? Have you brought him with you as well?'

'I thought he might have come here himself,' said Omnia.

'No, I don't think so. Winny, have we had another visitor?'

Winnicott shook his head.

'I suppose he knows how to get here, does he?'

'I think so,' replied Omnia.

'Well, I must say, this is all very confusing, Omnia. You can't accuse Cornelius of trying to kill you one day and then of saving your life the next. It's very inconsistent and quite exhausting for those of us who have to listen to you.'

'I made the assumption that it was him, Basilica, like you told me. It turned out to be wrong.' Omnia remembered the way Winnicott had tried to defend Cornelius when she had accused him of betraying her. Now it made sense. He was Winnicott's nephew, after all.

'I see. I take it there's another explanation. Was there something you overlooked?'

Omnia nodded. 'You remember if you asked me if I had told you everything? There *was* something I forgot. I'd seen someone following me.'

'And they knew where you were going that day?'

'They must have. It was a polisher. I thought Trimbleby had ordered her to follow me, but it turns out he hadn't. It must have been someone else.'

'So who was it, Omnia? Who was the one who tried to kill you this morning if it wasn't Cornelius?'

'William Bell.'

'Never heard of him.'

'He's one of the junior clerks in the Butlery. He locked me in a room in the Bright Tower and left me to starve.'

Basilica looked at her with interest. 'You're quite sure of that? You're not making another assumption?'

'No. I'm sure. I really would have starved to death. And Cornelius saved me, even after I told him I didn't trust him and I didn't want him anywhere near me. He still tried to protect me.'

'Well, that's what the Slinkers do,' said Basilica. 'You see the Slinkers, Omnia, are an ancient family of messengers.'

'The House's first family of messengers,' said Winnicott proudly. He leaned against the wall, arms folded, a serious look on his face.

'Exactly. The House's first family. And as a result, the First Captain gave them a second, secret role. They're not only hereditary messengers, they're hereditary protectors of Halibuts who are in danger. Those months when I was outside the wall, Winnicott was with me. In the first weeks, when no one trusted me, there were a couple of Evergones who might well have done away with me if not for him. Isn't that right, Winny?'

'Not for me to say,' murmured Winnicott, with just the same embarrassment as Omnia was accustomed to seeing from Cornelius.

'If I'm not mistaken, that's exactly what Cornelius has been doing too.'

Omnia looked at him. 'Is this true? Why didn't you tell me?'

Cornelius murmured something in embarrassment, just as his uncle had.

'It's supposed to be secret,' said Basilica. 'Even from the Halibuts themselves.'

'But you know!'

'Well, there are a lot things I've had to learn. Winnicott paid the same price as me.'

'A privilege,' murmured the old servant.

'No, Winny. It's a price you should never have had to pay.'

Omnia gazed at him. She had vowed to get the truth from Basilica and she had done that. But that wasn't the only promise she had made to herself. She didn't know how, she didn't know when, but she was going to bring Basilica's imprisonment to an end. And Winnicott's too.

Suddenly she turned back to Basilica. 'Why didn't you tell me any of this when I said I thought Cornelius was the killer?'

'What difference would it have made?'

'I would have known that he was really trying to protect me!'

'But he could have been the killer. Just because his name's Slinker—'

Winnicott coughed.

'Just because his name's Slinker,' continued Basilica firmly, 'doesn't mean he couldn't have turned bad.'

'He'd be the first in two hundred years,' said Winnicott, fixing Omnia with a meaningful glance.

Omnia nodded. Now she understood Winnicott's refusal to believe that Cornelius had betrayed her. Not only because he was his nephew – not even mostly because of that – but because he was a Slinker.

'Doesn't mean it couldn't happen,' said Basilica. 'Winnicott didn't believe it was even possible. We had quite an argument after Omnia left that time, didn't we, Winny? But he could have been the killer, Omnia. How did we *know?*' Basilica paused. 'How do you know even now that you can trust him?'

'You trust Winnicott, don't you?'

'Well, a man who's prepared to be imprisoned for seventeen years—'

'And a man who's saved my life twice and was almost killed in doing it – I trust him, Basilica. If you can trust Winnicott, I can trust Cornelius.'

Basilica cast a glance at Cornelius, as if appraising him. 'Fair enough,' she said, turning back to Omnia. 'There's no one I trust more than Winnicott Slinker.'

Omnia looked at Cornelius and smiled. Cornelius nodded silently in return.

'All right,' said Basilica. 'Let's think about this latest attack. It's an interesting way of trying to get rid of you. It wouldn't look like an accident, because no one would have known what happened to you.'

'I might never have been found. Not for years anyway. I would have been like your brother's parrot.'

'So it would have seemed to be a disappearance.'

'How would they explain that?'

'Maybe they don't care.'

'If they don't care,' said Winnicott, 'they must think they're close.'

Basilica nodded.

'You mean they think they've almost won?' said Omnia.

'Provided they get rid of you,' replied Basilica. 'They're obviously still concerned enough about you to want to make sure of that. But it sounds as if they're prepared to do it in any way now, whether it looks like an accident or not.' Basilica paused. 'That's worrying. That's very worrying.'

'The Butler thinks he has time,' said Omnia. 'I spoke to him in the Hold. He's not coming out. If you ask me, I think that's what the Evergones want. I think they want him to stay in hiding and for the House to fall into chaos. It's already happening, isn't it, Cornelius?'

Cornelius nodded.

'I think that's why they killed the UnderButlers. It wasn't a mistake. They knew exactly what they were doing.'

Basilica thought about it. 'It's possible, I suppose. They've never tried that way before.'

'And they've never succeeded, have they? Why wouldn't they try something new? I would.'

'What about Everdean?'

'Everdean's in the Hold as well. He just sits there. Most of the time I don't think he's even awake.'

Basilica heaved a deep sigh. She shook her head. 'This House . . . What's become of it?'

'I couldn't think of anywhere safer to come than here.'

'I agree, I can't think of anywhere safer either. We have room, we have food. The fishing's not great,' she added, glancing apologetically at Cornelius, 'but it's good enough.'

'She means birds,' explained Omnia.

'You can hide here, Omnia, but you can't hide forever.'

'I know that. That would be as bad as what the Butler's doing. I have to *do* something. Time's running out. I need a plan.'

'Which is?'

'That's what I've got to work out.'

'Well, let's think about it,' said Basilica. 'As Pedagogia would say, they may *need* the Butler and the Captain to stay in the Hold – but we have no *obligation* to allow that to happen.'

They talked about the possibilities. Winnicott went out and came back with a tray of pies. The conversation went round in circles. No matter what they thought of, there were two problems they couldn't surmount.

First, they didn't know who was leading this conspiracy or where he was hiding, apart from the fact that he was probably using the river to move between the Warren and the House. That didn't mean they couldn't find him, but it would take time. And second, the Butler refused to come out of the Hold in order to reassure the House and help gain the time that was needed.

Later on they had dinner. Winnicott set the table and came back with a grouse, pheasant and duckling stew in a huge dish that would have served sixteen. Omnia wondered where Evergrow was. All afternoon she had hoped he'd turn up. Now it was dark. Cornelius promised he'd look for him in the morning. And still they had no solution to the two problems.

'Omnia,' said Basilica eventually, 'this seems very complicated, but ultimately it's very simple. I don't know how you're going to do it yet, but there's one thing you must do – find the person who's leading this attack and kill him.'

There was silence in the room. No one had anything to say to that. The way Basilica had put it was stark, black and white.

'Let's think about this again in the morning,' said Basilica. 'Perhaps the way to do it will be clearer then.'

Omnia stared at her.

'Omnia, he's killed already, he'll kill again. I've seen too many things in Neversuch House. I've only told you some of them. Believe me, if you want to survive, you have no choice. It's you or him. Don't delude yourself. You must find him and kill him, before he kills you.'

26

Attack

The boat sliced through the water, riding low. Tobias Hildegrew pulled on the oars. He had left William Bell behind to guard Evergrow. In the boat with him were the three other young servants. They had never been to this river before, hadn't even known of its existence. Owens looked ahead with excitement, eagerly waiting for the journey to end. Alice and Robert exchanged glances, and looked at the axes lying in the bottom of the boat, and stared into the darkness ahead of them, wishing that it never would.

Hildegrew pulled hard. The boat moved fast.

At last, they came to the landing area. Tobias Hildegrew told them to get out. They splashed on to the rock. He pulled the boat out of the water beside the old vessel that lay there. Then he leaned into the boat and pulled out the axes.

'Here,' he said.

He handed them out, keeping one for himself. He had

brought the panther masks they had worn on Flip Day. Now he distributed them and watched as they put them on. He put the grey one on himself.

'Ready?' he said. 'Silence. Not a word unless I say so.' He picked up a lantern. 'Come on.'

They went up the spiral steps, along the passage, over the rubble, up the final stairs. Hildegrew shut off the light of the lantern and crouched to look out the door. Then he opened it, crept out and waited until all three had followed him.

'Silence,' he whispered again. 'Let's go.'

They moved off, a procession of two-legged, axe-bearing panthers marching quickly through the alleys. The moon was full and its light was strong, unobscured by cloud. They came to the Bridled Mound, scene of the trap that Hildegrew had laid for Trimbleby on just such a night as this, and skirted it. It was after midnight and most of the House slumbered, but here and there in the buildings around them lights glowed in various windows. Faces looked out. Did anyone see them? Did an axe glint in the moonlight and draw attention to the four monstrous panthers moving through the House? Hildegrew wouldn't object if it did. Whoever saw them would wonder whether what they had seen was reality or nightmare, and in the morning, the rumours amongst the Halibuts would fly.

At last, Hildegrew led them up a set of stairs. He stopped in the court at the top. In front of them rose a huge black arch. Alice knew where they were. Four times, over the past three months, she had followed Omnia Halibut here, each time after having seen her deposit her stone in the wall of the Captain's Keep.

Hildegrew pointed his axe upwards to a building beside the arch that was pale and stark in the moonlight.

'The Winter House,' he whispered.

Omnia put her head around the door. Basilica was sitting in her chair with a light beside her, working at one of her nets.

'Can't you sleep?' said Omnia.

'I don't sleep much,' replied Basilica. 'Haven't done for years. What about you?'

'Usually I do.'

'But not tonight?'

Omnia shrugged. She couldn't get to sleep. No one in the apartment seemed to be able to. In the next room, Winnicott and Cornelius were deep in conversation.

'Am I disturbing you?' she asked.

'Not at all.'

Omnia came in and sat down. She watched Basilica working. 'Do you have to fix your nets a lot?'

'Depends what I catch,' replied Basilica. She glanced up and smiled. 'Sharp beaks, sharp claws. They all do their damage.' She continued to gaze at Omnia for a moment, then turned back to the net. 'It's funny,' she said after a couple of minutes. 'Fishing wasn't so important to me when I was younger. Occasionally I'd go to one of the streams to catch trout, or to the Deep Lake if I wanted pike. Not very often. When we were children, I'd go with Evernow. He taught me.

And then, after they locked me away, I began to think of it all the time. Sometimes I thought, if only I could go fishing again once, just once, I'd be happy. Just to do it one more time in my life. It was a kind of symbol of freedom, I suppose. The freedom I'd lost.' She paused. 'Anyway, one day, Winnicott said if I couldn't fish where I wanted, then I would fish where I could. That's when he had the idea of fishing in the air. Of course it was ridiculous, and I told him so, but he kept telling me I should try it, he absolutely insisted, and it was so ridiculous that one day I did. And that's how I started.'

'Where do you get the nets?'

'Oh, the Butlers have always been very kind. Anything I want, I can have. Haven't you heard, Omnia? Each Halibut is like a prince or princess in their realm. Only my realm's rather small.'

'Didn't you hate them?'

'Who?'

'The Butler, Trimbleby, the Captain. They killed your brother.'

'Oh, I see. Yes, of course I did. I would have killed them if I'd had the chance. I would have throttled them with my bare hands. But I never did have the chance and after a while . . .' Basilica paused, frowning at the thought. 'After a while, I came to see that my brother was just as bad. It took me a long time to accept that, Omnia. It was very hard. But it was the truth. He had killed as well.'

'Do you know that for certain? Did he tell you?'

'He never did. But if he didn't kill with his own hands,

he killed with someone else's. So he was as bad as them, wasn't he? They had tricked him and he had paid the price – but he would have done the same if he had had the chance. I really believe that he would have. I don't know if I ever went so far as to forgive them, but I understood. They did it for the House. Just as Evernow, I suppose, did it for the House as well, in his own way – or that's probably how he would have put it. Everyone always thinks they're right, don't they?'

Omnia frowned. She looked out the window. She could see the full moon high in the sky.

Basilica sighed. 'I don't know. The old Butler was a good man in his own way. I suppose that's a funny thing to say about someone who helped kill your brother, but I don't think that's something he ever really wanted to do. Or to lock me away either. On the other hand, the old Captain, Everwise, was a spiteful man and got more spiteful with the years. He was kinder to his puppets, I would imagine, than to people. And Trimbleby... Trimbleby was another kettle of fish altogether.'

'He told me he regretted what had happened to you. I told you, remember?'

Basilica shrugged. 'Whether I believe it or not, I don't know. Words are easy. He's gone now so we'll never know.'

'Did you ever see them again?'

'The UnderButlers? Yes. Well, Winnicott saw them mostly. I had no desire to. Everything I've ever had was personally delivered by one of them. No one else knows, you see. Oh, and once a year the Butler and the Captain would come to see me. I'm not sure why. To make sure I was still here. To gloat perhaps. Maybe that's why the Captain came anyway.' Basilica paused. Then she forced a smile. 'Well . . . Anyway, what was I saying? Oh, yes, Winnicott insisted and I got these nets. It's nothing like fishing, of course. It's quite ridiculous. But it's all I can do, and do you know what, Omnia? I've quite got to enjoy it.'

'You'll fish again,' said Omnia. 'In the streams. In the Deep Lake. Wherever you want.'

Basilica shook her head sadly.

'None of this can go on, Basilica. Especially *this*. You being locked away. That's the worst thing of all.'

'After seventeen years, Omnia, you get used to it.'

'That's not true. I saw you when we were outside. I saw how excited you were.'

'I wish I hadn't gone out.'

'Don't say that.'

'Seventeen years to forget what it was like, Omnia, and one day for it all to come back. How long will it take me to forget again? I didn't fish today, do you know that? It's the first time in . . . I don't know how long. I just didn't want to.'

'Soon you'll be out for good.'

Basilica shook her head.

'I promise you.' Omnia said it solemnly. She had never meant anything more seriously in her life.

Basilica looked at her, with the expression an adult has for a child who promises to do something that they just don't understand can't be done. 'Do you have a plan for that as well?'

'Not yet. But I will.'

Basilica smiled.

'You told me I'm a Halibut who can *do* things.'

'Some things can't be done.'

'This can,' said Omnia. 'You will go out. I promise you that. And sooner than you think.'

Basilica lifted the net off her knees and put it on the chair beside her. 'I fear there'll be nothing left to go out to. I fear we're close to the end, Omnia. Closer than we've ever been before. The Captain sleeps, the Butler hides. The UnderButlers lie dead and the UnderUnderButlers fight among themselves, and the Halibuts live their lives in a dream and don't realise it's about to end. Isn't that right?'

'That's right. But I'm still here.'

'So you are. And all you have to do is kill the leader of this attack. One small detail.'

'Is there no other way?'

Basilica shrugged. 'You know as much as I do now, Omnia. What do you think?'

'I'm not sure.' She frowned. 'I'll do it if it has to be done. I'll do it or I'll die trying.' Omnia looked out the window at the moon. 'I just wish I knew who it is.'

Tobias Hildegrew stood at the entrance to the Snowflake, lantern in one hand and axe in the other. Moonlight came through the frosted glass roof, sending a pale light over the jagged shapes that filled the space, throwing others into shadow. The three young servants behind him gazed at the scene in wonder.

Then they were on the move. Hildegrew had no more idea how to find the door to the red corridor than Omnia had the first time she came back. He headed for the first door. A cupboard. He headed for another door. A narrow corridor that was so long he couldn't see to the end of it. Another door. Wrong again. The three servants followed him from door to door, around walkways, up and down stairs, wearing their masks and carrying their axes. They began to exchange glances, wondering whether Hildegrew had any idea where they were going. Another door. Another one . . .

Hildegrew stopped and lowered the lantern. There was something at the bottom of the stairs that led up to this door.

He knelt. Crumbs. He put down his axe for a moment, picked them up, felt them in his fingers, then let them drop. He turned to the others and put his finger to the lips of his panther mask. Slowly, very quietly, he led them up the stairs. He opened the door. In front of him was a window. Wrong again.

Inside the panther mask, Tobias Hildegrew frowned in thought. Then he went quickly towards the stairs to another door and found the telltale crumbs again. He went up the stairs and opened it, but this time expected to find that it was wrong. It was. The crumbs, he realised, didn't mark the right doors, but the wrong ones.

He moved more quickly now, the others almost running

288

to keep up. At each set of stairs he looked for the crumbs and moved on. Finally he came to one without crumbs. Again he put his finger to his lips.

He opened the door. Wrong again.

This time Tobias Hildegrew really was puzzled. The crumbs were definitely a sign. They were at the start of stairs that led to a door – nowhere else. There was only one door in this whole place that was the right one, that much he knew. And since so many doors had been marked with crumbs, they had to mark the doors that were wrong. Didn't they? But then he had found an unmarked door and it was wrong as well.

He gazed around the Snowflake. Maybe it was some kind of trick. Maybe one of the piles of crumbs marked the right door – a particular arrangement, or a particular size – and the others were all there to mislead.

Who had laid them? Omnia? Who else could it be? What if it wasn't a trick? How would she have done it? She would lay the crumbs until . . . she found the right door. Of course! She wouldn't have kept going after that. The marked doors were wrong. *One* of the unmarked ones was right.

'Tobias,' said Robert Gondolier, looking for an excuse to be able to turn around and go back to the river, 'do you really—'

'*Shhhhhhhhhhh!*' hissed Hildegrew and he raised his axe threateningly.

The young mason took a step back. So did the others.

'Now come with me,' whispered Hildegrew. 'We're almost there.'

He moved off and found stairs marked with crumbs, and again, and again, before coming to another unmarked stair. He went up and opened the door.

This was it. The small, blind, red space. The one from which Omnia Halibut had simply disappeared.

'Thanks for the crumbs, Omnia,' he whispered to himself. 'Hopefully, in another minute, I'll be able to thank you in person.'

He turned to the others. He held his fingers to his lips and beckoned them through.

'All right,' he whispered. 'Start!'

The others looked at him blankly.

Tobias Hildegrew raised his axe and swung it at the wall.

Winnicott stood at the door and cleared his throat.

Basilica and Omnia looked around.

'I don't mean to interrupt, but we have a disturbance.'

'A disturbance, Winny?'

Winnicott nodded. 'I think you should come and see.'

They went quickly to the entrance of the apartment. From the other side of the wall came a volley of thuds and the screech of cracking wood. Cornelius was looking through a viewing hole. Winnicott gestured towards another one.

Basilica looked. 'Oh!' she murmured.

Cornelius stepped back to let Omnia see. Her blood froze. Four people wearing panther masks were in the corridor, wildly swinging axes at the walls. Wood splintered and flew around them. The tallest of the four was the grey panther. As Omnia watched, he swung his axe and it thudded into a wall.

Winnicott had his hand on the big Bracketball stick he kept in the corner.

'Uncle, I don't think that's going to be enough,' said Cornelius.

'We'll see,' muttered Winnicott with an air of grim determination.

'Have you got anything else here?'

Winnicott shook his head.

Cornelius looked at Omnia. 'This isn't the time to stay and fight.'

Omnia nodded. She turned to Basilica. 'Don't you think we should—'

The blade of an axe came smashing through the wall two centimetres from her nose.

They ran. They raced to the room with the door that led to the chute. They didn't know how much of a head start they would have from the time it would take the panthers to smash their way into the apartment and find the exit. They didn't stop to think where they would go once they were out. One after the other they jumped into the chute and slid to the bottom, then down the stairs, flight after flight after flight, and into the tunnel that led away from the Winter House.

27

Out of the Warren

Evergrow kept his eyes on William Bell.

The junior clerk had taken off his walnut-coloured coat and was sitting at the table, scratching irritably at the wood with a knife. He didn't like the idea of going to kill someone, but he liked even less the fact that he had been left behind. He had always been Hildegrew's most trusted assistant, the only one who knew his identity before today. Now he didn't feel important at all. If he was really important, he would have been one of those chosen to go to the Winter House, not left behind to watch Evergrow, whose wrists and ankles were tied so he could hardly escape.

It was all because of today, he knew. Failing to kill Omnia. And being identified. He was beginning to realise what that meant. He had lost his usefulness for Tobias. He tried to keep his spirits up by telling himself that pretty soon it wouldn't matter that he had been seen. Soon enough it would all be over and everything would be different forever.

But then why hadn't Tobias taken him? There was one panther mask left on the bed. He looked at it resentfully. He should be out there with them now, wearing that mask, carrying an axe.

Lost in his thoughts, he was hardly aware of Evergrow watching him. Ever since Evergrow had seen Tobias Hildegrew and the other three conspirators leave with their axes, he had been thinking only of one thing, and at last, he had come up with an idea. He didn't know if it was going to work, but if he was ever going to find out, now was the time.

Evergrow took a deep breath. 'These ropes are too tight,' he said.

William ignored him.

'I said, these ropes are too tight.'

William looked around. 'Shut up!'

'They're too tight! I can't feel my hands.'

'Why do I care?'

'They're too tight.'

'Shut up!'

Evergrow watched him. The clerk went back to his thoughts.

'I can't feel my feet either.'

'Shut up, I said. You're getting on my nerves.'

'They're *too tight*.'

'*Shut up!*' The clerk held up his knife. 'You want to feel something? How about this? Now shut up!'

Evergrow waited a moment. 'They're too tight.'

William didn't respond.

'They're too tight.' Evergrow began shouting it. '*Too tight! Too tight! Too tight! Too tight! Too tight! Too tight!*'

'Shut up!'

'*Too tight! Too tight! Too tight! Too tight! Too*—'

'*Shut up! Shut up! Shut up! Shut up! Shut up!*' William paused. '*Shut up! Understand?*'

Evergrow stared at him. Then he began again. '*Too tight! Too tight! Too tight! Too tight! Too tight! Too tight! Too*—'

William Bell jumped up and ran over and slapped him across the face. 'You made me do that! Shut up and I won't hit you again.'

'But they're too tight!' said Evergrow, his face stinging. 'They're killing me.'

'Bad luck.' William walked away and sat down again.

'*Too tight! Too tight! Too tight! Too tight! Too tight! Too tight! Too tight! Too tight!*'

William ran back and held his fist in front of Evergrow's face. 'Are you going to shut up? Are you going to?'

'I *can't*. They're too tight.'

'If I loosen them, will you shut up?'

Evergrow nodded.

'Promise?'

'Yes.'

The clerk crouched in front of him. 'Put out your hands,' he muttered.

Evergrow put them out.

William began working at the rope. He loosened the knot. 'I don't know what you're talking about,' he said, examining Evergrow's wrists. 'There's hardly a mark on your—'

Evergrow jerked up both fists as hard as he could and smashed them into William's chin. The clerk tumbled backwards and Evergrow got to his feet, ankles still tied together, and jumped on him with all his weight. He pummelled him with his fists. 'That's for what you did to Omnia!' he yelled. 'And that! And that! And that! And that! And *that's* for hitting me.'

He stopped, breathing heavily. The clerk lay moaning. Quickly, Evergrow used the rope from his own hands to tie William's wrists. He untied the rope from around his ankles and bound William's feet. Then he stood up.

His knuckles were raw and stinging from the punches he had thrown. He looked down at the clerk. Bruises were coming out on William's face to add to the one he had acquired from Cornelius Slinker earlier in the day.

Evergrow turned and picked up the clerk's walnut-coloured coat from the bed. He put it on. Halibuts weren't allowed in the Warren, he knew. He grabbed the panther mask that had been left in the room as well. He didn't know if he would need it, but he might.

William's eyes were opening. After a moment, he struggled to get up, then realised that his limbs were tied.

'When Tobias comes back,' said Evergrow, 'tell him I'll be seeing him again. Tell him to be afraid.'

'Of you?' said Bell.

'Of me. And of Omnia.'

'Omnia? She's dead already,' Bell sneered, looking up at him from the floor. 'Didn't you see the axes they took? Be careful on the way to breakfast tomorrow. Her head will be in the Great Kitchen Court.'

Evergrow felt like giving William a few more punches, but he resisted the temptation. Who was the one standing up, free, and who was the one tied up on the ground?

'I'll be seeing you again too,' he said, and then he turned and left.

Down the stairs he ran. Along the gallery, down the next stairs and the next. He came out into a dark alley. There were balconies above him and hardly a beam of moonlight penetrated down here. Evergrow had never been in the Warren before and had no idea what to expect. He had no idea how deserted this part was and he ran, worried that William Bell would call for help and that someone would hear, expecting shouts and footsteps behind him at any moment. He stumbled down a step and just managed to keep his feet, realising that there was a whole flight of steps in front of him.

The alleys seemed endless, one dark, moonless passage after another. Evergrow felt a rising sense of panic. He asked himself what Everlook would do. His uncle would never have panicked. He'd stay calm. Even though he had never been in the Warren, he'd remember that it stood on two hills, Evergrow told himself, and there must be a valley between them. So, as long as he was going down, Everlook would know, he must be moving away from the place where he had been imprisoned. He would keep going down, staying calm.

Now there were lights in some of the windows. Evergrow went past a couple of dark figures and turned his head away. He kept moving down. Eventually the ground levelled and the alley opened into a broader passage. Moonlight lit up the scene. He looked around in amazement. There were grand houses here. Without knowing it, Evergrow had found his way to the main avenue of the Warren where the houses of the great servant families stood. He kept going, avoiding the few people who were out this late at night. He stayed in the wide street. He sensed that if he went into the alleys that led up either hillside, he would be lost. The wide street curved and he followed it. Now the grand houses had gone and there were only tall, close, dark buildings on either side. And then they were gone as well and he was on open land.

He was out. The Warren was behind him. Evergrow looked for the House. Far off, to his left, he could see a few twinkling lights. He looked up. In the moonlight he saw the black, soaring shape of the Great Tower.

He went towards it as fast as he could, not knowing what William Bell was doing behind him, not knowing what Tobias Hildegrew had already done ahead of him. Perhaps there would still be time to get to Omnia and warn her. With only the moonlight to light his way, he ran across the open ground of the estate. Fifteen minutes later, he saw the shape of the Great West Range above him and entered along the side of the West Stable.

He didn't stop. He moved quickly through the House, over the Mounted Bridge, past the Bright Tower, round the Purple Nave and on. His head throbbed, his legs were tired, but he kept going. Finally he stopped, with the inky black shape of the Granite Arch towering above him.

Here, for the first time since he'd left the Warren, Evergrow hesitated, remembering the axes that Tobias Hildegrew had taken.

Again, he thought of his Uncle Everlook. Everlook wouldn't falter, not at this point, not when he was so close. Evergrow nodded to himself. He clenched his fists for courage and then headed for the Arch.

He climbed the stairs and turned into the Winter House. A moment later, he opened the door to the Snowflake.

Above him, and to his right, a door stood open, letting out a single rectangle of light over the walkways and staircases.

His heart sank. He was too late.

Evergrow made his way towards the door. When he got there, a scene of utter destruction met him. The walls had been hacked to pieces. Splintered wood and shreds of red paper hung from the sides and covered the floor. At the end, the wall to Basilica's apartment had been totally hacked down.

He moved gingerly across the wood on the floor. He stepped on a piece and it broke under his weight with a loud crack.

He froze. What if they were still here, inside the apartment?

Evergrow listened.

Beyond the smashed entrance wall of the apartment he saw something lying on the ground. A Bracketball stick. He moved forward quietly and picked it up.

Gripping it tightly, he went in.

He didn't know what he expected to find. Bodies. Blood. Or Tobias Hildegrew himself and the others, waiting with their axes.

He stopped, took a deep breath and turned a corner.

Eyes! A face!

He almost jumped out of his skin. But it was a mirror. He was looking at himself.

Furniture was strewn across the room, plates smashed, rugs ripped. He went into another room and found the same sight. It was the same everywhere else. Everything had been destroyed. He wandered through the apartment, forgetting now about the noise he was making. They were gone, but what had happened? There was no blood, no bodies.

Perhaps they had been taken away.

The door to the chute stood open. Now Evergrow's fear came back. Had Hildegrew and the others left by the chute? Were they down there, waiting?

For what? Why would they wait?

Evergrow looked around and picked up a book. He tossed it into the chute. He heard it sliding down, then stop. He listened. Nothing.

Cautiously, still holding the Bracketball stick, he climbed into the chute. No one was there. He went down the stairs that led to the tunnel and walked away.

Evergrow didn't know where else to look. From the Splitted Stairs, he made his way dejectedly back to the Middle Range. He climbed the stairs to the third floor and went to his room.

The door was locked.

Evergrow looked around to check where he was. Was this his room? It was, wasn't it?

He tried the door again. Then, very quietly, he tapped. He waited.

'Who is it?' The voice was so low it was barely possible to hear it.

'What do you mean, who is it?' whispered Evergrow. 'It's me! Who are you?'

'Who are *you*?' came back the voice.

'Evergrow! You're in my room!'

The lock turned. The door opened a fraction, then all the way. Omnia stood in the doorway.

Evergrow went in. He stared. Basilica, Winnicott and Cornelius Slinker sat in various places around the room.

'What happened to you?' he whispered.

'What happened to *you*?' replied Omnia, peering at Evergrow's face. He had a huge, purple bruise on his forehead from the headbutt that had knocked him out. 'And what are you doing in that coat?'

Evergrow sat down on the edge of the bed. 'I know who their leader is. It's Tobias Hildegrew. He's back.'

Omnia stared at him in disbelief.

'I think you'd better tell us what happened,' said Basilica.

As Omnia, Basilica, Winnicott and Cornelius gathered round him, Evergrow told them the whole story, ending with his escape and attempt to find them at the Winter House.

'Evergrow,' said Omnia when he had finished, 'that's incredibly brave.'

Evergrow shrugged. 'I don't know if it's brave. It just seemed the obvious thing to do.'

'It's brave,' said Cornelius. 'Trust me, Evergrow – it's brave.'

Evergrow shrugged again. 'How did you end up here?'

Omnia told him about their escape. After leaving the Winter House, they had run through the tunnel and come out at the top of the Splitted Stairs. From there, still not knowing how close the panthers were behind them, they had moved rapidly through the House towards the Middle Range and Basilica had led them to the secret stairs that ended at the room behind the hole in his wardrobe.

'So everyone's safe,' Evergrow said with relief.

Omnia nodded. 'And now we know who's behind all of this.'

'And we know where he's hiding,' said Basilica. 'Evergrow, do you think you could find your way back there?'

'I don't know about that.'

'With some help,' said Cornelius, 'from someone who knows the Warren?'

'I could try.' Evergrow didn't say it with much conviction. He remembered the darkness of the alleys. He didn't think there was a single landmark he would recognise.

'This changes everything,' said Omnia. 'Now we have the advantage. Hildegrew doesn't realise it, but we know who he is. We know where he's hiding.' She glanced at Cornelius. 'We'll go after him tomorrow.'

Cornelius nodded.

'Certainly,' said Basilica. 'But this advantage – don't rely on it. As soon as he gets back and finds William Bell, he'll know that you know as well.'

Basilica was right. In fact, the advantage was already gone. At just about the time that Evergrow was telling his story, Tobias Hildegrew and the three servants were climbing the stairs to his hiding place above the quarry, where they found William Bell tied up on the floor.

Hildegrew let out a howl of anger.

He clutched the axe in his hand. 'This ends tomorrow!'

28

Riot

They were woken by a banging on the door.

'Evergrow? Are you in there? *Evergrow!*'

Omnia looked around blearily. People were strewn all over Evergrow's room. It must have been four or five in the morning before they had finally fallen asleep.

The banging on the door continued.

By now everyone was awake except Evergrow himself. Omnia crawled over to him and gave him a shake. He mumbled something, his eyes still closed.

'Evergrow,' whispered Omnia. 'It's your mother.'

'Where?' he murmured.

'At the door!' Omnia shook him again.

He looked around, saw everyone and immediately scrambled up.

'*Evergrow! Open this door! Open it now!*'

They all hurried into the wardrobe, leaving Evergrow by himself.

'*Evergrow! Open the door! Open this—*'

He opened it. His mother, Ribelia, peered around suspiciously, while his two little brothers ran in. It was they, at six o'clock in the morning, who had discovered that Evergrow's door was locked after he had failed to come home the night before, and had immediately run to tell Ribelia.

'Where were you last night?' demanded Ribelia. 'Why didn't you come home?' She strode across and threw open the curtains. 'Why are you still in your clothes? Why are you—' She stopped, seeing his face properly for the first time in the light. 'What happened to you? Where did you get that bruise?'

'I . . . fell over.'

Ribelia came closer to him, gazing at the huge bruise on his forehead. 'And did *that*? Where? Where did you fall over?'

Evergrow blurted out the first thing that came into his head. 'Bracketball.'

'Bracketball? You fell over at Bracketball and did that? How?'

'I don't remember.'

'You must remember. Why not? Did you knock yourself out? Is that what happened?'

'I told you, I don't remember.'

'You got into a fight, didn't you? Tell me the truth!'

'I didn't get into a fight.'

'Mummy!' called out one of his brothers.

'Not now, Everlight,' she snapped.

'But Mummy!'

'Not now, I said!'

'But Mummy, there's someone in here!'

Ribelia looked round. The two little boys had opened the door to the wardrobe.

'Is that true, Evergrow?' she demanded.

Evergrow stared at her, speechless. Facing Tobias Hildegrew in the Warren had been scary – in a way, facing his mother in this kind of mood was even scarier.

Ribelia gave him a searching glance. She went towards the wardrobe.

Omnia stepped out.

'Hello, Aunt Ribelia,' she said. 'I slept over last night.'

'Did you?'

Omnia nodded.

'Then I suppose you can explain where Evergrow was until all hours of the night. And why he's been in a fight. And who the fight was with.'

Omnia took a deep breath. 'I can try.'

'Try? Does your mother know you're here?'

'Possibly not.'

'Well, *your* mother may not care where you run off to, Omnia Halibut, but I certainly *do* care where—'

'Mummy!'

'Not now, Everlight.'

'But Mummy!'

'I said, not now!'

'But there's more people!'

'When I say not—' Ribelia's head turned towards him. 'What did you say?'

'There's *more* people, Mummy.'

Ribelia threw a mistrustful glance at Omnia. Then she stepped past her and pulled back the door of the wardrobe.

'Come out!' she said. 'Whoever's in there, come out this second!'

The others had stayed in the wardrobe, fearing the noise they would make if they tried to crawl through the hole into the secret room. Now they emerged. First came Cornelius Slinker. Ribelia's eyes went wide. Then came Winnicott. Her eyes went wider. And then her eyes went so wide that Evergrow thought the shock was going to kill her. Her mouth dropped and her head jerked back as if she had been hit.

'Basilica?' she whispered. 'Is that you? Basilica Halibut?'

'Hello, Ribelia. How's the knitting?'

Ribelia stared at her in disbelief.

Omnia didn't know what Ribelia was going to do next, but she had no intention of getting stuck here trying to explain things. There was too much to do. She looked at the door, then glanced at Cornelius and Evergrow.

They nodded.

Ribelia was still staring. Omnia and Cornelius Slinker slipped past her. Evergrow was already at the door.

Before Ribelia could do anything about it, the three of

them were gone. They ran along the corridor, down the stairs and out into the morning air.

They headed for the Bright Tower. They had no reason to avoid the Great Kitchen Court, which was directly on their way.

The fires in the ovens blazed. Pots boiled, sending plumes of steam billowing into the air. But half the ovens in the kitchen were empty, and half the pots had nothing in them but water, when by now they should have been full of the foods they were supposed to be cooking. Vast piles of oats waited to be boiled, dough to be kneaded, eggs to be cracked, meats to be fried.

'Get to *work*,' yelled the High Chef at one of the junior cooks, and he slapped him across the head. '*Work!*'

'Where's the Butler?' one of them demanded. 'Where's he gone? Why hasn't he been seen?'

'Don't you worry about that!' retorted the High Chef, throwing out another slap. 'He'll be at the Rinque tomorrow, just like he always is. Now cook!'

The Lesser Chefs slapped and yelled as well. But they were less forceful than the High Chef. Some were even beginning to wonder what would happen if things turned nasty. There were a lot of knives in the kitchens, not to mention choppers and cleavers. The place was full of tools that could turn instantly into weapons.

The High Chef bawled out a pair of kitchen hands. They scurried away from him, muttering darkly.

A few of the cooks still worked as they always did, their hands whirring and knives flashing as they chopped. Others looked around, toying with the food, chopping for a moment, kneading for an instant when they thought someone was watching, then stopping again. Up and down the benches strode the High Chef, shouting, prodding, anything to get people working. For the first time in his entire life, Thomas Coffier didn't know if he could. The kitchen seemed like one of his pots, simmering, ready to boil over if something happened to turn up the heat.

He turned and saw Owens coming in by a door on the other side of the kitchen.

'Where have *you* been?' he roared in a voice that carried down the benches like a fiery wind.

Suddenly there was silence.

'*Where?*' demanded the High Chef. Owens, he knew, was the worst of the troublemakers and Coffier was itching to make an example of him. He strode along one of the benches, knocking out of the way any cook who wasn't quick enough to jump.

Owens ran away from him. He was late, having been up long after midnight smashing into Basilica's apartment. But he hadn't come here to work. He had been sent back to make as much trouble as he could.

The High Chef lumbered after him.

Owens grabbed the closest things to hand, a big ladle and the lid of a pot, and began to beat them together, gazing defiantly at the High Chef. The High Chef growled.

Owens skipped away, beating the lid and taunting the High Chef. Every pair of eyes in the kitchen was on him. Others took up the beat, with knives, choppers, ladles, graters, rolling pins, anything they could find. The noise thundered around the kitchen.

Owens kept skipping away – straight into the arms of two Lesser Chefs, who held him tight.

The High Chef approached him. 'Now we'll see,' he muttered. He swung his arm, knocking the ladle out of Owens's hand and sending it flying along the bench. He grabbed Owens by the shoulders. 'You think you can make fun of me, do you?' The veins in his neck bulged above the buttoned-up collar of his white coat. *Do you?*' The High Chef gave Owens a shove, sending him sprawling under the bench.

Owens jumped back up and ran at him. There was a roar around the kitchen. The High Chef swatted him away and sent Owens sprawling again. Owens lay on his back, beneath a bench of bubbling, boiling pots. The High Chef knelt. He grabbed a fistful of Owens's jacket and pulled the kitchen hand up until his face was a centimetre from his own.

'Now you're going to *work*,' he snarled. 'If you think acting up like this is a way to get out of my kitchen, you're wrong. Carry on like this and I'll see to it that you stay here forever. You're going to *work*. You're going to *work*, and *work*, and *work*, and when you think you're too tired to keep going, you're going to *work* some more. You're going to work until I say you can stop! And if I never say you can stop, you're going to work until you drop down dead!'

The High Chef raised Owens further by his jacket and looked around.

'Does everyone understand? Well? Does *everyone* understand?'

Owens looked to his right. He saw the boiling pots. The High Chef continued to glare around the kitchen, still holding the kitchen hand up by the jacket as some kind of exhibit. Owens reached for the handle of one of the pots and tipped it over him.

The High Chef dropped him with a terrible cry and rolled on the floor, screaming in agony.

Suddenly there was pandemonium. Cooks and kitchen hands threw themselves at the Lesser Chefs. Others defended them. Fights broke out everywhere. 'No food for the Halibuts!' shouted Owens. 'No food for the Halibuts!' The cry was taken up by the attackers as they punched and kicked.

'Up to the Tempered Hall!' yelled Owens, and he grabbed a knife and ran for the exit from the kitchens. Some of the cooks ran with him, waving cleavers and shouting the new slogan. Up the stairs they went and burst out into the Great Kitchen Court.

Omnia, Evergrow and Cornelius Slinker had just come into the Court from the other side.

Owens spotted them. 'Get them!' he yelled, brandishing his knife, and he swung towards them, followed by the mob he had brought up from the kitchen.

'Get behind me,' muttered Cornelius. Eyes on the mob, he pushed Omnia and Evergrow back. 'Stay back. Stay here. Don't move!'

Then he left them and started to run, loping across the Court on his long legs. He gathered speed. Owens slowed, watching the oncoming messenger running at him in confusion. The mob stopped behind him. But Cornelius kept going, getting faster, aiming straight at Owens. Suddenly he put his head down, put his fists out and slammed into him.

Owens flew back on to the cobbles. His knife bounced away.

The mob stared at Cornelius in amazement.

Cornelius picked up the knife. He was bleeding from a cut that it had made across the back of his wrist when he had colided with Owens, and the blood ran down his arm as he held it up. His eyes blazed. 'Anyone else?' he demanded, looking around the crowd of cooks with the knife in his hand. 'Anyone else want to try it? Come on! I'm waiting.'

They backed away.

'Go!' he shouted.

They looked at one another for a moment, then ran.

Cornelius knelt over Owens. The kitchen hand been knocked out momentarily by the fall, but was coming to.

'Who are you?' demanded Cornelius. 'What's your name?'

Owens mumbled something.

'He was with Tobias Hildegrew,' said Evergrow, who had come across with Omnia.

'Are you sure?'

'He was one of them.'

Cornelius grabbed Owens by the collar of his white tunic. 'Is that true?'

Owens looked up at him. He was alert now. You could see from his eyes that he understood the question.

'Is it *true*?'

Owens smirked.

'I'm sure he was one of them,' said Evergrow.

Cornelius jerked Owens to his feet.

Omnia pointed at him. 'You're coming with us!'

29

A New Captain

One last time, Omnia went to the Hold. She had decided
what she was going to do – now she wanted to give the
Butler one last chance to play his part. This time, she didn't
leave Cornelius Slinker behind. The Master Filer didn't
want to take him, much less Evergrow and Owens. But
Omnia said she knew the way by now and they were going
to go there themselves, whether he liked it or not. At that,
he jumped up from his desk and insisted on coming – which
was just as well, since Omnia wasn't sure that she could
have found her way there without him. They put a blindfold on Owens and Cornelius dragged him along by the
collar.

'Mr Digby,' she said bluntly to the Butler when they had
arrived, 'you have to come out. There's no time left. With
you or without you, we have to finish this today.'

'That's very hasty,' objected the Master Filer.

'Let me say what I've got to say. Mr Digby, it's almost too late. Everything's falling apart. There was a riot in the kitchen this morning.'

'There'll be more riots too, don't you worry,' said Owens smugly. The blindfold had been removed and he looked at the Butler with a smirk.

'Who are you?' asked the Butler. 'You're wearing a kitchen hand's tunic. What's your name?'

'Owens.'

'He's one of them,' said Omnia.

'How many are there?'

'Hundreds,' said Owens. 'You'll never stop us.'

'Four that we know of,' said Omnia, 'in addition to their leader.'

'Four?' Owens scoffed. 'Don't believe her. There are hundreds of us, Mr Digby.'

'There will be if we don't do anything about it,' said Omnia.

'Do anything about it?' said Owens. 'You'll never do— *Ow!*'

Cornelius had gripped him hard on the shoulder. 'Quiet,' he muttered. 'Talk when you're spoken to.'

'I'll talk when— *Owwww!*'

Omnia went closer to the Butler. 'Mr Digby, the leader . . . it's Tobias Hildegrew.'

A spasm of dread flickered across the Butler's face. 'Are you sure?' he whispered.

'I saw him yesterday,' said Evergrow. 'I saw him together

with *him*,' he said, pointing at Owens, 'and William Bell and two others.'

The Butler was silent. He shook his head. Tobias Hildegrew . . . Digby slumped in his chair. His worst fear had come to life.

Owens glanced at Everdean, who sat slumped in another chair in the blue Captain's coat, murmuring something to himself entirely unconnected with what was happening around him. 'This is going to be even easier than we thought,' said the kitchen hand.

'You be *quiet* until you're *spoken* to!' said Cornelius and he shoved the kitchen hand into a corner. Owens crouched there, gazing resentfully at Cornelius.

Digby looked up for a moment, then stared at the floor again, his eyes blank.

Omnia knelt in front of him. 'Mr Digby?'

'I knew it was him,' murmured the Butler. 'I knew he'd come back. He killed my father. He smashed his head and drowned him in a puddle.' He paused. 'He was my friend. Supposedly. That's what he always said. But he never was. It was all a show. All a show to make me trust him. My father used to tell me, "A Butler can have no friends," he said, "that's the burden we bear." He tried to warn me, but I didn't listen.'

'I know who Tobias's father was,' said Omnia. 'I know what happened to him.'

Digby turned to her. 'You know that as well?' He smiled sadly. 'The UnderButlers used to tell me I shouldn't let him near me because of his father, but they wouldn't say why. The more they told me to stay away from him, of course, the more I wanted him to be my friend. So eventually they told me what happened to his father, and I went to Tobias and asked him if he knew how his father had died, and he said he didn't. He said all he knew was that it was an accident, but he had no idea what kind. I believed him. I felt sorry for him, having lost his father like that, and wanted to be his friend even more.'

'Basilica Halibut told me about it,' said Omnia. 'And don't tell me she's a ghost, Mr Digby, because I know the truth. She told me everything. And she's not in the Winter House any more. They found us there last night. We had to leave.'

'Where is she now?' demanded the Master Filer.

'It doesn't matter. Mr Digby, shouldn't Tobias pay? Shouldn't he pay for what he did? It's not only your father that he killed. It's the old Captain and the UnderButlers, and there's probably other people as well.'

'*Should* he pay?' asked Digby. 'What about *his* father?'

'Yes, and what did *his* father do? What about all the killings he helped Evernow carry out?' It was hopeless to try to find where the blame stopped, Omnia knew. One set of killings led to another. To reach the end of the chain you would have to go all the way back to the First Captain and his son, the first Evergone. All you could do, Omnia had decided, was to try to deal with what was happening now. 'He won't stop, Mr Digby. You know that as well as me.'

'That's right!' hissed Owens from beside the wall. 'He'll get you all! He'll—'

He fell silent, cowering, as Cornelius Slinker turned and glared at him.

'Mr Digby,' said Omnia, 'he won't stop. I'm not saying I'm not scared, because I am. Altogether Tobias Hildegrew has tried to kill me six times now and each time I've escaped. I don't know if I'll escape the seventh. But I have no choice. He's going to try again, I know that. He won't give up. So I may as well try to stop him myself, because that's the only way to put an end to it. And if you ask me, the same is true for you.'

Digby was silent.

'You have to go out. Tomorrow's the Rinque. If you're not there, if you and the Captain don't show that you're still in charge, I don't know what will happen. I think it'll be the end. In fact, I'm not even sure we'll last that long. You have to go out today. We have to find Tobias and do whatever we have to do to stop him.'

Digby nodded. 'Maybe I should,' he murmured.

'You must. Get the UnderUnderButlers, Mr Digby. Get them together and we'll go to the Warren.'

'Yes.'

'No!' It was the Master Filer. 'Now just you hold on, young lady. I've listened to everything you've said, like you asked. And when you put it all together, all you're saying is that Mr Digby should go outside, where you've just admitted there's a merciless killer on the loose. Well, if you ask me, that's the last place he should go. Mr Digby, you stay here.

You're safe, the Captain's safe. The keys are safe. The UnderUnderButlers will deal with this.'

'Like they've dealt with it already?' demanded Omnia.

'The servants of Neversuch House will know what to do. They're not going to be persuaded by a scoundrel like Tobias Hildegrew.'

'There was a riot in the kitchen. They *were* persuaded.'

'The kitchen!' The Master Filer snorted in contempt. 'I read the files. The way Coffier treats them, it's a wonder they don't riot every day.' He turned back to the Butler. 'Mr Digby, your place is here. Your safety and the Captain's safety is the first concern.'

Digby frowned. 'Maybe that's right.'

'Of course it's right! You can't listen to her. Who is she? A Halibut! And a child Halibut at that.'

'What's that supposed to mean?' demanded Omnia.

'If you go out there, Mr Digby,' said the Master Filer, ignoring her, 'you simply expose yourself to danger.'

'He has no choice!' cried Omnia. 'He has to be at the Rinque!'

'He can miss the Rinque,' snapped the Master Filer. 'I've seen the files!'

'I don't care about the files!'

The Master Filer stared at Omnia in shock.

'The files are the past. What about the present? What about the future? When was the last time you stopped reading the files and left the Bright Tower? Do you know *anything* about what's happening outside?'

'I know enough,' muttered the Master Filer.

'Then you should know the Butler can't continue to hide! He has to show he's still in charge. He has to—'

'*Who do you think you are?*' shouted the Master Filer. 'Well? Just who exactly? Who are you to tell the Butler what to do? Only the Captain has that right!'

Everyone turned to look at Everdean, who sat in his chair on the other side of the room in the blue coat, the big ruby ring of the Captain on his finger, muttering about rocks or sediments or some other geological nonsense.

Owens laughed.

'The Master Filer's right,' said Cornelius Slinker. 'Only the Captain can tell the Butler what to do.'

'See!' exclaimed the Master Filer. 'Thank you!'

Cornelius strode across the room. Everdean stared up at the messenger in surprise. Cornelius pulled the coat off the old man's shoulders and out from under him almost before anyone realised what he was doing.

'No!' cried the Master Filer.

Cornelius pulled the ring off Everdean's finger. He came back and held them out to Omnia.

Omnia shook her head.

'Put them on,' said Cornelius.

'You dare not!' cried the Master Filer and he threw himself at Cornelius, losing his raisin-coloured hat in the process. But he was a tiny man who had spent his whole life sitting at a desk, and Cornelius easily held him off with one hand while holding the coat and the ring out in the other.

Omnia stared at the coat. It seemed like some kind of deadly trap.

'She can't,' said Digby. He looked at Omnia. 'You mustn't.'

'Exactly!' said the Master Filer, still flailing at Cornelius.

'Who better?' demanded Slinker.

'This isn't how it's done,' said the Butler.

'Too late for that, Mr Digby. Too late when Everwise died. It wasn't how it was done then either, was it? Look who we ended up with!'

In his chair, Everdean was muttering something to himself, snarling and grinding his teeth.

Cornelius pushed the Master Filer away, put one of Omnia's arms into a sleeve of the coat, then the other.

The Master Filer stared. So did everyone else. Even Everdean seemed to be looking.

'This isn't how it's done,' murmured the Master Filer, but his tone had changed, as if, suddenly, seeing Omnia in the Captain's coat, it seemed that perhaps it could be.

Owens laughed maliciously. 'She looks ridiculous!'

She did. The coat was much too big. Cornelius pulled out the knife he had taken from the kitchen hand and grabbed the bottom of the coat.

'*No!*' cried the Master Filer and the Butler together.

Cornelius looked around.

'You can't cut it,' said Digby. 'That's the First Captain's coat. It's the original one.'

Cornelius examined it more closely. The material was faded, the gold braid hanging by threads. 'Why was

Everdean wearing it?' he demanded. 'It's only meant to be used for ceremonies.'

The Butler shrugged ruefully. 'He's only happy when he's got that one on. He didn't like the other ones.'

Cornelius threw a glance at Everdean, who was still snarling and muttering. Then he turned back, the bottom of the coat still gathered in his hand.

'It's just a coat,' he said. 'I'd trade a House for a coat. I bet the First Captain would too.'

And before anyone could do anything to stop him, Cornelius Slinker slashed at the bottom of the two-hundred-year-old coat of the First Captain, tearing through it. The Butler let out a cry. The Master Filer staggered backwards into a chair, clutching at his chest.

Cornelius dropped the material he had cut on the floor. Then he cut off the cuffs that hung far below the tips of Omnia's fingers. He stood up and stepped back. The coat on Omnia's shoulders was still much too big, but no longer utterly swamped her. It was ragged at the hem, ragged at the cuffs. Yet it still had the gold braid on the shoulders, the silver buttons on the front. It was still a Captain's coat. Anyone seeing it would recognise it.

Slinker put the ruby ring on Omnia's finger. It was much too big. He tore a strip off the material he had cut, threaded the ring on to it and tied a knot to close the loop, then put it over Omnia's head.

'There's meant to be a ceremony,' said the Master Filer hoarsely.

'That was it,' said Cornelius.

Omnia looked down at herself. She spread her arms. She saw the blue, gold-braided material coming down to her wrists. She caught sight of herself in a mirror on the other side of the room. The ruby ring glinted on her chest.

She threw a glance at Evergrow. He nodded solemnly.

Omnia turned to the Butler. 'Mr Digby, I don't know if this makes me the Captain. I'm wearing the coat; I've got the ring. You can listen to me because of that, if you want. But more importantly, you should listen to me because what I'm telling you is the truth. There's no time left. I'm going out there today with Evergrow and Cornelius to meet Tobias Hildegrew and whoever's with him and defeat them – or die trying. I think we'll have more chance of success if you're with us. I think that your just being outside will do a lot to save the House. I came here today to give you the chance to do that. It's up to you.'

Digby glanced at the Master Filer. The small man in the raisin-coloured coat silently shook his head.

Digby stood up. 'I'll come. Where do we go?'

'To the Warren.' Said Omnia. 'Hildegrew's hiding there.'

'Do we know where?'

Omnia glanced at Evergrow. Evergrow pointed at Owens. 'I think we ought to ask him.'

Suddenly all eyes were on the kitchen hand. He shrank into the corner.

Cornelius Slinker walked over to him. 'Where's Hildegrew hiding?'

Owens looked up at him, cowering.

'I'm going to ask you again. *Where's he hiding?*'

The fear in Owens's face grew.

Cornelius showed his wrist to the kitchen hand. It was still covered in blood.

'You did this to me. So I owe you something, don't I?' He took out the knife that Owens had dropped in the Great Kitchen Court and held it over the kitchen hand's wrist. 'Now tell me, where is Tobias Hildegrew hiding?'

Owens squirmed away, trying to get his wrist out of Cornelius's grasp.

Cornelius jerked him back hard. He put the blade on Owens's skin. It wasn't cutting him yet, but he could feel its sharpness.

'Where?' Cornelius waited. He pressed slightly with the blade.

'It's near the quarry!' cried Owens, trying to twist away again.

'Not good enough,' said Slinker, jerking him back.

'Above Higson's Jumble! Near the place where Arkwright fell!'

'Better,' said Slinker. 'Go on.'

Owens gave a description that Cornelius and the Butler seemed to understand. It meant nothing to Omnia, or to Evergrow, even though he had actually been there himself.

'Is there somewhere safe we can leave him until this is over?' said Cornelius to the Butler when Owens had finished.

The Butler nodded. He and Cornelius led Owens off to a room and locked him in, then came back.

The Butler glanced at the Master Filer. 'Go. Find the UnderUnderButlers. Tell them to be ready for me in half an hour.'

The Master Filer looked at him doubtfully.

'Go now!'

The Master Filer got up, muttering something, and left the room.

'Cornelius,' said the Butler, 'you'll come with me too. Omnia, you stay here. You too, Evergrow. You'll be safe until it's finished.'

Omnia shook her head. She wasn't going to let Digby try to finish this without her, even if he had all the UnderUnderButlers with him. Last time he and the UnderButlers said they had finished it and had done nothing of the sort. 'I'm coming too!'

'You can't. It's too dangerous.'

Omnia shrugged.

'You can't come even if you want to,' said the Butler. 'No Halibut ever goes into the Warren. That's a rule. If you want a riot, that's the best way to start one.'

'No Halibut but the Captain goes into the Warren,' said Cornelius pointedly.

Omnia remembered what she was wearing. 'That's right.'

The Butler shook his head. 'Omnia, don't make me order Cornelius to restrain you. I'll do it if I have to.'

'You try,' muttered Evergrow.

'And you too, Evergrow,' said the Butler.

'I'm going,' said Omnia. 'Cornelius?'

'Slinker!' snapped the Butler. 'Remember your duty. To protect Halibuts, not expose them to danger.'

Slinker nodded. Then he shrugged. 'I'll do what my Captain tells me.'

Omnia grinned.

'What about me?' demanded Evergrow. 'I'm coming too.'

Omnia looked questioningly at Cornelius.

He walked out and went to the room where Owens had been locked away. A couple of minutes later, he came back with the kitchen hand's tunic in his hand. He held it out to Evergrow. 'Put it on. While you wear it, you're one of us.'

Evergrow took it eagerly.

'Let's go,' said Omnia. 'Mr Digby, how long before you and the UnderUnderButlers get to the Warren?'

'I'd say within the hour.'

'Good.' She walked to the door. Evergrow and Cornelius went with her.

'I thought you were going with us as well,' said the Butler.

'We're going, Mr Digby. But not with you.'

30

Revenge

Tobias Hildegrew paced around the room. Through the window of the attic he could see the quarry and beyond that, the north of the estate and the wall that surrounded it. But everything he was interested in was happening in the other direction, in the House and in the Warren itself.

This was the day he had been waiting for, scheming for, for seventeen years. Hildegrew's father had died when he was eleven. Before he died, he had told Tobias that he had left him a letter to be opened in case anything happened to him, but no sooner than Tobias's sixteenth birthday. After his father's death, Tobias dutifully treasured the letter until his sixteenth birthday came. When he opened it on that day, he found that his father had written that if an accident ever befell him, then it would be no accident, but the doings of the Halibuts and he must avenge his father's murder. The letter then contained a set of instructions. He was to say nothing of this letter, make no accusations about his father's death, but befriend the Butler's son, making himself indispensable. All the time he was to hide his purpose behind charm and good manners. Then, when another twelve years had passed, he was to go out into the city of Pettifog and find a boy who would by then be eighteen years old. He would find the boy through the boy's mother, Elisabeth Felt. The boy would be ready to seek revenge for another death. It would be Tobias's mission to help him.

Tobias Hildegrew carried out these instructions to the letter, becoming first the acquaintance of the Butler's son, then his friend, then his indispensable assistant. He had hidden his purpose, denying knowing anything about his father's death when asked by the Younger Digby. When the time came, he went in search of the boy, finding the boy's mother, Elisabeth Felt, and then the boy himself. That had been six months earlier. Together they had plotted and planned their revenge. Tobias had recruited William Bell to be his assistant. Three months later, they had put their plan into action, only to be thwarted by Omnia Halibut and for Tobias to escape from the House, unable ever to show his face there again. Since then, he had hidden in Pettifog, communicating with William Bell through secret letters. No one believed he would come back, certainly not anyone in the House, he knew, and not even the Evergones outside. No one had ever done it before. All the better, he thought. If no one had done it, that would give him an even greater element of surprise.

That was when Elisabeth Felt told him about the underground river. It would enable him to move undetected between the Warren and the House. Her husband had told her about it, she said. His father used to take him there with his sister when he was a small boy to sing operas as they rowed.

So, three nights before Flip Day, Hildegrew had crept back into the House, up to the hiding place that William Bell had prepared for him, and on Flip Day itself, using the underground river to move safely between the Warren and the House, hidden under the mask of the grey panther, he had reopened the fight.

And now had come the day to decide what to do. All along, his plan had been to force the Butler and the Captain into hiding and keep them there as the House fell further and further into chaos, using his four young conspirators to stir up dissent. He knew the Butler well and didn't think highly of his courage, and Everdean, he knew, wanted nothing less than to be Captain of the House. If advised to hide, he was sure, they would hide, even on Rinque Day. When they didn't appear then, and if enough confusion had been created in the days leading up to it, the uncertainty would be so great that he could come into the open and lead a servants' revolt. After all, everyone still thought he had been a loyal servant. No one had been told the truth. In the past – before his supposed death – the servants had looked to him for guidance at times of difficulty. When he reappeared – alive – they would do so again. The great servants might try to oppose him – the Chief Mason, the High Chef, the Prime Plumber and the like – but the mass would follow. In the atmosphere of chaos that he hoped to create, with confusion and panic in the air, if he chose his words carefully, they would follow him without even realising to what purpose he was leading them.

But he had still failed to get rid of the one Halibut who always seemed to stand in his way. After his fruitless attack in the Winter House last night, and after Evergrow had escaped and surely told her that he had come back and was hiding in the Warren, Omnia would be planning something of her own. By now she had surely told the Butler about him. He couldn't ignore her. He had to act.

There were two possibilities. One was to go after Omnia, try to find her, and if he couldn't, take hostages – her friends, her brother, anyone she cared about – to force her to give herself up. But what if that caused the Butler to come out of hiding and announce that he, Hildegrew, had been behind the deaths of the UnderButlers? The whole House would turn against him. The second possibility was not to wait for Rinque Day, but to take a chance that the confusion was already so great that he could lead the servants in an uprising that would have such power as to make Omnia irrelevant. But was the confusion great enough? Uncertainty, doubt and rumours had been building for days, but were they sufficient? In short, would the servants join him if he revealed himself now?

He didn't know. That was the most difficult thing about

having to rely on others, not being able to see for oneself what was happening. He had sent Owens, Alice Bickerstaff and Robert Gondolier into the House to stir up even more discontent among the servants and discover what they were saying, then come back and report what they had seen. Now all he could do was wait.

As he paced the floor, he went over the two options in his mind. If he couldn't find Omnia, it would be easy enough to take hostages, but then what? What if that provoked Digby to come out? What if Digby finally found the courage to emerge and say what he must now suspect about the deaths of the UnderButlers? The second option, on the other hand, would require him to come into the open earlier than he had planned. But if he succeeded, he would lead a great wave of servants out of the Warren that would crash into the House and drive the Halibuts out.

And then he wouldn't need anyone else. Change the plan. Why not? The Evergones could stay where they were. Neversuch House would be his. And why shouldn't it be? He was the one who had done everything, taken the risks, committed the murders. Why shouldn't he be the one to reap the rewards? Perhaps Neversuch House would have a new Captain, after all. Him.

He continued to pace the floor. William Bell was with him in the room. Hildegrew was getting sick of the junior clerk, who had made up some unbelievable story to explain how he had ended up tied with the ropes that had bound his prisoner. William was useless to him at this point, unable to leave the room for fear of being recognised. Hildegrew glanced at him from time to time, but said nothing. He kept pacing.

The stairs creaked. Someone was coming up. Hildegrew waited impatiently to see who it was.

In came Alice Bickerstaff.

'What have you heard?' he demanded.

'There's chaos. I heard there's been a riot in the kitchen. The Halibuts have had no breakfast.'

'Where's Owens?'

'Making more trouble, I expect! No one's working. Everyone's saying the Butler's dead or has left the House or some such thing. People must have seen us last night with our masks and axes. There are rumours flying around about a panther army.'

'Are they scared?'

Alice nodded, grinning. 'The Halibuts are standing around talking, whipping themselves into a panic. The servants aren't sure what to do. A lot of them are coming back to the Warren.'

Hildegrew nodded quickly, greedy for the news. Robert Gondolier arrived with similar stories. All over the House, servants were stopping work and coming back.

'Where's Owens?' asked Hildegrew.

They didn't know.

He pondered the situation. Now was the time to decide. Should he take the risk, come out into the open? Would the servants follow him? Were they ready?

He asked the two young servants to tell him again what they had seen. They did. Robert said he had returned to the Warren through a huge crowd of servants who had abandoned their work and were coming back.

'How many?' asked Hildegrew.

'I don't know.'

'Think!'

'Too many to count. Just about everyone.'

'If we don't do anything now,' said Alice, 'they might decide to go back to work.'

There comes a point in every great endeavour when you must seize the moment or watch it pass away forever. The difficulty is to know when that point is reached. It was that one sentence of Alice's, more than anything else, that made up Hildegrew's mind.

Tobias Hildegrew stood. He grabbed the mask of the grey panther in one hand and an axe in the other, and headed for the door.

31

Baling to the Warren

They found the carving of the dancing clown. They turned the corner and there was the door.

Omnia carried the Captain's coat bundled up in a ball so no one could see what it was as she walked through the House. The Captain's ring was in her pocket. The Halibuts were already bubbling with alarm. She didn't know what they would do if anyone saw her wearing the symbols of the Captaincy. Some kind of Halibut-panic probably. Right now, that was the last thing they needed.

They went through the door, first Omnia, then Evergrow, then Cornelius bringing up the rear. Cornelius lit the lantern they had brought and down they went.

The old gondola lay on the rock beside the water. There was no sign of the other boat that had been there before.

'How long ago did Basilica say her father used to use this?' asked Evergrow.

'Forty years,' said Omnia.

'Do you think it still floats?'

'Let's find out.'

It had been Omnia's idea to come to the river. The most effective weapon she could use against Tobias Hildegrew, she knew, would be surprise. Although no Halibut but the Captain was allowed in the Warren, he might still be expecting her to come after him there. But even if he did, he wouldn't be expecting her to come by the river. Cornelius didn't know where in the Warren the river led. He hadn't even known it existed until Omnia told him. But Evergrow, who had been taken there by Hildegrew, knew that the exit from the river was close to where he was hiding, and from Owens's description, Cornelius knew where that hiding place was. The river had been Hildegrew's secret channel – now they would turn the very secrecy of it against him.

Or at least that was what Omnia thought. She didn't know that Hildegrew had realised someone had been there on the day they found his boat.

They dragged the gondola to the river's edge. Inside was a single, long paddle. They pushed the boat into the water. Cornelius held the boat's prow so it wouldn't drift away.

Omnia raised the lantern and peered inside. Some of the seams between the wood had darkened slightly, as if dampened. 'What do you think?' she said to Cornelius.

He stepped into the boat and walked along its length while Evergrow held the prow. He came back and stepped out again. He shrugged. 'Only one way to find out.'

334

If they sank once they got out into the river, Omnia knew they would have to swim for their lives. She had no idea how close they would be to the next place where they could get out of the water. They might have to swim all the way back or drown.

'What do you think?' she said to Evergrow.

Evergrow looked along the length of the boat uncertainly. Here and there a few drops of water had come through.

'Bale with our hands if we need to,' said Cornelius.

Evergrow glanced at Omnia questioningly.

She took a deep breath. 'All right. Let's go.'

She stepped into the boat. Evergrow followed her. Cornelius pushed it out a little further, entered the water in his boots and got in. The boat, being so narrow, rocked markedly with every movement. Cornelius stood at the back, trying to steady it, and slid the long paddle into the water. He pushed off.

They moved out into the water and turned into the current. At first, Cornelius used the paddle to push off the rock at the bottom of the river. Then the river got deeper and he used it to push the boat forwards with wide, sweeping movements in the water behind them.

For a while they went along smoothly. Water began to come through, but hardly enough even to form a puddle at the bottom of the boat. Then the leaks became bigger. The water sloshed at their feet. Omnia and Evergrow began to bale, cupping their hands and capturing as much water as they could and throwing it overboard.

Cornelius drove the boat on with all his strength, pushing it forward with the current.

The water in the boat got deeper. It was up to their ankles. They baled faster.

'We should have brought buckets,' said Evergrow.

Omnia nodded. Baling by hand, they lost as much back into the boat each time as they managed to get rid of.

The water kept coming in. Cornelius paddled. Evergrow and Omnia baled continuously, breathing hard with the effort, no longer bothering to cup their hands, just pushing the water up and over the edge as fast as they could. They didn't know how much longer it would be before the water sank them. Omnia kept the Captain's coat on her lap, trying to keep it dry. She peered into the gloom as she baled, hoping to spot a place where they could land. But as far as she could see, it was only rock, only walls of stone, with the water lapping right up against it.

Then they went around a curve and a little further along the river, tethered to the rock, floated the boat they had seen before, beside a ladder that hung from the roof.

'That's it!' said Evergrow. 'That's where we got out.'

Cornelius headed straight for it, Omnia and Evergrow still baling as they went. They drew up alongside the other boat. Omnia stepped into it, taking the Captain's coat with her. Evergrow followed. Finally Cornelius stepped out of the gondola and joined them.

The rim of the gondola was low in the water. Cornelius tried to tether it to the other boat with a rope, but now that they had stopped baling, the gondola was sinking. They watched it fill with water.

Silently, it disappeared below the surface.

They were standing in the rowing boat. Beside them was the ladder that led to the trapdoor above the river. Cornelius reached for it.

'Wait a minute.' Omnia looked at Cornelius. 'There's something I need to understand. I should have asked you before. Why are you doing this, Cornelius?'

The messenger narrowed his eyes. 'You still don't trust me?'

'No, I do. That's the point. That's what I don't understand.'

'I'm a Slinker.'

'Then why do Slinkers do it? Why did your Uncle Winnicott do what he did?'

'Duty,' said Cornelius.

'He's been imprisoned seventeen years for doing his duty.'

Cornelius shrugged, as if that didn't surprise him.

Omnia glanced down at the bundle in her hands. Here she stood with the Captain's coat and here stood Cornelius ready to help her. A Halibut and a servant – as Halibuts and servants had stood for two centuries – one expecting the other to help her, the other expecting to give his help.

'Why are you helping me? You're a servant. Why don't you want to get rid of me?'

'Omnia!' whispered Evergrow.

'Why don't you want to see us gone, me, Evergrow, all the Halibuts?'

'Omnia!' whispered Evergrow more urgently. 'Do you think this is the time?'

'Yes, Evergrow, it is the time. It definitely is. I need to know. Cornelius, you saved my life . . . twice at least. Maybe more. For all I know, you might have saved it other times without me even knowing. I don't understand. Why aren't you with Tobias? Why aren't you on his side?'

'Oh, this is great,' muttered Evergrow to himself. He threw up his hands. 'This is just what we need.'

But Omnia wouldn't be deflected. 'Well?'

'Loyalty,' murmured Slinker.

'Yes, but why? Why be loyal? We have the treasure. What do you have? Work.'

'I don't mind work.'

'Why not outside? Why stay here?'

'I go outside. Do you think it's better?'

'I don't know. Is it? Isn't it?' Omnia shrugged. 'You see? How would I even know?'

'Here or there, I'd still have to work. This is my home, Omnia. Not just yours, mine too.'

'But we have the treasure.'

'So do we. The treasure pays for our work. It pays for our lives.'

'But the treasure isn't yours,' said Omnia. 'It's ours.'

'Yes. It's yours. It's your curse.'

Evergrow looked at Cornelius in surprise. 'You think the treasure's a curse?'

The messenger nodded. He gazed at the two children. 'We pity you.'

'Who?'

'The servants.'

'The servants pity us?' said Evergrow. 'Us? The Halibuts?'

Slinker nodded. 'We see what becomes of you. Look at your mother, Evergrow. How many knitted saucepans can one person use?'

'For heaven's sake, she doesn't knit saucepans!' Evergrow paused. He frowned uncertainly. 'Does she?'

'And your brother, Omnia? Where is he nowadays? I used to see him outside all the time. Now? I see packages for him. Resins, waxes, oils. What for?'

'Hair gels,' said Omnia quietly.

'That's right. Hair gels.'

'He's happy,' said Omnia defensively.

'Do you want to be happy like that?'

Omnia was silent for a moment. 'No,' she confessed.

'Work isn't such a bad thing, Omnia. I'd rather have it than not. Look what happens without it.'

Omnia frowned, thinking of Eversmooth and of every other adult Halibut she knew, each consumed by his or her unrelenting obsession.

'Without us, do you think you'd survive? You ask why we do it. I'll tell you. It's not just for you, it's for us. If we don't protect you, everything goes. Not only the Halibuts, but the servants. Not only your home, but mine. I told you, this is my House, not just yours. I love it just as much as you. That's always the way it's been, ever since the first Digby came to my great-great-great-great-great-great-grandfather and asked him to come to the House. What do you think he said to him? How do you think he got him to come? That was the agreement. It's our House as much as yours.'

'What about servants who don't want to stay?'

'They can go. No one's keeping them. Just like you.'

'But they can't come back?'

Cornelius shook his head. 'Just like you,' he said again. He frowned. 'The House is the House. It's not anyone's to change, Omnia. Not you, not me. Not the servants, not the Halibuts. Right or wrong, the House is the House. You accept it or you leave it. Each one has that choice, but the House goes on.'

Omnia looked around at the light of the lantern flickering over the cracked rock above the river. She had heard that a number of times before. She repeated the words in her mind. *The House goes on* . . . But was it really possible that it would *never* have to change, that it could go on just as it was forever?

'Enough talking,' said Cornelius. 'We've got work to do.'

Omnia nodded. That was easily the longest speech she had ever heard Cornelius Slinker make. She had needed to know and he had told her. Now the time for words was past.

Evergrow heaved a sigh of relief.

Omnia unrolled the blue coat and put it on. She hung the ruby ring around her neck. Then she looked at the other two sheepishly.

Cornelius nodded.

'You look good,' said Evergrow, wearing Owens's tunic. He held up his arms. 'And me?'

'You could get a job in the kitchen any time,' said Cornelius.

Omnia smiled for an instant. Then she looked up, aware that somewhere above her, above that trapdoor, was the Warren. And somewhere in the Warren was Tobias Hildegrew.

It felt worse, somehow, that she hadn't actually seen him, that she only knew that he was there, waiting. Thinking of the moment she would see him again chilled her blood.

But she *had* seen him. Behind the mask of the grey panther.

She felt the fear again, worse than ever before. There was so much of it, as if the terror of each of Hildegrew's attacks piled on the others – the ones that had happened three months ago and the ones that had taken place in the last week – the terror of being flung from the top of Slate Tower, of the sound of footsteps waking her under the roof of the Ribbled Lodge, of the great black bird landing behind her on the roof of the Silent Cloister, of the panther-man chasing her on the stairs of the Snowflake, of finding his boat at the river and knowing that he might be coming back, of his axe slicing through a wall two centimetres from her nose. Of what might come when they found him in his hiding place.

She wanted to flee, to untie the boat and row away as fast as she could.

'Ready?' said Cornelius.

She looked up at him, frowning. There was no fleeing now. The time had come to face the grey panther, to face the fear of him, and to overcome it.

Omnia nodded. 'Ready,' she said.

'Should we sink this boat?' asked Evergrow.

They looked at one another. None of them wanted to say it, but if things went badly, this might be their only means of escape.

So they leave the boat when they might have sunk it. One after the other, they climb the ladder, the same ladder that Tobias Hildegrew has used on his murderous trips to kill Trimbleby, Withers and Dish. When they push the trapdoor open, they find themselves at the bottom of an old, wooden staircase, and when they look up they see that it rises seven storeys above them, with steps that are missing or rotten or cracked. They climb it carefully and finally, at the top, they push open a door that leads on to a roof.

And now Omnia Halibut, wearing the ancient blue coat and the ruby ring of the First Captain of the House, with Evergrow and Cornelius at her side, must once again march forward to face her nemesis, the man who has hunted her down and almost killed her on half a dozen occasions, not knowing whether her luck will hold, whether she will survive this time, or whether this will be the time that she won't come back.

32

March of the Grey Panther

Tobias Hildegrew strode down an alley wearing the panther mask and gripping his axe. Alice Bickerstaff, Robert Gondolier and William Bell marched with him. People who saw him stared in surprise and then pointed, shouting. Word flew from window to window. News of the panther-man swept down the alleys ahead of him.

The Warren was already in a fever. Servants had been streaming back from the House with news of the riot in the kitchen and of the breakfastless Halibuts. With each telling, the story grew more exaggerated. The High Chef had been killed by being boiled alive in a cauldron of soup. His six assistant Lesser Chefs had been boiled as well. The cooks and kitchen hands had invaded the Tempered Hall and driven the Halibuts out. Or beaten them. Or massacred them. It was all nonsense – the riot had fizzled out after the capture of Owens by Cornelius Slinker – but that

343

didn't matter. The truth was less important than the effect it created. Among the servants inside the Warren, as with the Halibuts in the House, excitement, fear, anxiety and bewilderment reigned. No one had heard of a riot of the servants before. What did it mean? What was going to happen? What were they supposed to do?

The appearance of the panther-man stoked the fire. As soon as he got out into the alleys, Hildegrew knew that his decision was the right one – this was the moment. In his mind, he could already see a huge mob of servants streaming out of the Warren with him at their head, flooding across the mile of open ground that separated them from the Halibuts in their buildings, slamming into the House like a storm wave and crashing through doors and windows and driving the Halibuts out with the sheer force of their energy until everything was theirs. He would only have to choose the right words to make it happen.

'You!' cried a woman, pointing at him from a window. 'Who are you? What are you going to do?'

'Come and see!' He raised his axe. 'Join us! Come! Join us now!'

'Join us!' shouted William and Robert and Alice.

People did. They came out of workshops and houses. Soon the procession filled the alley behind the panther-man. It grew from itself, as such crowds do. The more people there were, the more people joined, having no idea why they were marching or who was leading them. The mass of servants streamed down the hill and came to the valley where the main street of the Warren ran past the houses of the grand servant families and there they ran into the crowd of servants streaming back from the House. The two crowds mixed, bubbling and eddying, sharing rumours and raising anxiety still further. The street was teeming with people and more came towards it. Hardly a man, woman or child in the Warren wasn't in the crowd. The overflow of people backed up into the alleys that led the hills on either side.

Hildegrew saw the Butler's house in front of him. It stood sandwiched between the house of the Coffiers on one side and the Gondoliers on the other, the three grandest houses in the Warren with barely a finger's breadth of space between them. He leaped up the steps to the door and smashed it open with a blow of his axe.

The crowd stared. The panther-man had broken into the Butler's house!

He disappeared inside. William, Robert and Alice hesitated for a moment and then ran in after him.

Hildegrew knew the interior of the house well. He had been here many times in the years when he had deceived Digby into thinking that he was his friend. A moment later, he appeared at a balcony above the door that he had just smashed. William, Alice and Robert stood on the balcony beside him.

The people stared up at the figure of the panther-man, wondering what he was going to do next.

He tore the mask off his head.

A great, sighing gasp ran through the crowd, like a wind of amazement.

'Yes, it's me!' he cried. 'Tobias Hildegrew! It's me!' He paused, letting the crowd see that it was really him. 'Here I stand. I'm not dead. I never was. That was a lie. It shows what your Butler is really like, telling lies like that. I was outside the wall and now I've come back to help you!' Hildegrew scanned the crowd. He smiled and pointed, calling to several servants below him by name. 'It's good to see you again. Sometimes I wondered if I ever would.'

There were cheers. The named servants grinned. Some raised their arms and shook their fists for the crowd. People laughed and slapped them on the back.

'Listen to me!' cried Hildegrew. 'It's a difficult time. What to do? Listen to me and I'll tell you.'

He waited again, letting the suspense build. There was silence now. The crowd strained to hear more. No one understood how Tobias Hildegrew could suddenly have reappeared when everyone had been told he was dead, or what kind of errand could have taken him outside the wall for three months, but that didn't matter. All that mattered now was that he stood before them, the familiar, much-admired figure they all thought they would never see again, tall, handsome, curly-haired, saying he would help them, saying he would tell them what to do. In the confusion and bewilderment that reigned in the Warren, it was a relief to hear someone say that. The fact that it was Tobias Hildegrew made it an added relief. Tobias always knew what had to be done. Many of the people watching him had always wished that he would be the next Butler instead of young Digby. *He*, they thought now, would never have abandoned them as Digby seemed to have done. He would know what had to be done to make everything in the House go back to normal. The fact that he had returned was incomprehensible – the fact that he had returned at this moment, when he had never been needed more, seemed nothing short of a miracle.

'Listen to me! Where is your Captain? Where is your Butler? Are they even alive? Why don't they show their faces?'

There were murmurs in the crowd.

'I'll tell you why. They're not here!' He let the words sink in. 'They've gone. Yes. Let me tell you what has happened. They've left you. They've abandoned the House. Why? Because they know something you don't know and I'm going to tell you.' He paused again. 'All of this is finished. It's time for the Halibuts to go.'

The murmurs in the crowd grew louder. What did Tobias mean? Were the Halibuts leaving? When? Now?

'Where do you think I've been for the last three months? They sent me to make preparations. They didn't they tell you, did they? It was a secret. For months, the Halibuts have been preparing to leave.'

People in the crowd looked at each other, some frowning, trying to comprehend what was being said.

'Let's help them!' said Tobias. 'For two hundred years,

we've been loyal. Let's not stop now. Let's perform this last service for them. Let's pack their bags. Let's take them to the gate. Let's help them go! That's what they want. Help them go!'

'*Help them go!*' shouted a few of the people in the crowd, servants who had been persuaded by the agitation of Alice and Robert and Owens over the past few days.

'Let's help them go!' cried Hildegrew.

'*Help them go!*' answered more people in the crowd.

Hildegrew shouted it again. The crowd roared back the slogan.

'Wait!' shouted someone in a loud voice. 'What happens to us?'

The crowd was silent. With no Halibuts to serve, what would they do?

'What's theirs will be ours,' said Hildegrew. 'Didn't you know? That's been agreed.'

'When?'

'Now! Let's help them go!'

'*Help them go!*'

'Where's the Butler?' demanded someone else. 'Why isn't the Butler here to tell us this?'

'Because he's gone!' cried Hildegrew. '*I'm* here to tell you.' He paused. He could see people in the crowd frowning, murmuring. Some believed him, others didn't know what to make of his revelation. He knew that the next few minutes – the things he said, the claims he made – would determine the outcome. 'There is no Butler now! Who has seen him in this last week? Well? Anyone? Show him to me. Just show him to me and I'll step away.' Hildegrew looked around dramatically. 'Who can? No one. And I'll tell you why. Because he's gone, him and the Captain. They've left. They were the first ones to go. That was always the plan.'

'Not so, Tobias Hildegrew!'

People looked around. From the balcony, Hildegrew searched for the source of the voice.

'Here I am, Tobias! You want someone to show you the Butler. I will! Here I am!'

At the end of the street stood Digby, wearing his green coat of office, flanked by the eight UnderUnderButlers.

He came forward. The crowd parted to let him through.

'Here I am!' cried Digby again, standing beneath the balcony.

'Precious good it'll do you!' shouted Hildegrew in reply.

'You said you'd step away.'

'For you?'

'You break into a man's house, I see.'

'After today, this house will mean nothing.' Hildegrew looked around the crowd again. 'Where has he been for the past week? What has he been doing? He left the House. Why has he come back now?'

'I never left!' shouted Digby.

'Didn't you?' demanded Hildegrew. 'Do we believe that? Do we?'

People in the crowd exchanged confused glances.

'Grab him!' shouted Hildegrew suddenly. 'Bring him here!' He called by name to people in the crowd who had shouted the slogan. 'Up here! Here! Bring him up! Let's settle this now!'

Confusion had broken out around the Butler. Some people tried to seize him; others came to his defence. In the scuffle, Digby was separated from the UnderUnderButlers and suddenly he was being held by four men and forced towards the smashed door of his house.

They took him up the steps and disappeared inside. A moment later, the Butler appeared on the balcony. They pushed him forward. He tripped and fell at Hildegrew's feet.

'Look at your Butler!' cried Hildegrew. 'Look at him now.'

People looked.

'Get up!' said Hildegrew, gazing at him in disdain. He would show the crowd what this Butler was made of. And once he had finished, the crowd would be his. Then they would follow him, and the wave of servants would crash against Neversuch House and send the Halibuts running forever.

But first, he was going to enjoy this. He had never had the chance to really show Digby how much he resented having to pretend to be his friend, how he hated both the Younger Digby and his father, how he had been biding his time until he could take his revenge for his own father's death. Now the chance had come. He wasn't going to rush it.

'Get up!' he said again.

He leaned down and grabbed the collar of the Butler's Green Coat and dragged him to his feet.

'Here he is!' shouted Hildegrew, still holding him by the collar. He gave him a shake. 'Here's your so-called Butler! Would have been better if he'd stayed away, don't you think?'

A few people laughed. Most of the crowd stood silent, stunned by what they were seeing.

'Would you like to say something, Mr Digby?'

The Butler looked up at him. The last time Digby had seen Tobias Hildegrew, the other man was flying away on the wind, out of reach, revealing the true depth of his betrayal. That was three months ago, but the wound was still raw. He dug deep within himself to find the courage he needed.

'You'll pay for this, Tobias.'

Hildegrew laughed. 'I'll pay for it? And who'll make me? You? You, Mr Digby? Mr Digby, by this time tomorrow, you won't be the butler of anything. There'll be nothing left for you to buttle.' Hildegrew looked around at the crowd. 'Isn't that right? Let's help them go!'

'*Help them go!*' came back the shout.

'Do you hear that, Mr Digby? We'll help them go, and you with them. No one wants you any more. No one ever wanted you.' Hildegrew paused, watching the Butler, the smile on his face getting crueller and crueller. 'Take off the coat, Mr Digby.'

'I will not.'

'Take it off.'

'Never!'

'Take it off!'

In the street, the alleys, there was utter silence. The crowd watched, wide-eyed. Everyone sensed that they were about to witness something unprecedented, something that would mark the end of one thing and the beginning of another – that if Digby took off the Green Coat, everything would change forever.

'Take it off!' roared Hildegrew again.

'Not for you, Tobias Hildegrew!'

'Yes, you will!' shouted Hildegrew and he put both hands on the Butler's shoulders and began to pull at the coat. Digby resisted, twisting and turning and trying to get free of Hildegrew's grasp. William Bell and Alice Bickerstaff joined in, each seizing any bit of the coat they could reach.

Suddenly Hildegrew stopped. He had heard a voice. He looked up, his hands still clutching the shoulders of the Butler's coat.

Digby looked up as well.

So did everyone in the crowd.

Next to the Butler's house, on the roof of the house of the Gondoliers, above its pillars and flying buttresses and sculptures, stood three figures – a man and two children. One of the children was wearing what appeared to be the blue Captain's coat, or at least the remains of it. She was far too small for it and couldn't fill it out, yet that was what it appeared to be.

Omnia shouted again. 'Let him go, Tobias Hildegrew!'

33

On the Roofs

Omnia looked down from the edge of the Gondoliers' roof. Immediately below her were the flying buttresses, thin, bent fingers of stone jutting out into space and then angling down to the next level of the roof below, each with a sculpture of a beaver or a stork or a crocodile on its point. Below her and to the right was the balcony of the Butler's house, where Tobias Hildegrew stood with the Butler, and further below that, far below, stood the crowd, filling the street and the alleys as far as she could see.

She had come out with Evergrow and Cornelius from the underground river on the roof of a building halfway up the hill to the quarry. Immediately, they had seen the crowd milling in the alleys at the bottom of the hill and had guessed that it was too late to go after Hildegrew in his hiding place. Cornelius led them quickly through a series of narrow, deserted alleys to the back of the Gondoliers' house, to an entrance he sometimes used when Albert Gondolier, the Chief Mason, asked him to run errands. He knew that here was a staircase – built by a previous Chief Mason on an architectural whim, as so many features of the Gondoliers' house had been – that ran up the outside of the house to the roof, from which they would be able to see what was happening in the main street of the Warren.

It was there, when they got to the top, when they came forward to the edge of the roof and could see the balcony of the Butler's house, that Omnia caught her first sight of Tobias Hildegrew unmasked.

For a moment, she hadn't been able to speak. The sight of him froze her. But then she saw what he was doing and forced herself to shout. The first sound that came out of her mouth was hoarse and faint, nowhere near enough to be heard by the crowd. She filled her lungs and from somewhere, somehow, she found the strength to shout more loudly than she had ever shouted in her life.

Tobias looked up and suddenly Omnia found herself staring into the eyes that had last gazed at her from behind the panther mask.

She shouted again. 'Let him go, Tobias Hildegrew!'

Hildegrew shoved the Butler away as if he had suddenly lost interest in him. He turned and disappeared inside. For the space of thirty seconds, perhaps, he was gone and then he burst out on to the roof of the Butler's house, which was separated from the Gondoliers' roof by only the narrowest of gaps. William Bell, Alice Bickerstaff and Robert Gondolier followed him out.

Hildegrew strode to the front of the roof. He pointed at Omnia. 'This is a Halibut!' he shouted to the crowd. 'No Halibut may come into the Warren but the Captain!'

'Look at the coat she wears!' Cornelius Slinker shouted back. For someone who was habitually so quiet, his voice turned out to be exceptionally loud when he chose to raise it.

'Is this the Captain?' demanded Tobias Hildegrew with a sneer. 'This youngster? This child?'

'She wears the coat!' retorted Cornelius. He grabbed the ring that hung at Omnia's neck and held it up. 'She wears the ring!'

Hildegrew turned to the crowd, sensing how to use this to his advantage. 'This is a little Halibut in a Captain's coat. A child. Where's the real Captain? Gone, as I said. He's left. What more proof do we need? What has become of this House when he leaves behind a child as the Captain? The House is finished. The Halibuts must go.'

'The House is not finished!' cried Cornelius.

'The House is finished when it has a Captain such as her'.

'Then you admit I'm the Captain?' demanded Omnia.

Hildegrew hesitated for a moment.

Omnia glanced at the crowd. She could see faces, hundreds of faces, turned towards her. She sensed that they were wondering. *Was* she the Captain? And if she was, what did it mean? Could the House have a Captain who was so young?

'Is that what you say?' demanded Hildegrew, sneering. 'That you're the Captain? Is that the best the Halibuts can do? A little one like you? A child?'

'Why can't I—'

'A pipsqueak!' Hildegrew shouted over her, preventing Omnia from being heard. 'What have we come to when *this* is what we have? I told you! The House is finished. The House is—'

'What else have you told them?' demanded Cornelius Slinker, his voice loud enough to match Hildegrew's. 'That you killed Trimbleby? That you killed Withers? That you killed Dish?'

There were murmurs of amazement in the crowd. What was that Cornelius Slinker had just said?

'Did you tell them that?' demanded Slinker. 'Did you tell them how you killed the three UnderButlers?'

'Lies! Where's your proof?'

'Do you deny it then?'

'Yes. I deny it!'

'Liar!' shouted Omnia. 'Murderer and liar!'

Hildegrew snorted. 'Lies! Desperate lies from a child!'

In the crowd, looks of amazement were turning to looks of anger. There were many people there from the families of the three dead UnderButlers. All but the most gullible had their doubts that the three deaths in such quick succession could have been accidents. And how was it that Tobias

Hildegrew – who was supposed to be dead himself – had just happened to turn up again so soon afterwards?

'Tell them where you've been for the last three months!' cried Omnia. 'Tell them who you've been with!'

'I've told them!'

'Have you?' demanded Omnia. Every person in the crowd strained to hear her. 'Have you told them how you killed the Older Digby before that? Have you told them how you killed the old Captain?'

The crowd gasped.

'Lies! Prove it!'

'How have you come back?' demanded Omnia. 'You were meant to be dead. What happened that night, Tobias? Have you told them that?'

Hildegrew looked down at the crowd. The men who seized the UnderUnderButlers, restraining them from running into the house after the Butler was taken, were loosening their grip. Angry, hostile faces glared at him. The mood was turning. The accidents, the deaths, Hildegrew's disappearance for three months, his sudden return, the strange things he had been saying about throwing the Halibuts out of the House – suddenly they all seemed to fit together to make a different story than the one he had been telling.

'You aren't the Captain!' he cried. 'And him!' he added, pointing at Evergrow. 'He's a Halibut too. Do you know what the punishment is for a Halibut who comes into the Warren?' He turned to the crowd in desperation. 'A Halibut in the Warren! A second one!'

But there was no response this time. Faces stared up at Hildegrew stonily. He could see relatives of the three dead UnderButlers wherever he looked. Some were pushing through the crowd to get to the door of the Butler's house. In another moment they would be on the stairs to the roof.

'Tell them, Tobias!' cried Omnia. 'Tell them how you dropped the statue on Withers's head. Tell them how you set a trap for Trimbleby at the Bridled Mount. Tell them how you—'

Tobias Hildegrew ran. He leaped across the sliver of a gap between the two roofs and lunged at Omnia. Cornelius caught him round the waist and just managed to stop him getting to her as Omnia stepped back. Tobias pummelled him with his fists as Cornelius struggled to hold on to his cloak. William Bell, who had come over as well, jumped on Cornelius and poked at his eyes. Robert Gondolier and Alice Bickerstaff came for Omnia and Evergrow. The two cousins fought together, side by side, desperately pushing back as Alice and Robert tried to drive them to the edge of the roof. Omnia got her leg around Robert's and tripped him up. He hit the roof with a thud. She turned to Alice, and together with Evergrow, pushed her back until she tripped over Robert and went down as well.

Evergrow glanced at her with a grin.

Someone flashed past him

'*Omnia!*'

She was flying through the air. Then she was gone. Tobias Hildegrew had broken free as William Bell scratched at Cornelius's eyes. He had hurled her off the roof.

For an instant, it seemed that everything on the roof stopped. Hildegrew stood with a triumphant sneer on his face. William Bell and Cornelius, the one still on the other's back, stared with opposite expressions, one of glee, the other of dismay, at the place where Omnia had stood. Robert Gondolier and Alice Bickerstaff, still flat on the roof, looked up in surprise. And Evergrow stood, stunned, disbelieving. Omnia was gone.

As Evergrow would remember it later, it was as if the world stood still. It seemed that that instant lasted forever.

But in reality it was the barest, tiniest sliver of time. A servant burst out on to the roof of the Butler's house and there were more behind him. Hildegrew ran, heading for the other side of the Gondoliers' roof. He leaped across to the next building, the roof of the Grand Glazier. Cornelius shook himself free of William Bell and ran after him. The servants who had come out on to the roof joined in the chase.

Hildegrew kept running, leaping from roof to roof. Cornelius raced after him, followed by a crowd of servants. Hildegrew jumped over the slit-like gaps between the buildings, leaped over narrow alleys, ran up stairs where he could find them, scrambled up ladders, climbing the hill towards the quarry roof by roof. The buildings were so close that there was always a way for him to keep going. Cornelius and the others gave chase. Others followed in the alleys below, tracking the dark figure running along the rooflines, running ahead in case he tried to get down.

But he didn't come down. From roof to roof he went. Then he stopped, about three-quarters of the way up the hill, beside a door on a roof. Only now did Cornelius realise where he had been heading.

Cornelius stopped, breathless, on the adjacent roof. The other servants pulled up behind him.

'Come quietly, Tobias,' said Cornelius.

Hildegrew smiled, holding the door open behind him. 'Why should I?'

'You'll never get away.'

'Won't I?' Hildegrew sneered. 'You failed, Slinker. You were protecting her, your hereditary duty. Where is she now? Dead, that's where. *Dead.*'

Slinker clenched his fists. 'Come quietly, Tobias.'

'Dead,' said Hildegrew, taunting him. 'The one you were supposed to protect. Dead, Cornelius Slinker. Dead.'

The Butler appeared in the alley below the roof and shouted up at him. 'Surrender, Tobias. There's nowhere for you to go. It's over.'

Hildegrew looked down at him. 'Over? I don't think so. Look around you, Digby. Who can you trust? Who will be the one to betray you? Who will be the one to creep up on you one day and break your neck like I broke your father's? Over? No. Never. The Evergones *will* win!'

Cornelius Slinker ran at him. Hildegrew turned, threw a last, taunting glance in his direction, stepped to the door, spread his cloak and jumped.

A few seconds later, Cornelius was at the door. He

caught a glimpse of Hildegrew plummeting down the well of the staircase, his cloak spread to slow the fall, then heard the crash as Hildegrew smashed through the trapdoor and plunged into the river below.

Cornelius almost jumped after him. But if he did, the splintered wood of that trapdoor, he knew, would slice him to ribbons.

By the time Cornelius got down the stairs, there was no trace of Hildegrew, nor of the boat that had been tied to the wall.

Cornelius Slinker made his way slowly back towards the Gondoliers' house. All around him people were talking, shaking their heads, rolling their eyes, telling each other about the events that had happened. But Cornelius didn't listen, didn't speak. Sunk in despair, he was barely able to put one foot after the other. Usually so quick, so agile, he shuffled down the street in a daze.

He had failed, as Hildegrew had taunted him. It was his duty to have protected Omnia Halibut. Instead, Hildegrew had slipped through his hands. He would never forget those last moments, William Bell's fingers scratching at his eyes, Hildegrew's fists smashing at his jaw, the feeling of his hands clutching at Hildegrew's cloak and the knowledge that it was slipping out of his grasp and that, in an instant, he would lose his hold altogether. And then he had, and Hildegrew had run at Omnia and got to her.

Got to her, but . . . not killed her? Outside the Gondoliers' ridiculous house with its pillars and sculptures and flying buttresses, he found Omnia standing beside Evergrow.

He stared, uncomprehending.

'The coat caught,' said Evergrow.

'On a stork,' said Omnia.

Slinker looked up. On each of the points of the flying buttresses below the Gondoliers' roof stood a beaver, a stork or a crocodile, each in a different pose. Omnia pointed at one of the storks. Its carved beak was raised to the sky.

She lifted her arm and showed Cornelius the tear on the side where the coat had caught. Cornelius shook his head in amazement.

'They must have made those coats strong in the First Captain's time,' said Evergrow.

Omnia smiled at Cornelius. 'Lucky you made me wear it.'

34

Above the Rinque

'Look at that,' said Pedagogia. 'There goes another one!'

She pointed, and the other Halibuts standing with her – the gluttons Everfull Halibut and his wife Insatia, Omnia's parents and a number of others – all laughed. Below them, on a great wooden floor, teams of Halibuts on stilts were involved in a complicated dance and one of them had just fallen over, landing painfully with his stilts flying across the floor and knocking the stilts out from under another dancer, who hit the floor as well.

'Priceless!' said Insatia.

The Rinque was held in a vast, circular structure known as the Rinque Rink and consisted of a competition among teams of various Halibuts who were required to perform a series of dances that had been invented in the days of the Fourth Captain, Evercalm, who had been an accomplished dancer as well as a wrestler of some skill. No one knew if it was Evercalm or somebody else who originally had the idea to put the dancers on stilts, or what purpose they possibly hoped to achieve by doing it. The stilts turned the dancers into tall, stiff, birdlike creatures, plodding mechanically round the rink in a desperate attempt to keep the rhythm of the music, which was played by an orchestra of Halibuts, without toppling over. Eldred Sturgeon normally had to plaster at least half a dozen broken bones each year. No one knew how the scores in the competition were kept apart from Everstep L Halibut, the House's foremost dancing expert, and he refused to reveal the secret – if there really was one, which many people doubted. In any case, as usual, most of the Halibuts came less to watch the competition than to enjoy the feast, which was a unique one in the Halibut calendar because traditionally it consisted of fruits, jellies, syrups and sweets of staggering size and created in the most extraordinary combinations.

The roof of the Rinque Rink was an enormous dome made of glass, and the viewing area above the floor consisted of a series of large, curving platforms connected by stairs at various heights. The entrance was from a raised walkway that ran on stilts along the edge of the Long Promenade from the top of the Thatched Lodge.

Three of the platforms had been set aside for the feast and servers in scarlet tunics were busy setting out the fruits, jellies and syrups. The sweets were on their way. Everdean, wearing a blue Captain's coat, sat on the Rinque Chair where the Captain always sat, on the second highest platform, with an UnderUnderButler on either side in case he slumped too far in one direction or the other. The Butler in his green velvet coat stood nearby, as he always stood. Elsewhere, Halibuts gazed down at the floor from various heights. As they watched the dances below, and applauded or laughed according to merit, they talked. What had happened the day previously in the House, no one could explain. First, no breakfast! Then the servants had all disappeared, not returning until the afternoon, as if they had been washed away like jellyfish on a tide and then washed back again. And the nonsense they talked when they came back! Stories of a battle in the Warren, of the Butler being involved in a desperate fight, of Omnia Halibut – Omnia Halibut, of all people – turning up in the Captain's coat! And of Tobias Hildegrew – if you *please* – coming back from the dead and then falling off a roof and plunging to his death in an underground river, of all places. As if plunging to his death once wasn't enough, and he would want to come back and do it all over again!

No one knew what to make of it. They each heard only fragments from the servants, and often the servants themselves had seen or heard only a fragment of what had happened. And then they told each other fragments of the fragments of the fragments they had heard. Soon the versions of the day's events were utterly garbled, which would probably have been the case even if the Halibuts had not been such terrible garblers by nature, which they were.

By now they had all more or less all decided that what had

happened, whatever it was, couldn't have been too serious, and had begun to wish that they had been notified about it in advance so they could have taken picnic baskets and gone to watch. After all, the Rinque was going ahead as it always did, with the Captain and the Butler in their usual places and the servers arranging the food on the three platforms where the food was always arranged, so how threatening could the previous day's events have been?

There was another rumour as well, that Basilica Halibut had been seen by Ribelia, but that, everyone agreed, was so ridiculous that it wasn't even worth wasting one's breath on. Two people coming back from the dead in one day was just a little too much!

'Ribelia's always been prone to exaggeration,' said Everfull Halibut.

'That isn't so,' said Omnia's father, Evernear. Ribelia was his sister and he felt obliged to defend her, even though he privately agreed with Everfull.

'Sometimes she does exaggerate,' said Omnia's mother, Candelia. 'Let's be honest, dear.'

'Well, sometimes, perhaps,' conceded Evernear. 'Not often though.'

'Where is she anyway?' asked Pedagogia.

Evernear shrugged.

'Recovering from the shock,' suggested Insatia with a sly smile.

'What shock?' demanded Everfull.

'The shock of seeing Basilica.'

'My dear, if Basilica Halibut's come back from the dead,' spluttered Everfull, 'I'll eat my blue boots!' He pointed at the bright blue boots that he was wearing, which would be quite a mouthful, even for a glutton as accomplished as him. 'I'll eat them with anchovy sauce and mustard relish, and for dessert I'll have the bootlaces fried in—'

Everfull stopped. His huge mouth fell open, perhaps in anticipation of the bright blue boots and fried laces that he was going to have to eat.

At the entrance to the Rinque, where the raised walkway came into the building, not twenty metres away from them, stood Basilica Halibut, with Omnia by her side.

Everyone in the group round Everfull looked to see what he was staring at. One by one, their mouths dropped as well.

There was no mistaking her. Over seventeen years had passed since the last time they had seen her, but it was as if that had been yesterday. The same face, the same hair. Greyer now, but with the same lustre and sheen.

On every platform around the Rinque, someone saw, and pointed, heads turned, and conversation stopped. A hush fell over the great circular building.

The ancient music of the dances suddenly sounded much louder in the silent hall. One of the flute players, who was a cousin of Basilica's, glanced upwards. The flute dropped from his hands and clattered across the floor. The other musicians looked up and the notes from their instruments died away. There was a last, low groan from an oboe and then the music stopped entirely. Now the only noise was the clattering and falling of the dancers, who had finally looked up as well, seen who was there and forgotten utterly that they were on stilts – until they hit the ground. Finally, when the last of the dancers had fallen over and cried out in pain, the silence was complete.

'Basilica . . .' said Pedagogia. Her face had gone utterly white. 'Basilica Halibut! You're supposed to be dead.'

'Hello, Pedagogia,' she replied. 'Sorry to disappoint.'

Suddenly the Halibuts flocked towards her. They came from the other platforms, they climbed the stairs from the floor. The Rinque was forgotten as a typical Halibut clamour filled the air.

Omnia slipped away. She watched the commotion from another platform. Basilica was to say nothing about where she had been for the past seventeen years. The Butler had insisted on that condition. This was immediately after Omnia had insisted that Basilica was to be freed. She had told Digby as they walked back from the Warren the previous day. She wouldn't tolerate it if Basilica was imprisoned again. She would tell everyone the truth.

Basilica had agreed to the Butler's condition. Omnia didn't know how she was going to stick to it, but if anyone could, she thought, it was Basilica. Besides, the Halibut adults, thought Omnia as she watched them thronging around Basilica, probably half guessed at what had happened to her. Or at least *some* of what had happened to her.

On the three designated platforms, the servers continued

to lay the feast. Omnia was aware of them stealing glances at her. Many of them had seen her standing in the Captain's coat on the roof of the Gondoliers' house the previous day, and those who hadn't had certainly heard about it. They didn't know what to think. On one side of the Rinque sat Everdean in a blue Captain's coat on the traditional Captain's chair, and on the other side stood Omnia with nothing to show that yesterday she had apparently taken his place. Had it been some kind of joke? If so, it was a very peculiar one, without an obvious punchline.

Evergrow came to join her from another platform. He had been watching the Rinque with Eversmart and the twins, but they had gone to see what was happening on the platform where Basilica had appeared. They had no idea who she was, but, being true Halibuts, that didn't stop them running over excitedly. Omnia could see the twins' yellow sunhats bobbing up and down on the edge of the crowd.

'She loves the House,' said Evergrow, gazing towards the spot where Basilica, somewhere in the middle of the throng, was standing. 'Now she'll have a chance to enjoy it.'

Omnia smiled. At least one good thing had come out of all of this.

A few more minutes went by. The dancers who had run up the stairs began to return. Eldred Sturgeon and his helpers finished clearing the floor of the most severely injured. A few musicians were back in place. Everstep clapped his hands and the music started again. More musicians returned and joined in. Eventually one of the dancing teams formed up and started dancing. The others were getting on to their stilts. A cluster of Halibuts remained around Basilica, who came forward to watch.

Rinque Day, thought Omnia, just like a hundred Rinque Days before it. The music played. The dance continued. The feast was laid. People watched. Basilica, who until a quarter of an hour before had supposedly been dead for seventeen years, watched as well, now just another Halibut among a crowd of Halibuts. Everything in Neversuch House seemed to get swallowed up and incorporated in the life of the House, which seemed so solid, so dependable. And yet it wasn't. From the Gondoliers' roof, Omnia had seen how close Tobias Hildegrew had come to destroying it. At that moment, as he wrestled to pull the Green Coat off the Butler's shoulders, everything had hung in the balance – the House and the life that was led within it, two centuries of Halibutuation and the traditions and rituals it had created. If she had arrived a few minutes later, if Hildegrew had got that coat off the Butler, if he had put it on himself, if he had led the servants out of the Warren, what would be left today? Would there be a Rinque? Would there be a feast? Would the Halibuts be standing here as they had always stood, dancing on the floor as they had always danced?

After the chase across the rooftops in the Warren, the Butler had come back to stand on the same balcony where Tobias had almost vanquished him. He told the servants that this time Hildegrew really was dead. That he had killed the UnderButlers, but now he would kill no one else. That the House was safe. And that they should all go back to their work.

And they had. As if awaking from a strange, troublesome dream, to find that the world was quiet and peaceful, after all, they had walked to the House. Back had gone launderers and gardeners and glaziers and polishers. Back went the kitchen hands and cooks who had rioted to find the High Chef, heavily bandaged, standing at the kitchen entrance. Dinner came out as usual and through the night the Rinque feast was prepared.

Already they were being forgotten, the strange events of the previous day, or at least the fragments of the fragments of the fragments that the Halibuts knew. Or not forgotten perhaps, but swallowed up and digested and made part of the history of the House. The history as it was remembered, not as it happened. Those who had heard about the riot in the kitchen were told that it was the work of a kitchen hand who had gone mad. Perhaps Evermay would paint a picture called *The High Chef Heroically Stopping the Riot of the Kitchen Madman*, and Everset would tell him to call it *The Mysterious Riot of the Kitchen Madman*, and the story, in that form, would become part of the House's history as well.

Everything would become part of that history, thought Omnia. It would be redrawn, reconstructed, so that the House could go on, as everybody always said, and nothing would have to change – until the moment came when someone found a way to make everything change, which was the moment that had almost come as Tobias Hildegrew began to pull the green velvet coat off Digby on the balcony of the Butler's house.

And in the mean time, what had come out of it? Lies. Another packet of lies to add to the towering, swaying pile on which the House already balanced. The four servants – William Bell, Alice Bickerstaff, Owens, Robert Gondolier – had already been expelled from the House. People were being told they had all died in a terrible accident in the Warren, crushed under a wall that collapsed, and had been hurriedly buried during the night, so mangled were their bodies. Walls collapsed often enough in the Warren, but whether anyone but a child would believe it had happened this time, Omnia doubted. And Tobias Hildegrew? Dead, according to the Butler's announcement, having drowned in the river into which he had plummeted, his body carried away by the current before anyone could reach him. But Omnia, Evergrow and Cornelius knew differently. The boat was gone – the boat they had decided to leave in case they needed to escape themselves. It had been fastened to the ring on the wall and the only way it could have gone would have been if someone had untied it. Hildegrew, slowed in his fall by his outstretched cloak, had obviously survived his plunge through the trapdoor and into the water. Wherever the river flowed from under the House, Hildegrew had followed it in the boat to make his escape.

Cornelius had whispered the truth to the Butler even before he stood on the balcony. Yet the Butler went ahead and announced that Hildegrew was dead, his body washed away by the current.

The lies would go on, Omnia knew, and everyone pretended to believe them. Perhaps, after a while, they really did believe them. But what good did it do? Now there were four more people outside the House, as well as Hildegrew, to add to all the others who were already there.

Omnia had taken off the Captain's coat on the way back from the Warren. Cornelius had wanted her to leave it on, but she hadn't. She gave the ring to the Butler and was going to give the coat to him as well. But at that, Cornelius objected. 'Keep it,' he had said. And she had. She wasn't sure why. Having been cut down by Cornelius, it was too small for anyone else to wear. But that wasn't the reason.

Now it was hidden on a shelf at the back of the wardrobe in her room. Did she wonder if she'd need it again? Maybe she did.

Evergrow nudged her. 'Look up there.'

Another huddle had formed on the platform, this time of servants. In the middle of it was Winnicott Slinker, with Cornelius by his side.

Omnia caught Cornelius's eye. A moment later, he slipped away and joined them. He was dressed in his black messenger's clothes, as always, with his black messenger's cloak. The corners of four envelopes poked out of his pocket.

Death certificates, Omnia knew. Four of them. She didn't even need to ask.

They surveyed the scene, the teams of dancers on the floor, the Halibuts above them, Everdean sitting between two of the UnderUnderButlers, the feast being laid. Basilica on a platform, surrounded by excited Halibuts, and a little further away, Winnicott, surrounded by his own small group of excited servants.

'I have something to say,' announced Evergrow.

They turned to look at him.

'No more secrets. Between us, I mean.'

Omnia glanced at Cornelius. He had kept secret from her the fact that he was a hereditary protector of the Halibuts. But she had kept secret from Evergrow the truth about the Evergones, at least until she had been forced to tell him, and the truth of what had happened to Tobias Hildegrew three months before.

Omnia nodded. That was fair. Better than fair. There were so many secrets in the House, sometimes it seemed that the whole place was built on them. If they were ever going to do anything about it, between them, at least, there could be none.

She clasped Evergrow's hand and glanced at Cornelius. He clasped their hands as well.

'No more secrets,' she said.

'No more secrets,' they replied.

Omnia smiled. It was his House as well as theirs, Cornelius had said. She thought she understood what he meant by that. She thought that now she really understood.

She understood as well now what the House meant to her. She had taken it for granted, but in the last few days, she had come to realise how much she loved its buildings, its walkways, its places. Its traditions, even if they might involve watching a group of elderly Halibuts trying to dance on stilts. Even its people, with their inexplicable obsessions. Not only the Halibuts, but the servants too. There was something of the same obsessions in them, she realised. Perhaps no one living in Neversuch House could avoid it.

Why had she suddenly realised how much she loved it? I can't say for certain. Maybe it was seeing Basilica's face on the day she came out of her imprisonment and walked among the buildings of the House for the first time in seventeen years. Or maybe it was the fact that Omnia – and all the Halibuts – had come so close to losing it. Maybe that was needed before Omnia could understand how much she loved the place where she had grown up.

But if that was true of her, wouldn't it be true of the Evergones as well, those who wanted to come back? They *had* lost the House. Wouldn't their desire for it be all the greater? And would it ever go away?

And would the Evergones lack assistants, servants who could be persuaded to help them? Tobias Hildegrew had only been their mask. The Evergones stood behind him, as surely as he had stood behind the face of the panther that he had worn. The previous day in the Warren, when he had spoken, there had been people in the crowd who had come forward to join him. How many more would have stepped forward if he had succeeded in taking the Butler's coat? What would it take to make them step forward again?

Omnia didn't know the answer to those questions, nor would you or I if we had been in her place. She could only guess. But now, at the age of twelve and seven-sixteenths, she has realised the full enormity of the battle that has gone on in the House for two centuries. Would it go on for two centuries more?

She looked at Basilica, who stood gazing down at the Rinque as if it was the most exquisite spectacle imaginable. Perhaps it was, for her.

'What do you think?' said Omnia.

'Rinque Day . . .' murmured Cornelius.

'Do you think there'll ever be another?'

'Hildegrew's still alive,' said Evergrow. 'Will he ever stop?'

Omnia didn't reply. She remembered what Basilica had said to her during that last night in the Winter House. 'You must find him and kill him, before he kills you.' Well, she had found him, but he was still alive. News reached the Evergones from servants in the House. Soon he would know that she was alive as well.

Omnia looked up. Through the glass dome of the Rinque she could see the Great Tower soaring into the air. From the top of the Great Tower, she knew, you could see for miles, beyond the wall and around the estate of Neversuch House and right across the city of Pettifog. Somewhere out there were the Evergones. Somewhere out there was Tobias Hildegrew, and Evernow's son, and his mother, Elisabeth Felt, still plotting their revenge.

At that moment, Omnia realised something. It could never be ended from in here. Suddenly she understood that that was the mistake that had always been made, a mistake going back two hundred years to the First Captain and his son, the first Evergone. Omnia wasn't sure if the struggle could ever be brought to an end, but she felt certain of one thing. If there was to be even a chance of stopping it, someone would have to go out there, beyond the wall and into the world outside Neversuch House, in order to do it.